The Birds In Shadowed Trees

By Avi Pinkerton
First Installment of the Pact of Fate series

Copyright

Map created by Seth Tongkaw using mapeffects.co

Cover designed by Fieriz Designs

Warnings

This novel contains depictions and references to:

Physical injury, blood, animal death, abuse, including mentions of child abuse, gore, thoughts of suicide ideation and implications of depression, and eating complications.

Your mental health is important. Please take a moment to consider these warnings before reading. Put yourself first and take care of yourself in any way you need.

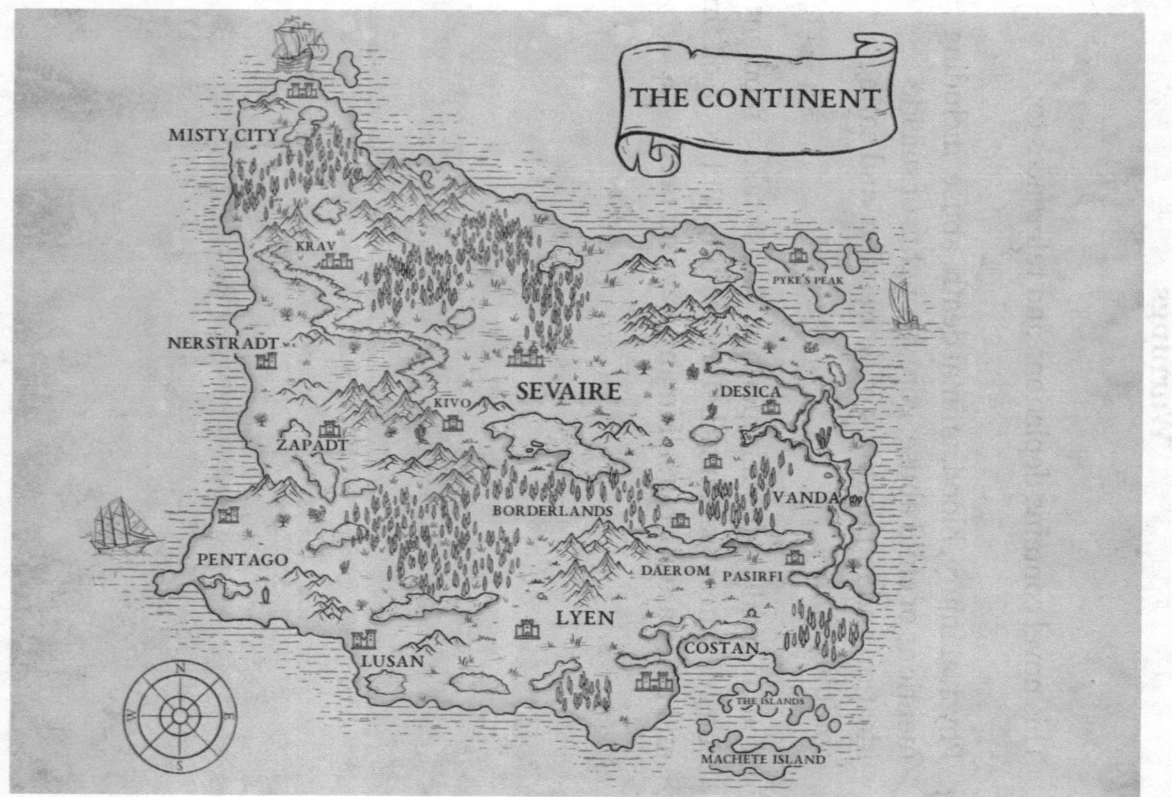

THE CONTINENT
MISTY CITY
KRAV
PYKE'S PEAK
NERSTRADT
SEVAIRE
DESICA
KIVO
ZAPADT
VANDA
BORDERLANDS
PENTAGO
DAEROM
PASIRFI
LYEN
LUSAN
COSTAN
THE ISLANDS
MACHETE ISLAND

Part 1
The North

ONE

I'd seen a woman die in a crown once.

Seven years ago, my mother collapsed behind me in a gown stitched with the finest gold, on the very steps we were meant to watch suitors parade their affections to my sister when she was just thirteen.

One moment Mother was chasing us through the rain, laughing like she'd never been a queen at all, but just our mother—and the next, she was a memory we couldn't outrun.

But tonight wasn't about scarring memories. It was about pretending we were still a whole, perfect, royal family.

Unfortunately, that meant wearing another dress and pretending I wasn't one breath away from setting this entire palace on fire with my spite and irritation, wishing I could be the next royal to die in a crown.

I scratched at the pins digging into my scalp and yanked a few out, dropping them onto the tufted maroon bench beneath me. Delicate snowflake clips—my sister's idea.

Royal flair for the Biannuals, as if matching accessories could make us look more united.

They didn't.

The tight bun made my head throb. The whispers behind the ballroom doors made it worse. Dozens of nobles waited beyond the iron barricade, likely praising Libby's taste while preparing to dissect mine.

As usual.

I was to walk in smiling, shoulders back, crown on, bowing to the same men who saw my sister as a prize and me as a problem.

I couldn't decide which was worse: being underestimated or being desired for the wrong reasons.

The black silk of my dress clung too tightly to my ribs, expecting me to be uptight. The satin bow was a ridiculous leash disguised as fashion presenting me as a wrapped offering from my kingdom. Almost a sacrifice.

A present for the princes.

Delightful.

I flicked the bow, ignoring the towering doors that loomed ahead like silent guards.

My father's crest sat carved into the iron—snowflake and antlers, frozen and brutal. Water and ice. My mother and father. The past and the...whatever we were now.

The waiting clawed at every decent part of me. I could already feel my sister's absence like a delay in a performance.

She was always late, floating at the last minute with her

radiant smile and perfectly measured elegance.

And I—

I was the storm that rolled in after her calm.

Gentle clicks echoed from the top of the stairs as Libby finally emerged. Her ruffled gown, in stark contrast to my dark attire, was yet another element, as to why she would be our perfect queen.

Our contrast in personality, looks, and the actual desire to rule were different enough.

She smiled as sweetly as ever, descending the stairs with measured grace to meet me at the entry of the ballroom. I greeted her with an exaggerated sigh.

Her gown sparkled with its jewels, stunning gold accents, and the complimentary jewelry that made her look regal yet youthful, in a very *Libby* way.

"You look so beautiful every time we do this. At least give me a heads up next time."

I brushed off some flecks on my skirt and joined her side, leaving the couch, the pins, and family portrait behind me.

The portrait of our *new* family, painted a year after Mother died, when our Father remarried Erie, a typical Northern Royal with no personality. But not my true family. Never again.

My father was seated in the center of the painting, stiff as ever. Libby was next to him, her smile as bright as her future. Me, close to her, off-centered, unbalanced. Our stepmother, Erie cradled baby Taroh on her lap when he was still a newborn.

I'd forgotten how long I sat for that painting. How long I was forced to sit before a painter and accept that my mother would never be in a family portrait.

Libby kissed my cheek, then quickly smudged off the lip paint.

"Me? You look like an evil princess—talk about looks that could kill."

She smiled cheekily.

I narrowed my black lined eyes and gave her a fierce look. "Let's hope the gentlemen think so."

She linked my arm and guided me down the next set of stairs. "If you were really *that* keen on scaring suitors away, you shouldn't have worn such a beautiful gown."

"Because you gave me so many options?" I narrowed my eyes at her.

However, I'd tried to wear the dress with pride, for her sake, if not mine.

I flicked the giant bow around my waist. "My personality would do just fine to repel the royals away."

Libby laughed her falsetto laugh, tilting her head back, her light, hazel eyes hiding behind her smile.

We reached the front of the doors, where two servants stood, waiting with our crowns on decadent pillows.

Libby's crown was larger than mine, as she was older. *Thank Heavens for that.* I tried it on once and didn't last longer than two minutes without ripping the tight combs off my scalp.

My own crown, another perfect fit to my personality, was a quaint little gold band adorned with three small prongs at the front, each embedded with a centered ruby, making them look almost like flames. I truly loved it.

Libby, with her tiny scrunched nose, perfectly full lips, and light sandy skin, shone brighter than the row of diamonds icing the top of the five prongs on her crown.

"Princess Libra."

The servant bowed to Libby after fitting her with her crown and left. Mine did the same.

"Princess Fiadh."

I sighed.

"Just Fia will do, Marily, how many times do we need to do this?" I joked with the expressionless woman, but she just nodded and left.

We waited before the towering iron doors, two stories high, metallic, heavy and intimidating for no particular reason. They loomed like silent sentinels. Guardians, separating the rich princesses from the rest of the North.

Even if it was installed after the marriage of my father to my mother, it still felt ancient to me.

It was still painful to look at, mainly for where my eyes drew to the center, where a circular crest embedded into the iron.

Subtle waves unfurled from the crests edges. Centered

in the circle were the subtle etchings that looked like a snowflake, but with jagged edges. Edges that mimicked antlers more than the ends of a snowflake.

The pain I felt from its looming presence was the way it symbolized my mother and father. My mother, because of her water powers—my father because of the ice in his veins.

I sneered at the barricade. Old and dark, ever since Mother's presence departed, along with all the light from the kingdom—and from our family.

"You know—" Libby whispered. "There is always a chance that one of these days you might just meet someone—" her ridiculous words shook me from my thoughts.

I clamped my eyes shut and held up my hand. "Libby, please. If I entertain these notions, Father will never let me go into the Warrior Guard. I'm not meant to marry and rule. He and I are lucky to have you because I can actually have a life I might actually enjoy. *Without all these ridiculous parties,*" I mumbled on.

She turned to me. "Oh Fia, you're too young to be so stuck on one path for your life. I thought similar things at your age, and if you just—"

"Not now," I scoffed.

Despite only being two years older than me, she always felt infinitely wiser. Or, at least, acted like it.

She might have been wiser, but her timing was as bad as her confrontations.

The guards from inside started to open the doors,

splitting the crest in half, filtering in the light from the ballroom and boom of the guard announcing us.

The door opened to groups of familiar faces parting in the center of the ballroom for us. My stomach turned in discomfort every time I entered a room full of people who'd never spared a genuine smile my way since my mother died. I might have groaned a little out of reflex, but kept my head high and my back painfully straight, acting like the crown on my head didn't bury into me like everyone's expectations.

Father and his wife, Erie, sat at the other end of the ballroom in their thrones upon a platform a step above the floor.

Two smaller thrones awaited us at the feet of Father's throne.

We bowed before walking in tandem through the hundreds of familiar faces to get to our seats.

Our little brother Taroh was already fidgeting in his giant chair next to his mother.

He turned six last week, and I was thankful for this stage in his life since it took a lot of Father's attention away from me. The less Father paid attention to me, the more likely I was to be on his good side—the more likely I was to get out of this palace sooner than later.

Polished, limestone brick lined the room, up to the curve of the domed ceiling. Yet I always felt confined in this room. Though I was only ever here for events or ballet lessons.

Even with the giant windows, boisterous chandeliers,

and sea of glittering gowns, it would always feel dark. Wrong. Most of the palace felt wrong without my mother. Even now.

"Do you think that handsome dancer from Pasirfi will come back for your hand?" I asked Libby from the corner of my mouth.

Southern Royals didn't usually attend Biannuals in the North. Some of that was due to the many cultural and political differences. Still, when they did make their rare appearance, it always left quite an impression—or rang some alarm bells.

Libby smiled sincerely to each person on her side of the ballroom.

My side of the crowd only offered me little nods at the slight tilt of my mouth. It was the most I could muster for what I hoped would be my last year of Biannuals.

Father and I had agreed if I could get through this year, he would finally approve my admittance to the Warrior Guard. He'd already pushed it back a year and I couldn't wait another, now that I had nothing to do post-Academy.

Children attended school at Academy starting at the age of five until they turned nineteen. In the final two years of Academy, students could choose one of five areas of study in which to specialize.

Warriorship wasn't popular in the North—just twelve of us in my cohort, and most never planned to join the Guard anyway.

But I had.

For years.

I eyed a few of Libby's friends near the front of the throne. I offered them a teasing, sarcastic smile.

They didn't return the sentiment.

They were her friends after all, not mine.

Instead, they scoffed and continued talking, most likely about me.

Our cousin Rosette was amongst them. I wouldn't call her a friend. Not anymore. Once upon a time perhaps, but she had grown into a real Northern Royal since we were kids.

If her stuck up nose wasn't evidence enough, her decadent blush-pink ball gown and giant diamond jewelry certainly were. As was the line of tiny jewels lining her eyelids.

Because diamonds on our clothes and accessories weren't enough—Northerners also needed jewels stuck to our skin.

"I'm not sure. I did like him..." Libby spoke through her smiling teeth, not moving her lips. "I haven't had the best luck the past few Biannuals."

I huffed a laugh.

That was how she saw it.

She had many suitors each Biannual, many had made it all the way to the proposal matches, but her poor decision-making always got in the way of her *actually* choosing someone.

I couldn't blame her though, men from the North were either ridiculously pompous, or related to us, or both.

Many did ask for our hands, mainly for political

purposes. Smaller, poorer kingdoms grew more desperate each year, it seemed.

We reached the end of the aisle and turned once more to the crowd to bow once more before taking our seats.

I glanced at my sister from the side of my eye. "Maybe that's because you're too nice to every boy that talks to you. Maybe this time *you* should go find one, instead of pitying the fools who have the ego to approach you."

Erie offered Libby a sweet smile before the speaker started.

Erie had shifted her focus away from me after many arguments and now devoted most of her attention to the future Queen Libby–and Taroh–making my life a little easier when it came to her.

"I hear he has a younger brother if you're interested," Libby whispered as the speaker of the kingdom began his usual monologue before them.

"You know what?" I turned, whispering harshly at Libby. "I am interested—*very* interested in which of the brothers I can make cry first."

Libby coughed to stifle a laugh as I straightened, pretending to pay attention.

"*As accustomed on this night, suitors of equal upbringing may show themselves worthy of the kindgom's heirs and their attention. We give our heirs the right to choose, the right to live, and the right to love those...*"

Libby and I mouthed the last words together, mocking

his almost singing voice. *"Who are suited by the Fates first, duty second, and love at last."*

He cleared his throat as I slumped into my seat, prepared to endure the rest of the decree I had memorized.

"For only the royal or warrior may present a hand to the heirs of the kingdom. But beware, if the King accepts the initial request, his test for his child's hand won't be easy to bear. So strap on the courage, show us your strengths, and move on with haste, until a final choice to last is made after the matches, by the Well."

I lazily clapped first to move things along. I could feel Fathers eyes on me, but I shrugged it off.

I had to sit through this twice a year—two events at home, and countless others across the continent—but he continued to act like I wouldn't do my best to hurry through it.

The same routine unfolded at every one of these dances. Suitors swarmed Libby while I found some other way to keep myself occupied.

Everyone wanted a Northern Royal in a marriage. But it was the ultimate dream to have someone like Libby carry an heir. To be able to parade her around like some prized trophy was a universal desire to men of all ages.

Over the years, my suitors grew scarcer the more easily I rejected them. Several brave souls approached, but the rare man I actually spoke to became easily frustrated at my ability to only talk about war, recent conflicts, and fighting until he realized I knew more than he did.

Then he'd quickly retreat to find a woman with lesser knowledge to impress.

I took pride in the growing lack of interest from boys over the years. My perpetually annoyed expression–thanks to my protruding lower lip and dark brows creating a face that seemed to rest in anger–were usually enough to make them second guess an approach.

Fortunately, my stepmother stopped trying to make me smile when she accepted that my passion was to be a warrior, not a wife.

I'd convinced my family the past several years that I wanted to be a warrior to the queen, defending our kingdom, the crown.

But the truth was simpler. I wanted to matter. I wanted to be seen, not for my tiara or clothes, but for strength, grit, purpose. I wanted the choice of who I'd become.

The line in front of Libby continued to grow, weaving through the set up of round, wooden tables. The overtly shiny marble floor squeaked and clicked with every shift of a heel.

I stood and turned toward the small crowd cowering in the corner, probably debating whether to approach me or not. A glare from me seemed warning enough.

I walked over to the table of drinks along the entire wall horizontally to the wall of windows.

The servants that were stationed at the ends of the narrow wooden table began to grab me a cup, but I quickly shook them off. They never gave me enough to drink.

I finished pouring the last scoop of wine, lifting it to take a sip.

"You still think you can handle your wine?"

A cocky tenor voice sounded from my left, making me almost instantly roll my eyes. I sipped the chalice for courage before I turned to him.

His dirty blonde, somewhat red hair was as unkempt as mine. His pale blue tunic sat uncomfortably beneath his folded arms.

He leaned against the table, keeping a safe distance, probably in remembrance of the last Biannual, when I punched him for taking my drink from me.

"*Jayce*. Of course you're here. I must have gotten my hopes up when I didn't see you on my birthday." I sipped the wine again, thankful I was nineteen now, of age to drink at parties without too many prying eyes questioning my choices.

"You can't get rid of me that easily."

Jayce perched an arm on my shoulder–something that he was only tall enough to do a couple years ago.

I rolled my eyes and pushed away from him to walk anywhere else but there. He jumped in front of me but didn't touch me—something he must have also learned from last time. "Fifi, darling, don't be so cold," he joked.

"Jayce, let's not repeat what happened last time."

I tried to step out of his path, but he matched my footing. I was not that fast in a dress.

"That's all in the past, Fifi. I can't lose you. I've yet to meet another lady who hates these parties as much as I do."

Jayce was...*kind of* a friend. He was actually one of my only friends, if I was honest. But that was all we were. Though we played this game every time before a few drinks brought us to our friendly selves again.

"How many have you had already?" I waved my hand in front of my nose to waft away the sour smell of the wine from his breath. "About two less from the last time we kissed."

"The *only* time we kissed."

"Semantics."

He waved a hand.

The kiss was a dare. A result of a moment of weakness and too much wine at my eighteenth birthday.

I supposed Jayce might have been viewed as handsome—by others—but I had always known him more as a brother than anything else.

He was my only companion at Biannuals, and during Academy. Growing up, we were practically joined at the hip until these past few years when he became more irritating and *royal* and I grew less tolerant of it all.

Perhaps I was a little too known for drunkenly kissing random boys at Biannuals the past few years, but most of those incidents stemmed from bets Jayce and I made—or from my ever growing desire to make Libby's stuck-up friends jealous.

They weren't my finest moments, but angering the Northern Royals was always a favorite pastime of mine. Only once or twice did I truly kiss a boy because I actually wanted to. I wasn't the romantic Libby was.

We walked away from the table, and I ignored Libby's pleading look for help, shooting her a thumbs-up instead.

I turned to Jayce, flashing a conniving smile.

"So...how many more glasses before I can convince you to dance for my sister again and make an ass out of yourself?" I hummed, swirled my goblet in front of him.

He rubbed his chin, pretending to ponder. "Maybe just a little sippy-sip."

His goofy smile made an appearance. As much as I hated showing any real enjoyment in a room of royals, Jayce had just the right level of ridiculousness to draw a chuckle from me at such inopportune moments.

I handed him my chalice, which he drained, ending with a smack of his lips.

"Ah. Now. Are you thinking something jolly, or—" He set down the cup, grabbed my hand, and pulled me by the waist into a dancing position. "...a waltz?"

His eyebrow shot up playfully while his eyes swept over me.

I knew how to dance; I'd been forced to learn despite my ever-stiff, awkward shoulders.

I rolled my eyes and stepped on his foot just hard enough to hurt him a little.

After wriggling free of his position, I returned my cup to my hand. Glancing over Jayce's shoulder, I noticed them—a group of warriors seated at a table near the door at the far end of the ballroom. I'd heard their laughter right before I'd seen them.

Even from this far, I could see them clear as day.

Many wore some versions of their fighting gear: shiny chains as vests, leather waistbands, corsets, and personalized metal shoulders that gleamed in the candlelight provided by the three giant crystal chandeliers above us.

I wanted my own shoulder protection...

They looked so cutthroat, yet relaxed–effortless in their confidence.

The other half of the group wore more palace-appropriate garments–decorated coats or tunics with patterns and colors that represented their kingdoms.

Except for one man, who had just enough clothing to keep him decent. Only a thin, leather vest on his back, showcasing massive, bronzed arms and a matching chest with a giant tattoo wrapping around his neck, exposed for all to see.

They were impossible to miss–tall, wide, and hairy. Many of them stood a head or more taller than even me. It was rare to see so many warriors at a Biannual, at least in this large a group. Usually I'd spot a pair or two that weren't there for business with my father, but that was the extent of it. I'd only ever seen one actually ask for a royal hand at a Biannual.

"Want to go see the Warriors?" I beamed to Jayce who was now shifting his weight to his unhurt foot.

Baby.

He grimaced. "Warriors are for our protection, not

dinner conversation."

My eyes started to strain at how often I rolled them around him. Many in the kingdom treated the warriors with respect, but maintained a firm separation between warriors and royals.

My father had many brave warrior advisors he was close to. The few I'd seen growing up were the reason I wanted to become a warrior. Though they rarely actually appeared in palaces, I had heard plenty about them.

I was raised seeing many male warriors, but the few women always looked stunningly lethal. Their rarity made them even more fascinating.

My eyes gravitated to a set of stunning crystal-blue eyes. A warrior that sat in the middle of the group. The group of warriors stood around him, blocking him from view. But when my eyes slid to his, I realized he was looking right at me.

Slicing through the veil of my composure, his gaze shone through a few tendrils of tussled, midnight black hair brushing the bottom of his temples—somehow perfectly imperfect.

He was as scruffy as most of the warriors, but the way he sat, and the slight trim to his shaded beard made him look more put together. He appeared far too handsome to blend in with some of the other warriors around him.

I couldn't look away.

Before I realized how long I was staring, my feet detached from my mind and began walking towards him.

I approached the group of half-drunken warriors, leaving Jayce behind to find another girl to annoy.

The group was composed of six men and two women, who quickly noted my presence the second I stepped into the group.

I smiled as sincerely as my mouth would allow, causing the group to fall silent.

Warriors didn't waste time at these parties, but over the past year, they'd been showing up more and more.

There wasn't anything I didn't like about them, about who I wanted to be.

They were brutal but honest and did their jobs so well that not many cared to correct them. Instead, people threw them dirty glances when they got too loud at parties.

"*Ah*, look what we have here—the wannabe warrior princess."

Reluctantly, I looked away from those impossibly blue eyes that grew more stunning and a little more silver the closer I got. I looked away from his slightly sun-kissed skin and subtle scruff that sharpened the sharp lines of his jaw.

Instead, I fixed my gaze at the giant, tan man closest to me. A slight beard stuck out from his strong jaw, and longer brown hair tangled in a knot over his head, away from the giant tattoo that looked more like a collar sitting in his neck and chest.

The man waved a goblet towards me, slurring his words.

"It's a pleasure."

I tried to maintain my royal smile.

It was hard not to wear a permanent sneer at these parties, but I made an effort to keep my attitude in check–*this last time.*

"On behalf of the kingdom, I want to thank you all for your service and —"

I couldn't finish the usual formal warrior greeting before one of the women interrupted. Her blunt, short auburn hair marked her as being from Kivo.

"Save your breath, Princess. We don't need all your required greetings. We're just here for the beer!"

She thrust her drink into the air with her thick, muscled arm and the rest of the group followed suit, cheering loudly enough to draw too much attention to us. I raised my goblet slightly to join them.

Just for a moment, I wanted to feel like one of them–a warrior. It gave me the smallest opening–a glimpse into the life I'd always dreamed of.

Camaraderie.

Loyalty.

Friendship.

My face relaxed with the drop of my shoulders. "I thought I would try to draw some wisdom out of you all since I'll be joining the Warrior Guard next year."

I'd be twenty by then. Older than most of the new recruits, but not as old for some female recruits.

The youngest someone can join is fifteen, but that was for the men, eighteen for women. I was supposed to go this year, but plans around Libby's *almost* engagement last year changed those plans.

A few of them snickered at me like I was still ten years old asking to go to the battlegrounds.

"Little Princess, the Warrior Guard isn't for the faint of heart—"

I tried to keep my patience. Warriors were allowed to be assholes with everything they went through.

So, I smiled tightly.

"I'm aware. I haven't been preparing all my life for nothing." I sneered at the drunken man, whose beard I hardly reached.

He guffawed before throwing up his hand. "Feisty as you may be, Princess, you need a little more to be a warrior."

I fought the urge to roll my eyes again. "How hard can it be if I can hold my liquor?" I muttered.

The other woman, with shorter blonder hair and a thick scar above her lip chuckled, "Can't argue there, *Princess*." She clinked her glass with mine, and I allowed myself a slight smirk.

I had always hated being called *Princess*, even if it was my technical title. Mother always shrugged off her title too, like it wasn't the most suitable title for her. The older I got, the more I hated my formality too. It wasn't the word, it was the way it was always said that gnawed at my irritation.

"How—" I cleared my throat and raised my chin, hoping to mask my nervousness. "How is the field nowadays?"

They muttered amongst themselves, presumably not wanting to give many details.

But I'd always been nosy, especially when I discovered how much of a threat creatures had become in recent years.

I found it fascinating, but no one talked about it—not in Academy at least. Even after I chose the warrior specialty.

I still didn't know if the silence surrounding the creatures was a result of a lack of knowledge, or fear of the subject overall.

But that didn't stop me from asking.

I never stopped asking, even when I received the same vague answers—*They're terrible—you'll never imagine—such evil things—you'd be lucky to never see one in your life.*

But I wanted to know.

I wanted to fight.

I wanted to feel what it would be like to kill something so evil. I wanted to do something that mattered, for once.

"Princess," a soft, husky voice crackled through the swarm of people. "The creatures are coming from places we'd never expect. We need our armies to grow, so we appreciate your desire to join the forces."

Wavy stone-black hair peeked out from beside the two women as the source of the voice rose to his feet. The same man with the blue eyes.

He was a warrior, still wearing most of his armor,

minus some bulkier pieces others wear on the job.

I had all the warrior gear practically memorized and if my seamstress—or Libby—had ever taught me their sewing skills, I would've made my own by now.

Sincere, calming eyes met mine as the man reached full height, towering over me. The group fell silent again, parting to make way for him.

He stood before me, and I could finally take in his full, powerful form. His eyes had already struck me, soft and approachable. But now, his stature and armored strength made him the most intimidating of them all.

His hair was pushed back in a way that made me wonder how often he ran his fingers through it. Even with a short, stubbled beard, he appeared almost regal.

His full lips peaked into a whisper of a smile. A smile that wasn't really sincere—one he didn't look like he used often.

I almost stepped back, overwhelmed by the quiet authority he seemed to place on the rest of the group.

"Th-Thank you," I stammered, struggling to keep my head high. I had to look at him—I wouldn't let myself falter— but grounding my gaze into his felt like I was standing in the path of a winding storm.

His eyes carried a weight that could make anyone cower in fear. Yet, a mountain of fascination held me rooted in place, unable to look away.

Heat crept into my cheeks as I realized we'd been staring at each other for too long.

Again.

The spell broke when a group of boys walked past, deliberately boisterous, laughing and chatting. I caught sight of one of them—Prince Ptolem from Vanda.

Ptolem shook his short brown hair before he glared at me. I recalled our last encounter and didn't bother hiding my annoyance. Being the royal-class jerk he was, he always asked for Libby's hand whenever he deemed himself worthy to appear at our kingdom.

His family wished more than anything that *they* were the grandest in the North, so naturally they wanted their boys tied to us.

He scanned me with a sneer and scoffed, whispering something to his friends. His attempts to embarrass me never went unnoticed—he made sure of that.

"Hey, weren't you the guy who threw up at his Biannual from crying too much?" I said loud enough for half of the room to hear.

He was an ass and deserved the punch to the stomach I gave him last year. Yes, I was in trouble for months, starved for a week as punishment, but I didn't regret it for a second.

The words hit their mark. His pale face flushed red, spreading over his freckled nose.

He took a few steps towards me, leaving his ridiculous posse of cousins behind. I turned to face him, but not before handing my goblet to the first giant man who had spoken to me.

I clenched my fist, ready to attack as I took a step towards him too. But his goons pulled his arm to leave, and I was sure his mother was sending him a scolding look somewhere in the distance.

I smirked and waved at him before returning to my goblet–now empty. My glare snapped to the giant man, who pretended to examine the goblet as if its empty contents were a mystery to him too.

The drunken woman from earlier threw her arm around my shoulder, her grip so strong it nearly sent me to the floor. "What are you doing making fun of little boys?"

The drunk man burped, and I caught a whiff of his alcohol-laced breath.

"Trust me, he deserved it," I said, sarcasm misting to hide my irritation.

The giant man's drunk laugh returned. "Well, sweetheart, if your father ever does allow you to join us, I will *personally* train you myself. Perhaps you have more in you than it appears."

He raised his mug for a cheer, but the rest of the group didn't return and instead watched him awkwardly.

I smirked in confusion.

"*If* my father allows? What do you mean?"

I wouldn't have given the phrase a second thought if it weren't for the sudden shift in atmosphere. The warriors around us avoided my gaze. All but that same pair of crystal-blue eyes I was reluctantly drawn to.

Those eyes locked onto mine, brows lowering into a stricter expression. If I had to guess, I'd assume he somehow outranked most of the warriors here.

It shifted his entire posture into something lethal, the kind of presence that could instill fear after fascination.

"Your father...he spoke to the warriors a few weeks ago —"

"Yes." I interrupted. "He attended an emergency update," *but he didn't tell me anything*.

"He seemed to have implied—" The man hesitated, shifting from one foot to the other looking almost...nervous?

Still, when he spoke, his voice carried an unexpected eloquence. His strong tone softened into something smooth, but it halted suddenly.

The crowd around us began parting. I felt it more than I saw it. The murmurs of those stepping aside grew louder, but my confused, defiant stare fixated on the man's clenched jaw and averted eyes.

That was when I felt my father's presence approaching.

"Warriors. Welcome."

His gravelly voice rang through the entire ballroom. He didn't need to speak too loud to be heard—his natural rumble always commanded silence.

A true king.

I winced as I felt him draw closer, his coldness sending shivers down my spine.

Somehow he always seemed to know when I was about

to get into trouble.

"Thank you for keeping my daughter entertained with all your war stories I'm sure she's asked you all too much about." His hand rested firmly on my shoulder.

"Father—" I began, turning towards him.

I wanted to speak, to ask, to beg for him to tell them they were wrong. That maybe they meant something else. Anything else.

But when I caught his eyes–those sharp daggers sent me a clear message to keep my mouth shut.

I was usually a coward in his presence, especially in public. Privately, I didn't mind challenging him–pushing him to his snapping point–at least a little bit.

Most times, it resulted with a simple beating, but I had become an expert at sensing when he was on the verge of snapping. I knew when to draw back and when to push further.

"Father," I tried again, my tone as patient as I could muster.

He turned his entire body to face me in a swift, deliberate move. The gesture alone silenced half the room.

It was answer enough, but I still couldn't stop hearing the gentle crackling I knew too well–the sound of his power.

That ice that–if I looked down at his fingers–I would see as a faint white tint creeping across his fingertips.

Father rarely threatened his powers at me, only when he *really* wanted me to understand the gravity of the consequences there would be.

For now, I would yield to the King in front of all his subjects. I had no real choice.

Family unity was a pedestal we were forced to uphold, and one I had grown afraid to challenge in public.

It had been easier when we were younger—when we were a real family. But once Mother had died and Father stopped looking at us the same way, everything changed.

He changed.

Irreversibly.

As his powers retreated, I had already turned to find my throne again, unable to say goodbye to the warriors.

Unable to do anything but obey, I slowly walked away, ignoring the chatter around me. I tried to shoulder off the embarrassment as I clenched my fists at my side.

It wasn't a true Biannual if I wasn't publicly scolded at least once.

This was still mild. The worst Biannual I ever experienced was when he backhanded me so hard for fighting one of the Krav princesses that I fell to the ground. Yet, I was forced to sit and endure a line of suitors, staring at the red mark on my face.

I glanced back at my father once more, but my gaze was intercepted by those crystal eyes again. I couldn't quite decipher the expression on his face. I'd never seen a man look at me with such...pity, perhaps?

His gaze quickly returned to Father as he spoke to the group.

The warriors stood at attention. No more leaning, no more smiles or relaxed postures—just pure obedience. I sat stiffly, watching them.

I was already on thin ice, needing Father to sign off on my papers to join the Warrior Guard. I'd been trying to be as good as I could be towards the man to win some favor.

As hard as it was, this was me behaving my best. I needed him in a good mood when the time came for him to stamp his approval on my submission papers.

Watching the warriors interact with my father wasn't all that different from my own exchanges with him. He had to see it—how so much of our interactions mirrored his with the warriors.

He had to realize how perfectly I would fit in.

How I was made for this.

How much easier his life would be if he didn't have me to deal with anymore.

It was perfect.

It was so close I could reach out and touch it.

TWO

Libby's beautiful smile wavered on the edge of concern as she met my eyes.

"Is everything all right?"

I felt weak. Confused under her stare, but tried to muster half a smile back.

"Fine. Talk about it later."

She sweetly nodded and refocused her attention on the gentlemen before her.

A few poor souls stumbled before me.

I hadn't noticed when the first boy started speaking. He looked too young to even be here. His mouth moved, but all I heard was *if*.

If my father allows... if... *if?*

If—if—if—

"Princess?"

I snapped out of my thoughts.

A nervous boy before me—barely a teenager—asked.

"Yes?" I replied, my tone sharper than I intended.

"Yes?" The boy's face lit up with excitement. "Could I ask for your hand?"

I hadn't registered his words as my attention drifted past him to where my father still spoke to the warriors.

My gaze slid to those blue eyes again that spared me one more glance.

"Sure," I muttered, despite being distracted.

The boy straightened up, puffing out his chest as he strutted out of my view.

Whatever.

I probably should have paid more attention. The poor boy had no idea what he was even asking. His parents clearly didn't know enough about me and had forced him into it.

Once a boy's request was approved, he became an official suitor. From there, the king of that kingdom gave the final approval to move to the proposal matches which happened every summer for us.

Not that I ever cared.

Not that I ever approved of a suitor.

Until now, apparently.

My eyes searched the group for the blue-eyed warrior.

I caught him, noticing him stepping away from the others with a stealthy grace, watching me while slipping away from my father's side.

I straightened up instinctively, leaning forward as he neared. The movement caused the next suitor in line to take a step back. Speaking to one boy brought a rush of others.

Not that I even noticed.

I couldn't have cared less.

The warrior stepped before my throne with purpose and power. We looked at each other for far too long.

I should have looked away. I'd never stared at a stranger for this long–not in this way, at least. Maybe in an attempt to threaten someone, but not whatever this was.

It just felt like there was something to look for in his eyes. I wasn't sure what it was, but I could have sworn I felt him looking for something in mine too.

He stepped before the suitor at the front of my line, towering over the boy.

Before he could interject, the warrior shot him a single glare. The poor lad whimpered away in seconds.

The warrior hesitantly dropped on one knee, as warriors customarily did when they approached a throne. I leaned forward.

"Rise, please," I responded.

He complied, quickly glancing over his shoulder to check on my father, who was still engrossed in conversation with the others.

The man turned back to me and took another step closer, lowering his voice.

My body leaned even closer, gripping the arms of the throne. I was practically off of my seat.

His breath was careful, but it was his eyes that captured

me. "Princess, if you share an interest in the happenings of the Warriors, perhaps I could offer you some assistance."

My hands tightened over carved wood as my head gently nodded.

He glanced over his shoulder again. Father was beginning to turn around.

My heart thudded in my chest. I couldn't comprehend why this interaction felt too fleeting, but my hands began to sweat as I feared it's end.

He whispered sternly, his serious, focused gaze returning. "I will be in your kingdom for the next few days. I often hunt in the forest at dawn."

Dawn?

What was wrong with this man?

I could only nod as I bathed the weight of his words.

"Tell me your name," I rushed, my voice breathy as my father glided towards us, completely at his mercy.

Maybe I shouldn't have been considering actually meeting with a strange man in private, but my head kept nodding against its own accord.

The King loomed behind him like a monumental shadow, stealing more light from the room than someone should.

The warrior tensed in his presence, halting conversation. His mouth shut before either of us could say anything more.

"I don't believe my eyes," Father's voice rumbled.

His dark, velvet robe dragged behind him like a trail of blood as he approached his throne.

I leaned back into my chair as I watched him, joining the eyes of the rest of the room.

The warrior knelt to him too, remaining until my father released him.

"Do my eyes deceive me, or is this brave Warrior truly asking for my Fia's hand?"

My face heated as Father's proclamation carried through the room, too loud for my liking.

This—so-called—shocking news apparently *had* to be broadcasted.

Father held his chin high.

"Father…" I whispered away from prying ears, trying to stop this spectacle. But the soldier's husky voice overpowered my attempt.

"Yes, your Highness," the warrior responded firmly.

My eyes shot to the man, but his gaze stayed locked on the King.

Why?

What was this intense gaze the two of them shared?

Father watched the man. His face portrayed no emotion as he slightly turned his stubbled chin toward me.

"And does the Princess accept this man's request?"

The question might have been directed my way. But it didn't feel like I was really being asked anything. As though someone else should have been answering instead of me. The shift in the air was unlike anything I'd experienced at a Biannual before.

I didn't know what was happening.

My acceptance was one small step for a suitor—admittance to the matches. That was all. It wasn't that big of a deal. Yet, something in the air tightened the muscles in my neck.

I scanned Father's gray eyes. No anger. No pleasure.

I'd grown used to his little expressions—an eyebrow perk, a lip twitch. Small movements were all he wore in public. Those I could read. *Somewhat.* This expression had me lost.

I didn't know what to say.

I didn't even know what to think as my lips parted.

"Yes?"

A moment of silence from everyone in the room grew so heavy and tentative that I instantly regretted my answer. A suffocating silence, as if I'd just ordered this man to be beheaded.

Father gazed back at the crowd to deliver a single nod. Like a snap of a finger, the room resumed their banter.

The warrior disappeared before I could take another breath or get his name or even process what just occurred.

My eyes darted towards the exit, catching a glimpse of him leaving, the rest of the warriors trailing behind.

What just happened?

I glanced towards my father, desperate for a clue to what he was thinking—what he was feeling. But he had mastered that careful, unreadable expression.

He didn't bother meeting my gaze. He probably wouldn't for the rest of the evening.

My stomach twisted into solid knots as my eyes continued to search for even a flicker of acknowledgement, something from someone to tell me I hadn't just made the worst mistake of my life. The silence I felt moments before still clung to me, choking every thought down.

The weight of fleeting sideway glances was heavy on my shoulders. Their unspoken judgment was expected, yet deeply unsettling.

Maybe this was some sick joke I wasn't aware of.

Father must have known me well enough to know I didn't truly mean it.

He had to know that.

Yet my chest tightened all the same, like I had unwittingly set an irreversible ploy in motion.

But that wasn't true. This could be reversed.

When a royal accepted a suitor's hand, it only allowed them a comfortable passage to the matches, where a suitor competed, only to permit them to the Well. Up until that point a suitor could be rejected.

Only after the Well decided a pair, was it irreversible. Because that was a decision of the Fates.

At least that was how it worked in my kingdom.

Libby had rejected her fair share of suitors. Many of them long before the matches. She'd done so twice at the Well.

Twice, she had gotten as far as taking a suitor to the Well, where the water would turn one of three colors to determine its blessing. If the Well didn't turn black for the final stage, then the Fates didn't bless the union.

Some might have rejected the Fates and continued with the marriage anyways. But not for Libby. Libby had never challenged the Fates.

Despite agreeing to the suitors before, she didn't go through with the engagement—the two engagements she actually said yes to. When the Well didn't bless it, she happily obliged with its decision.

My breath grew shallow under the scrutiny of the room. My nails scratched against the smooth wood of my chair as I fought to steady myself.

There was a feeling I couldn't shake—a heavy, gnawing that told me this decision carried more weight than it should. That the stakes were higher this time—that, somehow, this decision carried more leverage than I expected and I couldn't explain why.

I didn't look at Libby or her line of remaining suitors. However, my gaze briefly caught Jayce's as he hesitantly stepped forward. His unsteady movements betrayed just how tipsy he really was. Tipsy enough to cause a ridiculous scene, no doubt. I widened my eyes and shook my head ever so slightly, a silent warning for him not to approach.

He flashed his teeth in an awkward smile and pretended to dance as he jerked away from the thrones.

I suppressed any visible reaction as he circled back around and rejoined Libby's line.

I waited, tense and still, for the music to swell again and for the crowd to shift their attention elsewhere—to anything other than this unexpected spectacle I had made of myself.

By the end of the party, we stood by the palace doors to bid our guests farewell. A custom I never cared for, mostly because I didn't know, or particularly like, half the people who attended these Biannuals.

I only managed a smile after Erie nudged me—one of a hundred times that night—reminding me to keep up appearances. Since that was the only real purpose I had for attending these events.

Father escaped to his chambers before I could manage to speak with him, and no one was allowed in his private chambers after this hour. Not even his wife, unless summoned.

I sat at my vanity, combing through my hair after my shower. My thoughts wandered, restless and chaotic, as I stared at my reflection in the mirror.

No matter how hard I tried to distract myself, one sound from the evening refused to leave me—the gasps that had echoed through the ballroom.

Were people surprised that someone actually asked for

my hand, or that I had said yes?

I couldn't stand how much those in my kingdom judged everyone else. Their whispered opinions, their unspoken criticisms, their sharp, scrutinizing eyes—it all grated on me. The only thing I hated more was how much I let it bother me.

Most of my days, I wore my indifference as armor. The way I was convinced all royals did. But in the still of the night, when I was alone, my mind betrayed me. It wandered into places I didn't want to let it go, filling me with questions I didn't want to ask.

As I wiped the traces of black paint from my eyes, I wondered what my life might have been like if I were more like Libby.

I was usually a main topic of conversation during these events, as newcomers came and asked about my beautiful regal sister and found much to criticize about me and my *un-northern-like* ways. It was pretty well known that I had desired to be a warrior since I was young. But that didn't stop the rumors swirling that I only wanted that because my father couldn't marry me off to someone.

This, of course, still sparked relentless attempts from other families to sway me and Father to marry me off anyways. To anyone.

Through it all, I wore my desire for warriorship like a badge of honor. I preferred that identity, and I preferred how quickly it made the swellheaded dismiss me.

Libby wore her badges just as proudly. Intelligence.

Beauty. Kindness.

My family only needed one royal to carry the family name—that was enough.

As far as my family was concerned, they had two.

I wasn't the first female royal to desire to join the warriors, but I was the first female direct descendant of such a powerful king to do so.

In the meantime, I spent far too many parties pestering guards to take me on patrols.

That was the only taste of being a warrior I got besides the few nights I disguised myself and ran out into the town. A few bar brawls later, the thirst for fighting only grew.

Libby had already made her place on my bed when I exited my shower chambers.

"My finding of the night—"

Libby beamed as she held out a dangling earring pinched between her fingers.

It was a large, decorative piece. A thick gold disk with jangling pieces at the bottom. An ugly thing neither of us would ever wear, or desire to wear. But that wasn't the game. The game was to get the most extravagant trinket of the night.

"And who did you steal that from?"

Her jaw dropped. "Don't call it stealing. It's...misplacing."

I arched a brow at her.

"Some Daeroman prince," she shrugged in a scoff. "He had too much jewelry."

I chuckled as I grabbed the thing that took up half my palm.

"The men *do* like to be more decorated than their women nowadays."

I brought the monstrosity over to my vanity, opening the drawer that contained most of my trinkets.

"Unfortunately, I was a little too preoccupied to play, so I guess you win. *Again...*" I mumbled under my breath.

I turned back to see her smile all too knowingly. My eyes narrowed on her.

"Which suitor has you looking like that?"

I joined her on the bed, crossed my legs while hers dangled off the bed from excitement.

She sat up and raised her eyebrows at me. "You know who..."

I eyed her odd giddiness, expecting her answer.

"The warrior!"

The warrior?

Wait—was he asking for her hand instead of mine?

"He seems perfect for you!" she squealed.

I quickly rolled off the bed and walked back to the bathroom. "Stop it. You don't even know the man."

I grabbed my hair tie and brought it for her to braid my hair for me.

She grabbed the tie and patted the bed. I complied as she rose to her knees and began to braid.

"What are you talking about? You haven't said yes to a suitor in years and in one night you said yes to two?"

"Two?" I flinched.

"Yes. Him and the younger lad from Krav."

I'd already forgotten about him. "I was just...distracted. I didn't know what I was saying."

I recounted to her a vivid play by play of the conversation with the soldiers as she tied off one braid and started the second.

"I don't know what he meant by *if*," I sighed. "But I'm kind of freaked."

She hummed while she thought.

Libby was my best friend. I knew that people looked at us and assumed we were enemies because we were so different, but we had always been each other's person, as much as our own.

"I wouldn't think too much about it until you speak with Father."

"I doubt I'll get a chance to even cross paths with him. If I do, he might just tell me to steer clear and not listen to dirty soldiers..."

"Why were they even here?"

I tilted my head. I hadn't even considered that.

"What if they were here to speak with Father, to discuss some business? Or threaten him? You don't know who his enemies might be. Some warriors have whispered revolution against the royals in the past few years."

Her finger pulled strands of hair tighter into the braid.

"I doubt they would go through the trouble of coming here just to see Father during a Biannual."

"Wouldn't they? Maybe to...make Father mad, or tell him bad news?"

She paused her braiding, then continued, "Or do something more infuriating, like..." I waited. "Offering to marry his daughter."

I sat up straighter, pulling my hair out of her grip as I faced her.

"Right. Because the only way someone would marry the lesser sister would be because of political unrest."

Her face hardened. "Stop it! You are not lesser and how dare you think that was what I meant?"

I rolled my eyes despite the little pang of guilt at my outburst. She would never think that, but I would.

I knew the influence of royalty and beauty in our world. A fact she benefited from and often forgot.

I loved my sister to the grave, but at times I wished I didn't have to be associated with her. It wasn't the easiest, always being around someone so beautiful.

But I didn't think I was *that* unsightly.

I did have my mother's eyes, but I supposed any ordinary girl would see how lesser she was standing next to Libby.

"I didn't mean to insinuate anything, I just want you to be careful...you don't know this man."

I sometimes hated how kind she was when I got upset. At least I could count on her to calm me, almost instantly.

"I know. It's fine."

Though she was his biggest fan two minutes ago.

She scooted closer. "No, it's not. Please forgive me." Her kind eyes blinked down at me.

My shoulders dropped. I nodded.

"Now. If he *doesn't* have any other intentions then I think you'd make a great pair. He looks very strong and quite handsome."

I bit back my smile.

"He isn't too bad to look at...but I doubt he was serious."

I wasn't sure why but I didn't tell her about his conversation with me at the throne. She wouldn't have heard it over her conversation over her suitors. I hadn't considered his proposition to meet too seriously. So there was no point in telling her and giving her the chance to talk me out of it.

But I couldn't stop thinking about it. If Father continued to refuse talking to me, curiosity would eat me alive. *This* man had information I wanted.

"Would you marry him just because he's handsome?" Libby asked.

"No—I don't care about that...*much*. I just...noticed."

She tugged my hair playfully, finishing off the second braid. "I wonder what the Well will say."

Nothing.

The Well only informed those fated to be together and those who should never be. Most of the time it gave permission for people to choose. It was a ridiculous custom at this point, but Libby truly believed it. The Well was one of the final five Sigils left from the Fates in our world.

The Sigils were gifted to our world by the Fates, each with its own special purpose. Only three Sigils were said to still exist. There wasn't enough information taught on them to know what they all were—if they all even existed.

We were lucky enough to have one in the North, on our palace grounds, tucked far away inland.

Some believed it was placed there and that there was a force that pulled the people from other ends of the continent to start a life here.

Some believed the Well appeared here after my family established it.

And some believed the Fates put the Sigils as a curse. That one day the people would fight against each other to take its powers for themselves.

No one knew much about their history, and if anyone wanted to truly know, they would be stuck in archives for hours, if not days without a clear answer.

I never cared or had no time for such things.

Libby continued to discuss her night with the suitors while I considered what I was going to do tonight.

Was I to risk meeting a strange man, alone in the woods somewhere? I couldn't deny that Libby's words made somewhat of a dent in my perception of the man.

I didn't even know the man's name.

Our kingdom was quite the target because of its size and wealth. I couldn't even roam the streets of my own kingdom's towns because we were too powerful for anybody to not want to take a pass at us.

Or was I to leave this all behind me—explain to Father I would never actually marry and to formally reject the man? I fell asleep thinking about all the ways my life could potentially change after tonight, and how much I hated the lack of control I had over it.

THREE

I wasted the entire next day trying to find Father.

Erie was nowhere to be found either, and Taroh was off at Academy. Young children had ridiculously long hours in Academy here in the North.

I missed him.

Libby, I'd gotten used to her absences after her graduation. She was always busy with events or parties or royal duties. But Taroh used to always be here when I was and now that he wasn't. There was no one else I wanted to see.

I didn't meet the warrior at dawn.

But not only because I slept in.

When I finally woke up and looked out my window, I stared at the plain beyond the limestone gate. The plain that blended into an emerald forest of tall, pointed trees. It was the secret window I often escaped out of.

But when dawn came and I looked out onto the void, something didn't sit right with me.

I wouldn't call it fear, per say, but I couldn't get myself to look past the birds flocking my windowsill.

I couldn't leave.

Maybe Libby's words dug deeper than intended, or maybe I'd be risking too much to get out on my own, with no one's knowledge. I decided I'd rather face my father in his home first, before running into a forest to meet someone who definitely had skills to kill me, if he suddenly felt inclined to.

If he did have bad intentions, it would leave me exposed since I couldn't take any guards with me. Father would find out if I did.

However, I couldn't wait until the proposal matches to see this man again either.

I had to know more.

Hopefully Father would be more informative, and I wouldn't have to risk my life out in the woods.

But I didn't find Father until dinner.

Even at dinner, he brushed off everything I tried to ask. I was stubborn, but I knew when he would act on his anger and I wouldn't risk ruining the little bit of peace between us. I'd been given enough backhands to learn what would set him off.

I wasn't too angry yet, since he didn't confirm that he forbade me from entering the Warrior Guard.

Though he didn't deny it either.

He just vaguely pointed to the fact that *time will tell*. That was one of those vague phrases he used to tell us when we were children to get us to stop asking questions.

His dismissal irritated me enough that the queasy feeling of uncertainty was too much for me to live another day with.

I'll go.

I'd take precautions, but I'd do it. I would go see the warrior and pray to all Fates that this little rendezvous wouldn't lead to my death, or worse–that my father wouldn't catch me.

I knew if I left my window open a bird would fly in at dawn. My saving grace in remembering to wake up early were the birds pecking on my window in the mornings.

A few years ago I had discovered the birds would fly in if the window was open.

I learned that the hard way when I broke my window after tying a rope to a beam and swinging from it.

It shattered on impact, along with my knee. The window was broken for weeks, and birds flew in every single morning at dawn, right on schedule, reminding me of my carelessness. I started to hate birds when they woke me every morning before the sun.

There were only two birds today. At times I've had nearly ten hopping around my room. Their nests were scattered throughout the tall tree outside my window. The tree I usually sneaked out of my room from.

I already had on the underclothes for my daily trekking gear, which had been made for me at the beginning of my two years in my warrior specialty. It was a decent uniform, though we didn't actually spend much time outside.

On top of my fleece one-piece were some common clothes I'd bought myself on a secret trip out into the town. Royal clothes were too obvious—bright and heavy and tailored, so these were my only saving grace.

My wide, dark green pants wrapped around my waist. I slipped on a short, brown leather corset over the gray sleeves of my fleece, topping all of it with my dark overcoat.

Two holstered daggers rested on a belt over my waist. Daggers I couldn't use too well, but were enough of a weapon if needed.

I perched up on the window and looked for the loose brick a few feet down. I hadn't gotten caught sneaking out this way. It had been a couple years since I had discovered this escape route.

It was one of my only secrets from my family, including my sister.

My foot found the notch, and I reached for another little hole below my window.

I only needed to climb down several feet before the tree branch from the giant white oak under my window expanded close enough for me to grab.

It was about a floor down from the tree branch, but I had learned my lesson too many times to not jump down ever again and just climb the entire way down.

Small buds dotted the tips of the tree branches. Now that winter was ending, spring was on the cusp.

The sun hadn't peaked into the gray sky yet, but the lighter shade was starting to tease at its approach. Dimmed illumination guided my path towards the hills.

I only had to pass the two guards stationed at the front gate. At night, I could slip out with the servants, but in the mornings it was harder.

The guards wouldn't necessarily stop me from going just past the gates. I was outside often enough, taking my horse to the lake, running along the forest line. But on the off-chance they felt like my actions were off, and they wanted to alert Father of my whereabouts, I didn't want him to send a guard with me only to learn I was meeting up with a man. Not just a man—a suitor.

I really didn't want to get his hopes up about me marrying and shutting my dreams down.

My cloak kept me hidden in the dim light. Maintaining some stealth, I crouched low as I walked along the palace walls, reaching the corner where the bricks seemed loose enough for me to climb and slip past the gates.

Beyond the gate lay sprawling hills on the other side of the gate that spanned for a sliver before the ever-ending forest seemed to swallow up the rest of the world.

After a few attempts, I found a decent spot to scale the wall. My grip faltered as I climbed down the other end, falling a little sooner than I planned—but I shook it off, ignoring the faint sting.

I jogged into the fields, crouching until I reached taller grass. I walked a few minutes before the edge of the forest came into view.

Almost half an hour later, I drew one of my daggers when the cold and hollowed silence pressed in around me.

Unnerved, I kept it gripped at my side—the sapphire blue dagger, a Yuletide gift from Libby last year.

Warrior lessons at Academy only taught me a few basic stances with swords—rarely practiced. Daggers should be easier to handle, and I didn't want to risk being caught off guard by a rabid dog or a creature.

The scent of the forest greeted me, wood and wet grass, but a faint hint of burnt wood teased my senses. I stilled for a moment, scanning the surroundings for any signs of fire.

Perhaps the warrior had set up camp nearby. Though it would have been odd to camp near a palace. In hindsight, he should have clarified a location, but there hadn't been time for that.

I kept trudging deeper into the forest. Amongst the branches I started kicking along the ground, a small winter ferret curiously peeked its head up from behind the root of a nearby tree. I smiled at the critter. They were definitely the cutest animals in the kingdom.

I even had one as a pet my eighth year in Academy after I'd found it wandering outside during recess.

Some boys had been teasing it, so I kicked the boys where I knew it would really hurt, then snatched the creature up and hid it in my sack for several days, feeding and caring for it in between classes.

But those same boys, Ptolem among them, found out the same girl that embarrassed them was fond of the critter.

They killed my ferret during a lunch break and nailed his body to my desk. I was sent home the rest of the week for my *reaction*.

Since then, I was quite the expert of the tactics of northern boys, and I never regretted making those enemies.

I took a step towards the critter, wondering if this one might have been as friendly as some of the others. Its pure white fur looked impossibly lush and soft against the iced-kissed grass riddled with tree branches and roots.

The ground here was a mixture of mud and short grass, yet the ferret was impeccably clean. It wiggled a few steps from me before it turned around and hopped the other way. I followed.

It stopped every few steps and glanced at me, as if it waited for me to follow.

Its little body waddled behind another giant tree and I crouched to peek around, closer to ground level.

A small crack of a sound came from the trees. I froze in my tracks, fearing what larger animal might be around. I took a slow, steady step around the tree the ferret had disappeared behind.

My eyes shot wide open when I saw a black arrow pinning down its now-dead body. Its pure fur began growing a red ring around the center of the arrow. Its immobile body staring up at me.

My palm found the tree and I looked up to find a figure a few trees away from me and the ferret. I froze as my eyes focused on two figures instead of one.

Two people.

One stood stoically, bow in hand, positioned from shooting the arrow a second ago. Another figure sat on a log in front of a small boiling caldron with rocks underneath a slab of wood.

The smell of burnt wood thickened in the air, yet I saw no fire. The two appeared like phantoms, materializing out of nowhere. We all stood frozen from the moment, studying each other.

The figure closest to me was a woman. Armed. A bow resting in her hand. Standing in a stance I'd expect a warrior would.

She was a warrior. But not exactly. She wasn't fully dressed in the standard warrior's garb.

She looked worn, like she'd been out here for weeks. Her coat was dirty, frayed at the edges, and underneath it, a tattered shirt clung to her boney frame. Yet her waistband appeared to be made of a military-grade leather. Along with the strap across her chest—her quiver.

Her bow looked too precise, a particular design carved into it that hinted at her origin from some far-off region I couldn't decipher. The man beside the fire looked just as worn down, just as filthy.

The air between us swelled with unspoken questions. But as baffled as I might have been, I wouldn't let it show. As much as I hated killing innocent animals, I didn't need potential comrades to see me frightened at the sight of a dying critter, no matter how sudden and sad.

"Warriors, welcome."

My voice was steady, despite the aching in my chest.

The two warriors exchanged glances.

"No need to bow—" I interjected, cutting through the silence. It was custom for warriors to initially bow to royals, but something told me formalities weren't necessary right now. I also wasn't dressed as a royal.

I cleared the lump in my throat. "Proceed with what you were doing."

I took a slight step back, trying to figure out what exactly two warriors were doing out here, so close to the palace without many supplies.

The woman had black hair, cut in the messiest way possible, like edges were burned off in areas around her face.

She walked towards me, a glint of amusement flickering in her eyes. There was a chuckle teasing her face, directed at me. She threw the laugh over to her counterpart, who mirrored her expression.

I took another step back, giving the woman space as she neared the ferret.

With a perfected motion, she pulled it from the earth, along with her arrow.

She turned without a word, heading back to the fire where something was cooking though the flames remained invisible.

The sun had risen slightly higher, making their skin more visible, dirtier. The man stood up and grabbed a knife from near the fire.

He was going to—

Oh no.

He pulled the skewered ferret off the arrow then backed towards the fire.

He began to skin the carcass. I looked away.

It was normal to hunt while on assignment, although I didn't know what assignment a warrior might have possibly had so far from the borderlands, looking so…unprepared. And alone.

I looked at the woman while he skinned the carcass. "Is —" I didn't know if I had the right to ask, but my curiosity took over my reasoning. "Is there an assignment for warriors this far from the borders?"

They exchanged another silent glance. "It's a different kind of assignment." His eyes pinned me as he spoke to me. "*Princess.*"

The way his eyes scanned me itched at my skin. It was enough of an alarm that made all of this feel too deliberate. It hit me like a blow to the gut.

I swallowed hard, feeling as though my silence was giving away more than I'd wanted. There wasn't a possibility that they would know I would be here.

Was there?

They couldn't have known about this...

Whatever was happening, I knew I couldn't be alone with them.

The man threw the skin aside and placed the ferret onto the grill. The snap of the sizzle sent a jolt of heat down my spine. I felt that sizzle shoot down my spine. It felt too real, too irksome. I started to turn.

"Say—Princess."

I froze but didn't change my stature as I glanced back over my shoulder at him. "What are *you* doing wandering out here all on your own?" His gaze locked on mine. The woman gripped her bow in her hand, her eyes fixated on me too.

"I am not wandering. I hunt in the morning sometimes–" I lied, ignoring the quickening of my pulse. These weren't warriors I had seen at the Biannual. They seemed... unprepared. Which could have meant that these warriors were...inactive?

"How long is this assignment you're on?"

My voice rose slightly, as I tried to back away without being noticed. My hand began slowly creeping toward the dagger at my waist. My head was spinning, the uncomfortable possibility gnawing at me like a sharp ache. A feeling I didn't want to explore, but couldn't ignore.

Was the warrior from the Biannual involved with them? Had his invitation been a trap all along? My chest tightened as the questions flooded through me. Was he truly a warrior with a vendetta against the North? And if so, what did that mean for me? Kidnapping? Execution?

Whatever it was, I wasn't going to wait around and find out.

My head snapped back, scanning the trees for a clear path. I steadied my stance, muscles coiled back, ready to spring into motion. I couldn't fight them—not both. The woman was my height but broader, stronger, even through her visible bones.

One of them would already be a challenge. Two? Impossible. I had no chance of winning a fight. But maybe... maybe I could manage a distraction. Just enough to get away.

The man raised his hands, flashing his palms to me, trying to look harmless. But the air suddenly felt thinner, muting the sounds around me. Even the birds above us had gone silent. My entire body braced, every nerve screaming to run.

"No problem here," he said, his voice calm but unnervingly sharp, the edge of a blade. "I've just always been curious as to whether the princesses were as...*knowledgeable* about the King's tactics as some people assume they are."

I squinted.

"Tactics?"

It wasn't the best time to interrogate for my own benefit, but apparently I was easily goaded.

"You know—" He took a step forward. I, one step back. "With all the unrest the other kingdoms suffer...You would *have* to be aware."

Unease prickled at my chest, mingling with my growing caution. I kept my distance, step for step.

"Because of the creatures?" I asked, my voice betraying my uncertainty. I hated how unsure I sounded, but I needed answers. That was why I was here, wasn't it? It didn't matter who they came from. I'd ask my questions and run.

The woman scoffed from behind him, stepping forward to join his side. "Is that what *he* tells you?" she bit through her teeth. The trees seemed closer now, their branches curling inward, closing off my path. Even the earth beneath my feet felt restless, groaning faintly as if warning me to flee.

My fingers slowly wrapped around the hilt of my dagger. The air grew heavy, my lungs straining against the weight of it.

"I wonder," she mused, her voice biting and calculating, "if we held the little princess for ransom, would big, royal daddy actually listen to reason?"

Her words froze me, but only for a second. I didn't know exactly what was happening, but the ground beneath me seemed to scream in unison with my instincts, pushing only two words through me: *run* and *now*.

My feet shifted before my brain could process the man lunging at me.

FOUR

An eruption of screeches echoed from birds up ahead, shooting into every direction. I sprinted beneath them, my heart as frantic as their wings.

I raced to retrace my path, trying to head back towards the palace–or anywhere my feet could take me.

I made the mistake of glancing back, when a sharp snap captured my attention. The man had tripped, his body tumbling over something I luckily avoided. Relief couldn't register before the woman ran into view.

Her bow gripped tightly in her unwavering grasp. She halved the distance between us when I ducked as an arrow whistled past my ear, so close it might have grazed my breath.

There wasn't a second of relief.

She was already re-loading her bow.

My legs started to burn. The earth was hot below my feet when I veered sharply from my course.

My feet were trapped in a pool of sweat, but the fire in my lungs was what threatened to take me down. Every breath an arrow through my ribs.

The end of the tree line broke.

The faint silhouette of the palace's peak loomed in the distance. So close yet so impossibly far. It would take too long to run to it.

I wouldn't last that long, but I couldn't stop now.

I couldn't believe any of this was happening.

A scream howled from the forest behind me, raw and sharp. Hers.

I kept my gaze on the promise of my palace. I vaulted over a massive root, my body ducked when I landed, to avoid a low-hanging branch. I turned again, desperate to carve a path that could buy me a few seconds.

Then—

I slammed into something solid.

The force knocked me to the ground in a tangle of limbs. The impact rattled my bones. I rolled a few feet before hearing the grunts of someone else.

A body had fallen with me.

My breath came in sharp, hurried gasps as I squirmed away from the other body, equally as impacted by the fall.

I scrambled away, dirt and leaves clinging to my palms. My eyes darted frantically when I realized—I'd lost my dagger.

Before I could react, the male warrior rose from his cough attack on the ground.

I reached for the spare dagger at my waist, but only managed to grip the hilt when the woman's shoulder crashed into my stomach out of nowhere and I was plowed into the ground once again.

Pain exploded through my gut as she pinned me to the ground. My back hit the muddy earth with such force that the air fled my lungs, leaving me choking in stunned silence.

Then something pressed against my throat. My hands flew up instantly, trying to push the curved bow off my neck.

After little relief, one of my hands started jerking around, trying to grab my dagger.

Panic surged, but my hands worked instinctively— desperately. One hand clawed at her bow, straining to shove it away from my neck, the other abandoned its search and swatted to scratch her face.

She was faster, flinching away. The only mark I left on her was a slight scratch to her neck.

Her unsettling smile brought the panicked realization that I was about to die, and the annoyed horror that this would be the last vision I had on this earth.

Her face hovered over mine. Her evil smile carved into her face. Her unnerving eyes—I didn't notice them before, but as my last sight, all I could see was the shade of her eyes. A tint of white painted over the color beneath.

Her body pressed all its weight onto the bow, blurring the edges of my vision of everything but her sharp face. I only prayed that this attempt was only to render me unconscious instead of kill me.

But that didn't stop me from squirming my entire body

in hopes to find even a second of relief, bruising my palms as much as my neck.

But blinks slowed as the bow grew heavier. Air was a distant memory drowned beneath the crushing weight on my throat—until she was ripped away. Until something pulled her off of me with a quickening force.

My lungs seized the instant opportunity to suck in a breath as deep and desperate as I was.

Her body flew off and slammed against a tree with a sickening snap. I forced my eyes open and only looked through my cloudy vision for my next step.

I forced myself upright with a stumbling attempt to lean towards the palace. But my path was cut short.

Her accomplice stood before me and potential freedom. My shallow breath caught for a moment, but a fleeting second later, his eyes widened, fixed on something behind me.

Whatever it was, I hoped it was enough to distract him because I wasn't going to fight him. Not with my hands clutching my throat, my body screaming for air.

So I stepped to the side, ready to plunge back into the forest if need be, but my head turned into the direction the warrior was looking.

Then I stopped.

A tall figure stood several feet before me, his back to me, encased in gleaming metal catching the thin shein of sunlight streaming through the trees. His shoulders were broad, his dark, wavy hair tousled in the breeze. His stance was rigid, unyielding...familiar.

He raised his sword in a finalizing motion. Its tip aimed directly at the woman sprawled at the bottom of the tree. He was ready to plunge the blade into her, intent on finishing her.

Something caused him to stumble back—as if an invisible arm was pulling him away from the woman.

He staggered, momentarily off balance, snapping his head back. Then those familiar, piercing blue eyes flashed at me beneath his dark gaze.

Those same eyes I'd been so keen on seeing just hours ago—now burned with a darkness that made my stomach twist.

A raspy gasp fell from my lips as the tip of his sword shifted, pointing directly at me. As my heart fell out of my chest, his eyes narrowed and jerked to the warrior behind me. He began to close the gap, stepping towards the warrior, causing me to wobble away.

The two of them locked eyes before they charged at each other. They took their attention away from me, and I went back to forcing breath into my lungs.

If these two wanted to battle it out—I had no problem with that. They could kill each other for all I cared. I was getting out of here.

My knees hit the ground as the two men collided. The ground trembled beneath their clashes, colliding metal rang through the air. I scrambled out of the way, leaving the shouts and clangs behind.

Blood curdling cries sounded from one of the men—the

weaker, older warrior who was no physical match for the other.

I gripped my chest as I tried to get away. Clawing for a full breath while I clasped my free dagger. My lungs hadn't resumed their normal movements. My feet had only gotten heavier. I stumbled like a sack of potatoes weighed on my back.

The palace was in clear sight. My limbs were harder than chains, but I still ran. Or attempted to. Because stopping wasn't an option. Not when one of them could already be focusing their sights on me.

I tripped over a stump in the ground I must have missed. Not that I was really looking. But tripping at the treeline caused me to roll down the small hill dropping off from the tree line until I landed on all fours at the bottom.

Coughs and breaths escaped me, but no amount of oxygen would re-fill my lungs.

Desperation clawed out of me as I collapsed onto my side. My hand grabbed an exposed tree root next to me to hoist myself up. I gripped it like it was the only thing keeping my heart beating.

My eyes fluttered open, and I glanced back. Two figures fought at the top of the hill, swords swinging. Bodies lunging. The trees behind them seemed to sway in tandem with their movements, an eerie rhythm to the chaos. I convinced myself I was hallucinating—dying, maybe—as my breaths came in wheezes.

Through my haze I saw a figure fall, the other jammed

his sword into him. But between my rapid blinks and my pounding skull, I couldn't make out who was who.

Not that it mattered.

I had been killed, and there was no one in those woods I could trust. I was stupid for leaving the palace, and I was stupid for trusting a stranger. I was stupid for thinking my life could be anything else than what it was.

One blink later, the two silhouettes disappeared from the top of the hill. I didn't feel enough guilt at the relief that surged through me when I gasped my first full breath. I sucked in one more steadying breath before shakily pushing off the ground.

The cold air bit into my lungs, sharp, but healing. I sheathed my dagger back in my belt and scrubbed off some of the mud on my pants, tousling the bottom of my coat.

My fingers reached to touch my throat once more to confirm nothing was obstructing it. Breathing had never felt so good.

I was alive.

The world tilted. My head spun. But I was alive.

A group of birds clouded overhead, flocking over me. Their frantic wings drew my gaze upward. They brought them to a figure at the top of the hill. Standing at full height, sword in hand, his silhouette cut an imposing outline in the treeline. I could feel those crystal blue eyes glaring down at me.

He yelled something, but the wind muffled his words. Still, I wasn't going to risk getting attacked. Again.

My legs moved before my mind caught up, and I sprinted toward the palace. It felt miles away, and my feet weren't mine. They belonged to someone slow and heavy as they shuffled through the tall grass that just about reached my chest.

I dared to look back.

He'd already scaled the hill, closing the gap at a ridiculously alarming speed. He was probably ten steps from me.

A groan escaped me as pain flared in my thighs. I swung my arms wildly, in hopes that the movement would magically propel me faster.

The ground felt like it rumbled beneath me as he drew closer.

I couldn't outrun him. He was mere steps behind me. So if I couldn't run, I had to fight. That much, at least, I'd learned at the Academy.

I quickly twisted, throwing the dagger from my waist towards his stomach. Without waiting to see if it hit, I spun back and bolted.

Two steps.

I didn't even make it to three when the neck of my cloak yanked me backward. I turned to see my bloodless dagger lodged into the ground, pinning the garment to the ground.

I didn't waste time trying to free it.

I tore off my coat and let it fall.

Some balance remained in me as I tried to run again. I would cry for weeks for losing both of my daggers in one day. But if the alternative was staying alive, I was sure Libby would understand.

I needed to survive first, or make it close enough for palace guards to hear me scream.

I tripped over another bump and fell to my knees again. Fury and desperation bubbled into the little energy I had left. I yelled when I turned to throw a nearby rock at him, using whatever energy I had left to pray that it would hit him with enough force to incapacitate him.

It hit him in the chest and fell. I may as well have thrown a slipper at a wall.

Damn warrior gear.

His strides didn't falter as he closed the gap, his broad shoulders and metal armor making him look impossibly massive. My eyes fixated on his hands, so large they could snap my neck with a single twist.

I watched him come closer, growing larger and larger. I was trapped again, as helpless as that ferret. Soon, I would join it.

I pushed my body onto my elbows, crawling away from him, inch by inch...like that would do anything.

Logic had no place in life and death situations. I shook my head and shot my hand toward him, causing him to slow—slightly.

"Please don't kill me. *Please.* To be honest, my Father

wouldn't be that affected by my death," I blabbered desperately. "You have a better chance just taking a finger or a toe and asking for ransom."

It was probably what the warrior wanted.

This had to be about money. Or power. Clearly his kingdom was suffering—growing poorer. Or his leaders sent him to bring me back for ransom.

All of our history classes drilled it into us: the poorer a kingdom, the more desperate and vile its actions became—stealing, ransoming, plundering from neighbors.

He took another step to stand directly over me. "Or even an arm, if you're that desperate!" I blurted.

His face darkened, but I didn't give up yet. "We can work something out." I huffed out as I pressed on, crawling deeper into the tall grass.

Why did these warriors want me? Pirates and thugs targeting royalty for ransom were common enough, but this felt different—more serious, more political. Something darker.

To my shock, he actually halted in his tracks. I took a breath, thinking that I might have actually convinced him.

He shook his head, almost in disbelief before reaching down to grab me. If I couldn't convince him, at least I wouldn't go down without a fight.

I kicked him as hard as I could in the chest. He stumbled back, only a little, while I tried to get my feet back under me to run again.

As useless as it might have been, I had to try. I didn't

know his intentions and whether they'd changed or not. But the second I reached home, I would be sure to have him hanged for his crimes–whatever they were.

I nearly tripped again. All hope vanished when a strong grip closed around my bicep, yanking me toward him.

"How much more fight could you possibly have left in you?" he snarled through clenched teeth.

"You have no idea."

The words came out as more of a breathless whisper. I raised my arm to strike him—or grab him, or do anything remotely useful—but his grasp was stronger. My remaining strength was nothing against the sheer force of his hold.

He grabbed my flailing wrist, taking control of my entire arm. It didn't stop me from struggling in his firm grasp.

His nostrils flared in frustration, and I debated spitting in his face as a final encore. I'd love to spit in that strong, symmetrical face.

I could only breathe or move my head while locked in his embrace.

But before I could act, he wrapped my arms behind me, pinning me, leaving me fully at his mercy–vulnerable to be taken advantage of. Against my squirming, his grip tightened, pulling me closer until we were a whisper apart. I could see every detail of those deep, piercing eyes.

He didn't move.

He just held me.

It somehow calmed me. *It shouldn't have.* Maybe it was

the calm before the storm—peace before it all fell apart.

We breathed heavily as I suffocated in his arms. My chest rising and falling against his. Every attempt to struggle only caused him to lock his grip tighter until I couldn't move anywhere but closer to him.

He was a hand taller than me, glaring down with unbending will. A massive force I couldn't escape. Not a completely threatening force, right now, but a vast one.

A hint of a smirk appeared on his lips and suddenly the warmth of his breath brushed against mine. It felt...different.

A gentle, annoyed chuckle escaped him. "If you would stop for just a moment and listen—you would notice that I was trying to save your life, not end it."

"Excuse me?" I snapped. "I'm ambushed in a forest, you point a sword at me, you chase me down, you throw a dagger at me—" His face drew closer, stopping my words.

"You threw it first," he interrupted quietly, lowly. "Didn't you?"

I leered, trying to draw back an inch, but didn't make it far in this grip. So I stuck my chin up closer to him, defiantly, forcing him to slightly straighten.

"Of course I threw it first," I bit out. "I have a line of warriors apparently open to the idea of killing me. So do me a favor and just tell me what on earth it is you want from me."

He sighed.

"All right. I'm going to let you go. Promise me you won't throw another dagger at me?"

My eyes narrowed. I waited for a beat, but nodded curtly.

His strong grip loosened, and my arms slid free. His fingers lingered just long enough to make me hold my breath until we fully parted. With a short nod, he turned to retrieve the dagger I'd dropped, handing it to me, handle first.

I hesitated, keeping as much distance as possible between us, and grabbed only the tip of the handle before pulling it away from his hand.

He nodded in truce and took a step towards me. Without thinking, I lunged forward, pressing the tip of my blade beneath his scruffy chin, just shy of breaking the skin.

"Now, tell me *exactly* who you are and what you want from me."

He sighed as if I were a child butting into an adult conversation. "What did I *just* ask?"

I tightened my hold on the dagger. "You asked me not to throw my dagger. I didn't."

A low, unsettling chuckle rumbled from his lips. "You think you're clever, Warrior Princess?"

The mocking use of my dream title stirred something in me that it shouldn't have. The feeling pressed in my stomach.

No—not just the feeling. A dagger—my dagger.

"You dropped this earlier?"

I looked down.

He took the second of distraction I fell for and in one swift motion, leaned back and kicked the foot I had all my weight on

I fell again.

It didn't hurt as much as earlier. My hip took most of the impact, but I winced at the thud.

His body quickly pinned me in place, straddling me. Surprisingly, he didn't look too threatening from this angle.

I hated that.

The waves in his stone black hair framed his face like a wispy halo. That hint of a smirk returned, making me seriously consider spitting in his face.

He should be so lucky.

I would have, if he hadn't slid my own knife to the top of my neck. The tip pushing my chin up, angling it to look at him better.

"As a warrior, I'm trained to kill in many, *many* quick ways. One small jab..." He pressed into the pulsing vein in my aching neck. "...and the blood would be too quick to stop. You wouldn't have time to scream, or run. You'd be dead within a minute." His low voice was blood boiling, but something about his gaze was not...that frightening.

I clenched my jaw shut, keeping still as he studied me. Staring like he couldn't decide whether to do it or not. The uncertainty stung my eyes with tears.

A deep breath deepened my voice too. "What. Do. You. Want." Each word pushed my neck against the blade, daring him to act, because either I'd stopped caring or I'd stopped believing he would.

If he wanted to hurt me, he probably would have by now, if only to prove a point. Warriors were usually known for their cunning brutality, not drawn-out hesitation. If I didn't know any better, I'd say his surprised look was almost pleased at my outburst.

The cool steel slid to the base of my neck. "I want you to accept that if I wanted you dead, you wouldn't be breathing right now."

After a tense moment, his eyebrows perked up as a final *okay*? Then he stood and extended a hand.

I didn't accept as I scrambled up to my feet.

"Now..." He crossed his arms. "Please explain why you were so eager to listen to me a few nights ago, and now opt for murder?"

I clenched my teeth, refusing to hold back any response. As if I hadn't given him reason enough. "I don't need to explain myself to someone associated with those animals."

Animals was too kind of a description.

"Associated?" He sounded almost offended. "How is my killing them for trying to hurt you—*associated* with them?"

I sheathed my eye daggers and glanced at the hill again. It felt like hours ago, though it had been mere minutes.

"You...k-killed them." I confirmed. Testing the truth on my tongue. My hands clenched my coat and took another half step back. "Why? They're Warriors."

"Were," he corrected. His arms tensed, even through his gear. "Don't worry. It was quick."

My eyebrows shot up. "You think the speed of the killing is what's bothering me?"

"They weren't warriors anymore." His voice trailed off.

"They weren't active? Or were they discharged? How did you know they were here? Why were they here?" The questions tumbled out of me.

"If you'd like me to keep talking, perhaps we could find somewhere to sit and have a civil conversation?" He waved to an empty spot in the grass behind him where a few tree stumps resided. "Or do you still need proof that I mean you no harm?"

I stuck my chin out, regaining composure. "Your name," I demanded. "Tell me your name."

His arms relaxed slightly as he slightly bowed his head, but not enough to hide the color in his eyes.

"Kallias."

His eyes met mine again.

I waited. "Your full name," I demanded again.

"Let's sit first." He replied tightly, motioning to the tree stumps behind him, barely visible by the tall grass.

"Here is fine." I plopped down, bending the grass around me, ignoring how childish I might have looked.

I crossed my legs, setting one of my daggers on my thigh. I'd almost forgotten my carving tools in the pocket of my pants until one poked my leg.

"Ask the questions you really have first," he grunted as he sat his tall self down, the metal on his body creaking with his descent. He joined me on the ground, keeping a safe distance.

My mind raced. There were too many questions, and I had half an hour at most to return before breakfast to avoid any suspicions.

"Why did you want to meet me? I mean—why me? Why answer my questions, if that was indeed your intention? What questions do you think I have?"

He muttered, "Um—One at a time."

His alarmed expression eased some of my tension after what had just transpired.

He copied how I sat. Crossing his legs to mimic me, he finally answered, "The end goal is to make a deal with the King."

As impressive as this specimen seemed, he clearly wasn't the brightest if he thought to come to me for a favor with my father. That was foolish. Or perhaps...desperate. "You are the rumored Warrior Princess, are you not?"

I sat up a little straighter. "Yes," I responded quickly, accepting the title I'd always dreamed of. I craved it more, knowing it was potentially growing further from my reach.

He nodded stoically. "I thought so. Therefore, I assumed you would be more interested in news about the battles the Warriors have been facing. Those who want to become Warriors aren't faint-hearted and care about what happens to the people of the continent. The whole continent. Not just their Kingdom."

I shrugged. "Of course, everybody does."

He sighed. "I think everyone thinks they do. A lot has happened this past year that might suggest otherwise."

"Because of the creatures?"

Discomfort flickered across his face as he shifted in his seat. "Yes. Somewhat." He cleared his throat. "I can tell you the truth, Princess, if that's what you desire, but not everyone can handle the truth they think they seek."

I didn't even care what that meant. I just wanted answers. I started to nod but he cautioned me once more. "But I believe everyone deserves to know the truth."

"Tell me."

I prayed he wasn't manipulating me into some political scheme, because with those enchanting eyes and the gravity of this information...I feared I might fall for it anyway.

"The creatures are getting worse by the day, it seems. We've seen more attacks in the past few months than ever before. As if one dies and two take its place. Some are worse than you'd imagine. Others hide in trees or part of the earth. A warrior could be on a walk then the grass folds in over itself and tears him to shreds. They seem to be getting harder to kill too. Almost as if they learn our strategies and come back stronger. I don't know how it works. Most of our theories haven't panned out."

He looked so hurt, so frustrated—and yet so calm. I leaned in, wanting to understand what could reduce such a great warrior to this pained state. I wanted the weight in his gaze to dissipate.

"After a few months we started noticing a shift in the minds of some Warriors upon return from assignment. Many creatures are near the borderlands. Some kingdoms have cut off supplies to my kingdom since they need to go through the center, where most sightings have been."

From the whispers I'd heard, most of the effects on creatures were in the borderlands, near the South and the West.

"We've become the main source for many of our neighbors, but at this rate we'll only last ten years, maybe, until we run out of supplies for our neighboring kingdoms. We've already cut back. Our palace began taking in fewer goods and giving back to the people while we still can."

I didn't hide my shock.

Kingdoms never compromised in this fashion. Even in great wars of the past, the Capital Palaces always maintained their status. Something about *morale*. I couldn't imagine how desperate they'd become if their kingdom began rationing.

"Some of the Warriors...changed." His eyes locked onto mine, sending unease rippling throughout my body.

"I don't know how, or why, but even my closest comrades that fought the creatures hand to hand–they would return from an assignment and would be...thinking and acting differently. They confessed to hurting people, women. Some of them would make plans...terrible plans to take over kingdoms. They spoke of their desire to hurt children. Not just kill them, but–"

"Stop." My stomach churned. "I get it."

I grasped my dagger out of comfort. I needed to hold something. The sapphire on the pommel grounded me as I rubbed it with my thumb. He waited patiently for me to meet his eyes again.

"My kingdom and my Warriors have sent many inquiries to your King and have yet to hear an acceptable answer. That's why I came to the Biannual. We have to begin finding a path to get supplies in and keep the creatures out, otherwise it will be inevitable for our kingdoms to starve."

"My father wouldn't let that happen. He respects some of the Southern Kingdoms. My..." I almost didn't want to say it again. "My mother was from a Southern Kingdom."

The Northern disdain for the South was common knowledge, but I'd always thought it was more about pride than a true barrier to cooperation.

Kallias paused, watching me fidget with the grass at my feet, pulling out a few blades by the roots.

"I know," his low voice tried to comfort. Hearing someone else acknowledge her felt foreign.

I glanced at his face again, wondering which kingdom he was from. Vanda was known for taller people—taller than most Northerners—and they made up a mixture of the Southeast. Kallias was quite tall, but so were many of the Easterners. Where men were statuesque while the women were petite.

The southeastern and coastal cities possessed men

more tan, with longer hair from their work near the ocean. Northerners often looked down on them, though I wasn't sure how else they would get their intercontinental supplies.

Kallias didn't quite fit. His hair and beard weren't long enough for the coasts, though his skin held a faint sun-kissed hue, it wasn't permanent, just barely noticeable. Western coastal cities and the islands were home to people with much darker skin, and sometimes reddish-brown hair from the intermingling with other Westerners.

"I'm from the Southern kingdom, Lyen," he said proudly.

My eyes widened at his words, scanning them—confirming their truth. *Lyen was near Mother's kingdom.*

I almost smiled. *Almost.* Technically, now Mother's kingdom was merged and considered to be part of Costan. What once was a small kingdom along the water, was absorbed into Costan shortly after my mother married my father. Still, to ignore it completely felt like letting her go. Her memory. Her legacy.

"Why didn't you tell me sooner?"

I wondered how he'd look with slightly shorter, trimmed hair. His appearance did make him look how any warrior should, but I couldn't help but want to see the hair away from his eyes and strikingly perfect cheekbones, clean with no scruff.

"Was I supposed to say that before or after you threw the dagger at me?" He slightly smirked.

"No. Nothing like that. I just like to see if there are any similarities to my mother in your people." I kept looking at him.

"Your mother was a loved ruler, in all of the South."

I wished I knew more about her kingdom. I'd always planned to visit.

"How so?"

Father said I could visit when I was older, though I suspected it was his way of brushing me off and avoiding the topic. I could never talk about her around him.

I loved hearing about my mother.

"Did you ever meet her?"

Kallias's age was hard to place—he seemed wise beyond his years, but the youthfulness in his eyes gave me pause.

"Not personally, I heard a lot about the princess that brought life back to her land since the alliance with your kingdom brought us more opportunities, more than we'd ever dreamed of having. We gained more supplies, academics, and so on. If it weren't for her, we never would have grown so much as a kingdom."

Was that it? Was my incredibly brave and beautiful mother only known for her marriage?

"My brother spoke of her kindness and beauty more than anything."

Brother?

"He said even after her new residency in your kingdom, she would come at least once a year to be with the people—

meet with them, celebrate, and listen to their needs. She was a kind princess, an even kinder queen."

A faint smile escaped me. "Thank you." I whispered, unsure why I kept going. "No one talks about my mother anymore."

"I find that hard to believe. Lyen mourned for months after her passing."

I met his gaze, noting the warmth in his eyes. There was something familiar about them. "How did your brother know my mother? You never told me your full name."

As he opened his mouth to speak, the loud echo of a creak from the palace gates snapped my attention away. I quickly grabbed his arm. "Quiet. Follow me."

I pulled him deeper into the tall grass, crouching behind a tree.

"What are you hiding for?" He asked at normal volume.

"Shh!" I hissed. "It might be–somewhat–frowned upon for me to be running about the grounds without protection... *which I now understand*," I mumbled as I peeked over him to where the dead bodies probably now lay.

He brought his voice down to a whisper. "I'm sure running around to meet a man wouldn't be as enjoyable for your father to find out either."

I kept one eye on the gates. "I'm sure if I was caught with a man, my father might actually be pleased." I felt his gaze on me.

My face warmed instantly when I noticed how close we

were. "Um—I just meant, I don't have as many suitors as my sister, so any interest I show in a man is breaking news to my family."

"I saw many suitors approach you at the Biannual."

My eyes narrowed at him. He noticed the men that approached me? "I wouldn't call that many."

"You danced with a man."

My eyes moved into a roll. "We didn't dance. He annoyed me and I gave him a moment of attention. *I can't stand Jayce*," I finished with a mumble.

A merchant carriage pulled by a small dragon exited the gates, followed by a guard on horseback.

I winced at the snap of a whip against the dragon's leathery back. Its clipped wings jerked. I hated that we used dragons for merchant trips when horses did just fine.

Dragons were beautiful and rare. The smaller ones, slightly smaller than horses, were a little more popular in the North but didn't live very long and were subject to the same fate as this one.

"I have to follow the carriage," Kallias said, his breath grazing my ear.

I shivered at the sensation. "Why?"

"I need to confirm if shipments are being lost in the journey or if they're being diverted somewhere else."

I was still surprised he even answered me. I'd gotten too used to asking *why* and being ignored. I appreciated his honesty a bit too much.

"Will you be here tomorrow too?" I whispered, gripping his arm before he could stand.

His eyes searched mine for too long of a moment. I slightly feared he would leave without speaking to me again.

"Yes, I will be here, but perhaps you shouldn't come all the way to find me."

"I can handle myself," I said, looking away from his warm gaze.

His voice dropped into a teasing tone. "What did you handle? Nearly being strangled to death?"

I glared at him, all warmth evaporating.

He sighed again. "I could meet you closer to the palace gate. I noticed no one guarded it *there* this morning." He pointed to the end of the fence, nearest to the trees.

"They do every other day. Tomorrow *that* will be open," I said, pointing to the other corner of the gates, now closing after the carriage rolled out.

"You do this often?" he asked, almost impressed.

"Only when necessary."

I smirked, but quickly looked away when I caught him glancing at my lips.

"I will see you tomorrow then?"

I nodded, perhaps too eagerly.

"Wait. What about the..." I glanced toward the hill again.

"I'll deal with the bodies, Princess. Just stay out of trouble until tomorrow."

I scoffed. "Stop calling me that."

He looked at me once more before turning away.

"Then what *should* I call you?"

"Just call me Fia."

He rose to his feet and smirked at me once more. "Whatever you say, Princess."

I grunted at him.

He disappeared almost instantly up the hill towards the forest. He moved with an elegant strength. I couldn't imagine his gear was light, but he wore it with ease.

Just like that, my day was officially wasted from thinking about anything else but him.

No—not him. Just the information.

I didn't care about him. He was simply the only person who spoke to me about something important. I just needed to find out more. I wanted to hear about Mother, and I wanted him to be the one who told me.

FIVE

Father decided to grace us with his presence at dinner. My stepmother, Erie, spent the first part of dinner hounding him with questions about his frequent disappearances the past few weeks. I hadn't noticed, but I was *lucky* if we crossed paths more than twice a week.

We usually had at least one dinner together, but occasionally he'd be off on his convenient duties, and we'd be in Academy.

This year was a change. Libby had graduated from Academy two years ago, and I had finished a few months ago.

The reality of what came next hadn't kicked in yet. Technically, I was supposed to be starting Warrior Guard in three months, but Father hadn't signed my approval yet.

Erie complained while Father carefully chewed each bite of meat, little by little, focusing all his attention on his plate.

He was never in a rush, or very reactive, or nervous, and rarely looked anyone in the eye unless he had to. Unless he was threatening them.

I was always sure he liked Erie enough, but I was not sure how much she liked him. I wasn't sure how any could like him unless they had to.

Erie, on the other hand, was enough of a personality. They had started out as a good enough pair in the beginning. Now they just seemed like acquaintances who occasionally dined together and shared a child. Always civil though, which was something to note among royals. Apparently Father possessed the ability to be civil with others. Even only those he was sleeping with.

Taroh played with his food. I occasionally tossed a pea at him when no one was looking, making him burst into his infectious childish giggle.

I loved that, even if it only infected me. Father never cared for distractions, or noise, or anything to do with me, but that didn't stop me.

Much.

"Father," I began, working up the courage, hiding my trembling hands below the table. "When should we discuss my duties before I leave for the Warrior Guard?"
He silently chewed. Erie shot him an odd glance, but said nothing.

"Father?" I pressed again. Libby watched in such suspense that provided little to no comfort.

"Fia, we're not having this conversation right now." His tone was shaper, rubbing his brow in dismissal. He normally didn't show this much annoyance so early on in my pestering. I'd be lying if I said I wasn't a little scared.

"When *should* we have this conversation?"

My jaw clenched, but I kept biting the anger that was threatening to be released.

He huffed a stern sigh that stretched all the way to me at the end of the long table. "Let's forget about it until after the matches."

"After? That's months from now, I have to leave long before then."

"Fia, maybe this isn't the best year for this. Maybe you should wait to see how the proposals work out for you."

His white eyebrows creased against his square face. Objectively, he was old, but he looked stuck in time from the day my mother died. His wrinkles weren't deep. His smile lines disappeared, and he always looked a little younger than he actually was.

"Why are we pushing this back?" My voice strained. *We* haven't made a decision in years. *He* made them all. But right now, I needed some semblance of control, and that was the only hope I had to fool myself with.

"*Fia.*" Libby's gentle voice caressed over me along with her hand on mine. I released a little tension in my body, but my jaw remained locked, as sharp and immovable as stone. I sat back, waiting for his answer.

"Fia…" He hesitated.

My Father *hesitated*. I'd never seen my father hesitate.

"Fia," he said firmer. "You should strongly consider a suitor first, before settling for anything else."

Time stopped.

I sat frozen, a porcelain doll in a glass case, locked inside a bullpen all alone. Everything around me slowed to a crawl.

My father blinked.

My stepmother poked idly at a piece of food.

Taroh sat oblivious to the world around him. My heartbeat climbed into my throat, rising to hammer at the base of my skull.

I clawed, begging to release in a scream. But Libby's hand on me was the only tether to reality I had.

Because this didn't feel like reality. It couldn't be.

"Excuse me?" The words fell like gravel scraping from my mouth. "Settle?"

Time felt impossibly slow. I wasn't even in my own body anymore. I couldn't be. This had to be a dream I was a bystander of.

We were a painting: frozen, silent, unreal. My nails sliced into my palm as I clenched my fist to keep myself from screaming.

"Father," I forced out, "when have I *ever* led you to believe I would choose any other path for my life except becoming a Warrior? Never have I expressed this, have I? Never once during the last two years of Academy did I ever share an interest in anything else. So, please, tell me what I did to make you think otherwise?" I forced a sharp breath into my lungs, breathing for composure more than survival.

The room expanded in the deafening silence. The grand dining hall stretched infinitely, its space swallowing every sound. No silverware clinked, no footsteps sounded from the servants, not a whisper of a breath left anyone.

"Fia," Father said at last, "You do not understand what that life entails."

I couldn't take my eyes off of him. I couldn't think of which word to say, which curse to expel.

His voice lowered into a tone only he would consider soft. "We hoped that with time, you'd realize how dangerous these times are for Warriors."

We.

The word skittered across my skin. He knew there was no *we* in his kingdom or this palace. No partnership, no mutual agreements. Only him—and his decisions.

I wanted to bring change. To make a difference. To unite and protect the continent. Protect the kingdom. Protect my family—my brother and sister.

Never did I desire a life filled with parties with meaningless appearances. I wanted more. I had *always* wanted something else. And now, I needed to know why my father had let me believe in a future as a warrior for so long, only to crush it—in a day, in an hour, in a single, shattering moment I didn't know how to recover from.

"Most students abandon warriorship after Academy,"

he began in that maddeningly calm voice. "The horrors are too much. They settle in different royal roles. Roles in their palaces, kingdoms, even going past the continent. I expected you to change your mind before you graduated...but you didn't."

He sighed in irritation, as though it was my resolve that was the inconvenience. But I didn't. I didn't change my mind at all.

If anything, it fueled my desire to protect those during war. Those brutal lessons, sleepless nights I spent studying, the collection of scars I'd gathered during Academy—it built that desire to protect those who couldn't protect themselves. The powerless. The hopeless. Those trapped in their own torturous, inescapable realities.

Was Father so hungry with power that he couldn't fathom his daughter seeing how damaging those disgusting ambitions were?

Apparently it was unbelievable that a daughter of a Northerner was hungry for something besides the status, the money, the power. He couldn't fathom his daughter not buying into his disgusting desires to rule the entire continent.

I scoffed, a bitter disbelief pulsing through me. "I don't believe what I'm hearing." My grip on my composure was slipping. Fast.

"Who's we? Who the hell is the *we* that thought all of this?"

I didn't look at my stepmother, though I figured she

played a role. She was a traditionalist, a perfect, very stereotypical wife that expected all women to follow in her example. She probably wanted me to be right by their side, keeping the image of our family as squeaky clean and controlled as any other Northern family.

"We, as a family," Father said calmly. As if the phrase would pacify the thoughts bubbling in my blood.

The heat rose to the top of my head. If I'd been wearing my crown, it would've melted into my scalp by now. I searched to find Erie's light brown eyes, but her head was fixated downward.

Taroh's wide, confused expression mirrored the storm I felt inside, and for a fleeting moment, I envied him. His innocence, his ignorance—they were a gift at a time like this.

I tried not to—I told myself not to—but I carefully glanced over to Libby. Her head was also bowed. Her warm hand turned to ice over mine. It was her silence that crushed me more than anything Father had said.

I wondered if anyone would hear if the daggers in my spine were to fall to the ground.

"You can't be serious," I whispered, the words pulled out of me as a painful exhale.

Had my family—*my sister*—been humoring me for years? Were the dreams I'd poured everything into, nothing more than a joke to them?

"I've never been taken seriously. Have I? Not for one day in my life," I murmured to myself, the truth cutting deeper into my chest.

My life's purpose—my dedication, my hours, years, the near-death-experiences, my hopes were a joke.

My voice rose, trembling with unease, but booming in fury. "I can't believe this. How could you all think this? How could you not tell me?"

I shoved my chair back as I shot to my feet. I kept my clenched fists at my side, because if I got my hands on anyone I wouldn't let go until there was blood.

Every instinct screamed at me to do *something*, to make them listen. I fought it back, just barely.

Taroh's widened eyes met mine, so confused. Innocent and lost. For a moment, I considered grabbing him, whisking him away from all this—this terrible family. But there was nowhere to go. Nowhere that would make us feel less small.

"I worked tirelessly the past years to study, practice, and prepare myself for this. I'm mentally prepared—or preparing to be prepared. I started training my body." It was only a little, but it was something I was working towards. It was all I was working towards.

"I've talked to every warrior I've met . I've made lists of nearby stations to train at and work in so I wouldn't be far from home. It's the only thing I've thought about for *years*. This is my *life*."

This past year, my mind had been consumed with spending time with Libby and Taroh and training, with every waking thought devoted to the Warrior Guard. For the past thirteen years, I had lived and breathed the future I had worked so hard to build for myself–a world away from all of *this*.

When something encapsulates your mind so completely, so constantly, it becomes a part of you–body and soul. *That* was what my family was asking me to let go of. They wanted me to let go of *my soul*.

Libby slowly lifted her sad, big eyes to my flames. "Fia, please just listen. It's not what you think."

Her usual calming voice was fuel dripping into my fire.

She reached out her hand to touch my arm, but I jerked it away from her. Her face twisted, stunned. How dare she be surprised right now?

"How stupid do you think I am, Libby?" My voice croaked with the weight of my anger. "Because I'm younger? I'm not as smart as you so you think I won't have an opinion on this?"

Her shock deepened, but I didn't care.

"Fia...no. How could you—"

"How could I?" My voice rose, cutting her off. "How could you? Any of you—"

I was so close to breaking, I could feel the splintering in my control. I was ready to scream, I could feel it rising in my lungs. My emotions swirled in chaos, words I'd regret perched on the tip of my tongue, begging to escape.

I turned to my father, the source of all this betrayal. My breath caught in my throat as his booming voice shattered the silence, rattling the very walls of the dining room.

"Sit. Back. Down."

I froze.

If I were honest with myself, I'd been waiting for this moment. Waiting for years. A moment where I had nothing to lose. A moment where I no longer cared to stay on my father's good side. A moment I could truly challenge my father.

"No."

The word left my lips before I could stop it, trembling but defiant—for once. I took one more step away from the table before Father's body rose with a force that shook the very air around us. Not in a commanding way, not in a way that demanded respect—but in a way that should have sent me running in fear. His chair clattered to the floor behind him, echoing like a warning that rang through the palace.

"THAT'S AN ORDER!"

His voice was a crack of thunder, drowning out everything but the heartbeat roaring my ears. If time was slow before, now it was frozen.

My eyes locked on his, searching desperately for a way out. Anything—a lightning strike, an earthquake, a miracle, an aneurysm. I begged the universe for something, anything, to shatter this moment.

But nothing came.

I would not yield.

My gaze drifted to the window, catching the faint movement of a flock of birds in the distance. They flew through the shadowed forest, their silhouettes fading as the last light of day slipped away.

I could hear the birds in shadowed trees, faint and fleeting. The window's sliver of freedom was too small to leap through, even if I wanted to—but that didn't stop me from considering it. Shards of glass in my skin and a hard landing on gravel didn't sound much worse than this.

I would not yield.

Not this time.

Not when he'd laid all his cards on the table and I knew I had nothing left to lose. I'd take the beating. The starving. I'd take anything right now, but I would not yield.

A sharp, familiar crackle of frost interrupted my thoughts. It came from the window—at least that was where it started.

Slowly, it crept from its base, spreading unnaturally fast, its jagged edges splitting upward before crackling outward, frosting the walls.

Breathing was an afterthought. As was moving. As if my feet were unwilling to break from his command.

Time itself resisted me. I turned to face him.

My head turned so slowly, time resisting me as I met my fathers eyes. Ice coated those hazel, lifeless eyes.
I couldn't hide my fear.

He never used his powers on us. He'd flaunted them, put them on display to his rivals and allies alike, but never like this. Never towards us—towards me.

He wouldn't kill me.

Would he?

He'd beaten me before—plenty of times—but never enough to leave lasting damage. Not like his powers would.

Every muscle in my body became hyper-aware of the danger of my father. This was a side of him I'd only glimpsed before in small tastes of the monster beneath the man—but now, I was threatened with the entire feast. His dead eyes shot me one final warning.

I. Would. Not. Yield.

My foot shifted, fighting the tension, fighting time itself as it shifted. His hand twitched.

A sharp, cold pain grabbed my ankles in an icy grip of death. I inhaled sharply through my nose, refusing to give him the satisfaction of seeing my pain. Not pain from the cold or fear of losing a toe. I'd heard of what his powers had done to others—the whispers of the lives lost in its grip.

But the pain was from my father doing the one thing he had silently vowed never to do. He was using his powers to hurt me. His child.

Something inside me cracked, a deep, permanent fracture. This was no longer an argument between a father and child. This was a king threatening to eliminate a subject disobeying the royal order. A sovereign enforcing his will.

Nothing more. Nothing less.

The man who'd hurt me so many times over the past seven years had finally found a way to cut deeper than I thought possible.

Moving felt like wading through icy water. Slowly, painfully, I turned my head to my chair. Ice clung to my boots, splintering off chips with every shift of my feet as I forced myself to obey my father and return to my seat.

My hands shook as I reached for the table. One by one, I pried my fingers apart, biting back the pain from the ice teasing their tips.

My chest strained to rise with each cold breath. I felt every heavy gaze on me as I shakily sat back in my chair. The blood in my ears blocked out all sound around me as I bit back the tears burning in the back of my eyes. My palms stung as they flattened against the table's even colder surface.

I sat, rigid against the chilling chair, willing myself not to scream or cry or shiver.

Maybe someone spoke to me. Maybe they didn't. It didn't matter.

My eyes fixated on the table.

I would never look at this table the same way again. It had seen arguments, punishments, years of tension—but this... this was desecration.

My breaking heart twisted as I wondered what he would do if I froze to death.

Would they all just sit there? How quickly would they have quietly removed my frozen corpse and resumed their dinner.

I wished Mother was here.

Would she be saying the same things? I couldn't imagine her telling me to let go of my soul, to surrender my dreams. I couldn't imagine her standing by, watching this unfold–watching me lose my voice like this.

Then again, I hadn't thought Libby ever would have either.

Movement stirred at the edges of my vision. From the corner of my eye, I watched everyone return to their dinner. A servant scurried to bring Father his chair again. Someone's voice droned on into the void. Probably justifying their reasoning.

But I didn't listen.

I was still drowning, submerged in this choking silence.

But beneath me, that fire still burned, even more so now. I fought everything in me not to fly across this table and show my father just how much of a fighter I could be.

A servant reached for my plate, signifying dinner was over.

I bolted out of the room before anyone could stop me. I didn't turn to see if anyone followed.

My footsteps thundered through the halls, echoing into a cacophony of steps. I slammed my bedroom door shut with a rattling force. My chest heaved as I grabbed the edge of my massive dresser, pouring every ounce of strength and anger into dragging it across my room. It wasn't much of a barricade, but it would buy me a moment to breathe. To *feel*. Alone.

Gentle knocking wrapped on my door. Growing louder

and more frantic.

"Fia, open up. Please. Let's just talk."

Libby's muffled voice filtered through my barricade, her tone pleading, but I didn't stop moving.

I grabbed the first coat I saw in my closet. The familiar fabric was heavier than I remembered. It was one of mom's old coats. A velvet green cape—not really a coat, more of a covering. I rarely wore it, mostly because of Erie. She always looked at it a little too long whenever I wore it, as if my mother's spirit had woven itself into the threads and offended her by existing on me.

Libby kept knocking, louder and louder, pleading for me to open. But I had already pushed the window open and slipped my foot into the first notch below my window. Birds flitted around me, as if sensing my panic.

I climbed down faster than I ever had before. I remembered how I used to be afraid of falling. Now, there was one thing left to fear: being trapped in this palace for another nineteen years.

SIX

I climbed down the wall as fast as my shaky grip would allow me, my fingers scraping against the stone.

My breaths left me in faint bursts of clouds, wafting in the cooling night air. Gripping the nearest branch by the wall, I pushed off and swung until my other hand joined, and I climbed to the trunk of the tree.

It was muscle memory. Climbing to the trunk, wriggling my way down, knowing when it was close enough to jump.

The vast palace loomed behind me, still dark, still oppressive. For all its grandeur and space, it had an impeccable way of making me feel like a bird trapped in a too-small cage. But tonight, I was breaking free.

I pressed myself against the wall until I reached the corner. After a scan showed no guards in sight, I ducked into the shadows, my cloak—my mother's cloak—was enough to keep me hidden.

My eyes locked onto the corner of the fence, where a few small trees bunched together. The trees were probably twice my height, but they would provide me enough cover.

I crouched as I darted across the frost-tipped grass, the dark, emerald cloak billowing behind me.

Sliding underneath the nearest tree, I pressed my back against the trunk, closing my eyes for a moment to catch my breath.

Maybe I should go back.

Maybe I should talk to Libby.

The thought was a driving nail in my skull. Yes, I was angry, but I'm sure this was all my father's doing. Maybe he manipulated her into thinking a certain way. She was around him more than I was.

I couldn't let myself believe that she'd ever go against me. Father was amazing at convincing people with his tone. Maybe he planted these ideas in her mind. He was the one that twisted her loyalty.

Maybe I was the one who misunderstood.

I shook the thought away. A problem for later. I'd find her later tonight, or tomorrow, when I'd calmed down. She could handle my anger—she had before—but I couldn't let myself lash out too much. Not like I had in the past.

I took another slow, deep breath, letting myself breathe in the cool air, ground me to earth.

All I could hear was the forest trees rustling in tune with my rapid-beating heart. The moonlight illuminated the

dusting of frost on the grass. The forest spoke to me like a call
to join. A bird flew overhead, its shadow cutting across the
ground like a fleeting omen.

I wanted to stay here, under the stars, dreaming of a
future where I was free to choose my own path. Where I didn't
need to seek permission through all those above me. I didn't
understand why I couldn't. What would be so wrong with the
future I had planned out? Why wouldn't anyone tell me *why*?

My shoulders sagged under the weight of open
questions. I couldn't decide whether to go back and try to
reason through this horrible day or to run into the night and
never come back. But I wouldn't do that to Libby. I couldn't
leave her. Not forever.

Even though I planned to join the Warrior Guard, the
plan was to stay close by. The dream was never about leaving;
it was about earning my badges, winning my own battles,
doing what was right, and being her right-hand warrior.

The Queen's Guard.

That was how I wanted to live out the rest of my life.
That was my version of living up to my royal duties—
protecting my sister, our family, standing by their side, and
fighting for the people. But now, without that dream, who was
I supposed to be? Someone's wife?

Technically if I married Northern, I'd be living on the
palace grounds. Any one of our neighbors would desire to live
on our lands. I would be able to see Libby and Taroh every day
if I wanted to. But even with the promise of seeing her every

day, would that be enough of a reason to choose an unfulfilling life? A life I'd worked so hard to build.

The impending swarm of questions would have to wait. If I went back, I'd figure all of this out. Somehow. And I would go back...eventually.

My eyes landed on a small hole at the base of the fence wall.

I'd never noticed it before.

I usually escaped through the gates by bribing a guard, scaling the wall, or sneaking out with the servants before the sun set. But my usual spot was guarded, all the servants had already left the palace, and nowhere else was unguarded, besides the corner I was in.

I crawled over to the hole to see if I could fit through. It was a little smaller than expected, like an animal might have clawed through it. Tugging at the loose grass and dirt around the edges helped widen the gap for just enough space to crawl through.

Wrapping myself in the cloak, I slid my hands through first, wriggling my torso forward until I could grab the ground on the other side. The dirt scraped my arms, and the grass tugged at my clothes, but I kept pushing. With one last forceful shove, I pulled my hips through and tumbled into the clearing.

Then I ran.

The wind intensified into a thrashing push. I began to shiver. More so from the wind than my anger.

I wasn't going home tonight. If only it was a little warmer, sleeping outside might not have seemed so unbearable. A month from now would be perfect, but a month from now was when I would have started choosing which station I wanted to apply for in the Warrior Guard.

My foot caught on something loose in the ground. I tripped in the tall grass, falling into the sliver of open field before the forest—close to where Kallias and I had agreed not to kill each other.

The grass behind me swayed wildly in the growing wind as I knelt to catch my breath. When I looked up, a massive tree stood ahead in a commanding presence.

I hadn't noticed it before. I hadn't noticed most of my surroundings until now.

It loomed like the guardian of the forest, barring passage to the dark expanse of a forest beyond, as if silently demanding a summons for passage.

I was far enough from the palace now, but not too enraptured by the darkness of the forest in the distance. Not yet.

Exhaustion overtook me, and if I was honest, I didn't want to run. I wanted to be gone.

But I had nowhere to go.

Not really.

Still, I found my way to the guardian of a tree and

slumped against it. I let the weight of my life pour over me as I slid down the trunk and buried my face in my knees.

Soon, the few hot, angry tears escaped against my will, but who did I need to hide from in my loneliness? Even alone, I didn't feel in control.

Physical pain didn't spur tears from me for the longest time. Not since my mother had died. Even then, my tears had been driven more by anger than grief—anger at my father's cold refusal to speak of her, to let me learn about her. He never spoke of her to me after she died. Ever.

That was when I started hating my father. That was when he started to beat me.

I let myself sob, my head buried into my cloak. Until, a hand pressed on my arm.

I stilled, fearing a guard would drag me back and bring me back to the palace.

A heartbeat passed. I lifted my head slightly, hesitating to face whatever was here.

Then I saw him.

The same eyes I'd seen yesterday. There they were again, glowing brighter than the moonlight, brighter than the stars.

The world stilled again, in a completely different way. For the first time tonight I took a normal breath. A breath of relief.

I sniffed, quickly wiping at my face to erase any trace of

tears. His voice, low and careful, broke the silence. It was so soft that I almost didn't believe it was his.

"Tell me what happened."

He spoke the words as a soft command—a request from this kneeling warrior.

I wiped my nose once more. "What are you doing here?" I asked.

My voice came out shakier than I intended. I couldn't believe how embarrassed I was. I didn't know who it was worse to cry in front of—my father or Kallias.

"I wanted to—" His voice cut off as his eyes shifted over my shoulder. They widened, and he went completely still.

I almost turned to see what stole his attention, but his whisper stopped me cold. He whispered so quietly, it was more mouthing words than speaking.

"*Don't. Move.*"

My muscles locked into place, obeying his command. The two of us moved with agonizing slowness. As I began to turn my head, Kallias reached behind him, his body utterly motionless. Only his arm. Only my head.

Four steps behind me stood a silver wolf. It nearly towered over me. I sat frozen on the ground from where it gazed at me. Its eyes were such a pale blue, they may as well have been white.

They weren't that different from Kallias's. But as I stared into those eyes, I had the same thought I had when I looked in Kallias's eyes—Why was I not scared?

I must have lost all hope to live, because not a shred of fear dwelled in my body. Staring death in the face wasn't as terrifying as I had imagined.

The wolf studied me with something more than predatory intent. It looked...curious. Familiar, almost.

The way it looked at me reminded me of how Taroh did when he'd ask me to chase dragons with him in the courtyard—like it saw something in me worth chasing, too.

After a blink, a different kind of fear began to take hold. Kallias silently drew a short crossbow from his back, already loaded, and slowly raised it toward the animal.

I turned back to the wolf, now baring its teeth. My eyes shot open, and I stopped thinking. I just dove at it.

"No!"

I fell forward, throwing myself between the arrow and the wolf, my arm was the only shield.

The arrow sliced cleanly through my arm.

The wolf swiveled its body before it disappeared into the forest like a shadow. The arrow hadn't even struck the ground before the wolf was gone. A sharp yelp burst out of me when burning pain seared through my arm. I gripped my arm, clutching the wound, holding it to my chest.

I collapsed onto my side.

The tears from earlier were replaced with the blood gushing down my wrist.

Kallias grabbed my uninjured arm, pulling me upright, closer to him with a firm urgency. I clenched the giant slice on my forearm, refusing to let go.

Kallias's eyes widened in shock. "Why would you do that?" His grated voice mixed with shock and frustration, demanding an answer.

I opened my mouth to respond, but only a brief grunt of pain escaped. My entire arm was on fire, and when I finally pried my hand away to reveal a gash several inches long across my forearm. Dark blood stuck to my fingers, pooling inside the gush.

"Let me see."

His command grew sharper, but his hands held my wrist and elbow gently, carefully analyzing the blood pouring through the gash, then from the source, down to my fingers.

The blood was hot against my palm as I reflexively tried to pull my arm away from him, pained at the exposed air brushing against the wet skin.

I looked up at the sky, trying to ignore the pain. I didn't know who I was kidding. I couldn't possibly distract myself from this.

The pain in my shoulder from falling to my side was somewhat of a distraction to the cut. Not an effective one. I bit into my lip, trying to even out the pain.

He sighed, low and measured. "I told you not to move."

I couldn't decipher if his tone was more concerned or annoyed. I wanted to snap back at him, to argue, but the words died beneath the weight of the pain.

Was it as bad as it felt?

Kallias darted those blue eyes around us. Before I could reprimand him for touching a royal without permission—*again*—he crouched next to me and met my eyes before speaking again.

"How attached are you to this dress?"

"Excuse me?"

He didn't wait for my answer.

Bending down, he tore the hem of my burgundy, muslin dress with startling ease, pulling a thick strip from the seam.

My breath hitched, but I couldn't protest, despite wanting to. Every glance at the gash sent fresh waves of blood—and panic—shooting through every muscle. It felt like the more I thought about it, the more blood willing to spill out of it.

With practiced efficiency, he wrapped the fabric tightly around my bloody arm. I clenched every other muscle in my body, refusing to wince too openly in front of a warrior. Instead, I focused on his face, hoping for some distraction from the pain.

Lines of silver moonlight streaked through his stone-black hair, softening his overly-sharp appearance. I marveled at his tenderness in his movements.

His large, strong, and very experienced hands didn't seem like they should be capable of being this careful, but they worked intentionally, neatly around my wound.

"I'm sorry," he breathed out. "This is all my fault. Let's get you back to your palace and I can explain everything to your family."

I scoffed. "No. I'm not going back there tonight." Though I wanted a distraction, the mention of my family was definitely the best worst choice. I'd have to sleep here tonight if it was the only option. If he was worried about me telling on him, he had nothing to worry about. It wasn't like my opinion held any weight in my family anyway.

He analyzed me with that sharp gaze, though my focus was on clenching my jaw to suppress another wince.

"Where do you plan on going, Princess?"

"Fia," I corrected with a grunt.

I pulled away from his grip, slowly lying down and shutting my eyes, making my intention to stay here the rest of the night obvious. A soft, low laugh escaped him.

Though I wanted to look at him—to see if this armored warrior actually smiled at me—I stayed focused on the makeshift wrap around my arm.

"Being eaten by wolves sounds that appealing to you?" Though there was nothing serious in his tone, he still spoke with such assertion, I felt I needed to answer.

I glared at him before sitting back up, a gentle wince slipping through. "The wolf didn't do anything. You shot at it. Maybe it's you I should stay away from." I closed my eyes from the pain.

"Forgive me...Fia," he said in soft solemnity. I hated how nice he made my name sound. The softness in his voice shifted. "Next time, I will wait for it to finish its attack before I pry it away from your body."

"You didn't know what the wolf was going to do," I muttered as he sat down beside me. "Don't sit down–if you have nothing else to say, *or shoot*, then you may leave."

I shut my eyes, pretending to sleep, waiting for him to leave. As much as I might have liked to voice all that was unsaid between us, I wasn't going to be the first to bring it up.

"All right. Goodnight, Princess. Try not to die from infection."

I scoffed but kept my eyes closed. When I heard him stand, I cracked one eye open a peek, just in time to see him turn and stride away.

"Wait!" I called out, but he didn't stop. His long legs carried him away quickly.

I scrambled to my feet and ran after him. "You're really going to leave me to die from infection after trying to kill an animal for my sake?"

He kept walking, unwilling to glance in my direction. "I didn't say it was for your sake. The wolf could have killed me too."

I slowed.

"Oh. Right."

He slowed too but didn't stop.

"Fine."

I spun on my heel. "Then I'll go back to the palace. I'll rest and rest for days until you're long gone." I stormed off, throwing my voice over my shoulder. "Good luck finding someone to talk to my father."

Perhaps I didn't have the leverage I wanted, but he didn't need to know that. He had information I wanted to know and if we were going to be in cahoots together, he needed to understand just how stubborn I could be.

I heard his footsteps falter.

A small smile crept onto my face, but I kept walking, the pain in my arm nothing more than a stinging afterthought.

"What do you want?" His gentle, irritated voice called over.

I shrugged without looking back and sat back down at my tree. He pushed out a frustrated sigh.

"Hurry up and tell me. I don't have all night," he said, closing the distance between us in a few long strides. His mood was etched into every crevice of his face, but somehow even that looked indifferent, yet handsome.

I rolled my eyes. "How busy could you possibly be if you're out here at this time of night?"

"You'd be surprised," he replied, folding his arms.

I crossed mine too, ignoring the flare of pain upon impact. "I wasn't planning on coming, but I did need to hunt, since I was distracted this morning," he added, his tone dipping into low accusation. "And *that* could have been a week's worth of food." He pointed to the space in the forest from where the wolf disappeared from.

I arched a brow at him. "If it was food you needed you should have told me at the party. I would have brought you some."

He eyed me skeptically. His eyes really burned into me, intense and sure. Even in the chill of the night, his stare made the air feel warmer.

"Where are you going now?" I asked him.

"You tell me," he said, stepping closer.

"I meant—where are you staying?"

His eyes studied my face with careful precision, as though searching for hidden intentions. He had the kind of eyes that hid so much behind them, that even if he spoke everything he thought, I'd be convinced there would always be something unspoken.

"I'm staying at a home on the corner of Capital Town," he admitted.

I nodded. The kingdom didn't have any inns close by. Nothing affordable, at least. Most people in the North relied on family for housing, and not many moved away.

Costs were too high, and the kingdom's laws only allowed a limited number of North-born citizens to settle elsewhere.

"Take me there," I said with a shrug.

He tilted his head slightly. "To where I'm staying?" His inclination on the last word was too implicative.

"I—I just need somewhere to stay for tonight." My head dropped as my voice faltered. "I can't go home."

He sat down across from me, folding his legs like he planned to stay here. "You still haven't told me what happened."

I rested my head on my free hand, letting it shield my flushed cheeks. "I tried to speak to my father," I mumbled beneath my breath.

He waited patiently, his silence urging me to say more. I wanted to, but the lump in my throat returned. I shut my mouth, clenching my jaw to fight the tears threatening to spill. I'd never earn a warrior's respect if I cried in front of him.

My eyes flitted back toward the palace, it's cold walls were far away, yet weighing on me like a chain. Then I glanced down at my feet and for the first time tonight, I noticed I was barefoot. The chill hit my toes immediately.

Embarrassed, I tucked my freezing toes beneath my cloak almost immediately. "He won't tell me much—I don't want to talk about it," I added swiftly.

He let a moment of silence settle between us before asking, "Are you still wanting to be a warrior?" He asked in a low, calming purr that could have lulled me to sleep.

What kind of warrior spoke so softly?

"Of course I do! But..." My words faltered as my doubt took over. "I'm not sure I have much of a choice now."

"What are you going to do about it?"

I wish I knew.

Somehow when I looked into his eyes and basked in his attention, I didn't know what to say.

Me... I was never at a loss for words. Yet the weight of his questions pressed down on me.

"Maybe we can help each other." His tone shifted, more cordially, more inviting.

I wouldn't let him get off that easy. "You still haven't told me anything either," I said, narrowing my eyes at him. "I guess you're more of a shoot-first-ask-questions-later type of guy."

He sighed regretfully. All traces of his earlier quips escaped from him. "Princess, please forgive me, it wasn't my—"

I cut him off with a chuckle.

His eyes met mine again in a fleeting moment. I thought he'd smile too if his eyes hadn't danced down to my arm.

I followed his eyes to the bloodstained wrap. A small tang of dizziness overtook me. I blinked a few times before forcing my eyes open. I got hurt often, but the sight of this injury made my stomach tighten. I rarely saw this much blood leave my body.

Shaking my head to clear the dizziness, I looked back at him, trying to regain some semblance of composure. His expression was unreadable, but there was something in the way he observed me that tightened my stomach in a different way. He looked at me as if I were a puzzle that needed to be solved—like *I* was the question mark here.

"What?" I snapped, wanting him to voice whatever it was he was thinking. I feared the more I was around this man, the more I'd want to know what he was thinking.

I wanted to demand an answer, to know what he

thought about me. Was he curious? Fascinated? Frustrated?

But before I gathered myself enough to bother him, he simply smirked at me, leaving me with nothing but increasing questions and a growing uncertainty that Kallias had more about him than he let on.

"We should go before it gets too late. I'll take you with me, but you must be subtle. I won't be arrested for kidnapping a Northern Princess of all things," he said flatly, his gaze flickering over my attire. "You can't come dressed like that."

I frowned, crossing my arms. "I could climb back and grab—"

He didn't wait for me to finish. "How are you going to do that while injured?"

The glimmer of anger returned. "I'll have you know I can do whatever I want. Who are you to tell me what I can or can't do? If I'm going to be a warrior, I should learn how to push past a little injury."

Some blood returned to my face as I threw my words at him.

"Fine."

He stood and scanned the area around for a moment. Then, he pointed toward a tree at the edge of the clearing, its spindly branches swaying slightly in the breeze.

"Climb that tree. If you can, then I'll let you go."

I glanced up at the small tree that suddenly looked gigantic. Forcing a cool mask of indifference.

"No problem." I shrugged. But then I seethed as I

walked over to the tree, wincing a little from pain as I approached.

Once I stood before the overwhelming barrier, I grabbed the lowest branch with my uninjured hand, ignoring the smear of blood on my palm. The realization was more irritating than embarrassing, since I couldn't even reach up my other arm.

Refusing to look back at him, I focused on the task above. I didn't think about how I wanted to see if he was wearing that smug smile he held back earlier.

A bead of blood rolled down my arm as I slowly lifted it. I watched as it trickled down to my shoulder. I needed something else to focus on.

My gaze landed on a bird's nest a few branches up. That was my new goal. I just needed to make it there.

Placing my foot on a notch on the trunk that seemed to appear out of nowhere, I pressed up and jumped slightly to lift myself higher.

My good arm strained as I pulled myself away from the ground. Reaching as much as I could, my fingers grazed the branch just above me, and I stretched the last bit of space I had left, finally wrapping my hand around its rough surface.

With the growing grit of my teeth, I pulled myself halfway up the trunk, my feet scrambling for a hold. Each jerky movement sent a little ripple of pain through my arm that I was convinced I could push myself through.

Both arms wrapped uncomfortably around the branch

as I looked to the bird's nest–so close above me. I could reach it if I could get one more push.

I hooked a leg around the branch and kept myself close to the wood before I reached up for the next branch. My fingers brushed the underside gently. All I needed to do was grab it.

With a shaky exhale, I reached as much as I could. But the moment my other arm shifted from its position, the pain shot through me too suddenly. My arm shook, I was too far from grabbing the branch above.

Bark scraped against my skin as I sucked in a breath in a short burst. I closed my eyes, preparing for my fall.

Strong arms caught me mid-fall, holding my back and legs effortlessly. The lack of gear on Kallias revealed a fitted, dark gray long-sleeved shirt clinging to his lean frame almost as tightly as I was to his neck.

He looked at me, pleased with his point being made. I, however, was far from amused.

My gaze flickered to his sleek collarbones, then upward to his slender, strong neck. I didn't think a neck could be so beautiful. The thought made me swallow a quick breath and look back at his eyes and push away the unwelcome admiration.

"Put me down," I snapped, masking the flushing in my face with irritation.

An annoying hint of a smirk tugged at his lips. "What were you looking at?" he asked in a tease.

I felt my cheeks burn as I fumbled for a response. "Where are your clothes?" I shot back, ignoring his smirk and ready to yell *pervert* if necessary

He set me down cautiously, the smirk never leaving his scruffy face. "As much as I enjoyed your failed efforts, we should get moving and start disguising you a little."

Before I could add any input, he crouched to my feet, grabbed the frayed hem of my skirt, ripping a section from the middle.

I gasped at his lack of manners. "You could ask..." But my nagging was easily ignored.

"Pants?" he questioned, pausing as he noticed the loose pajama pants beneath my skirt.

My arms crossed in indifference. "I like to wear pants under my dresses. I've had plenty of scandalous tree-climbing incidents. What did you think you'd find down there?" I quipped, raising an eyebrow.

He shook his head. "Pants are good," he said, standing. Then with that typical maddening calmness, he added, "Take off your dress."

I eyed him through slitted eyes. "Is this usually how you undress strange women in the dead of night?"

He cleared his throat at the question, clearly unprepared, which pulled a little, pleased smile out of me. My lips twitched as I bit back a giggle.

"You're not strange," he mumbled, bending to retrieve his pile of gear. "You can wear this back to my room."

His underclothes still looked warm enough to keep him comfortable, and I wondered how he managed to wear so many heavy layers day after day without complaint.

"You want me to wear your warrior gear?" I asked, trying not to smile at the idea of wearing what a real warrior did. It thrilled me more than I'd care to admit. "If you promise not to bleed on it."

He handed me the chained vest with its attached metal shoulder guards, making it seem as though it wasn't as heavy as it really was.

"I make no such promises," I said with a grin.

Without too much excitement, I began tugging at the bottom of my ripped skirt absentmindedly, crinkling it up to my waist. But I stilled when I realized I was undressing. Alone. In the dark. In front of a man...

I shot a look at him. My eyebrow struck up at his presence. He stiffened immediately, before awkwardly turning his back to me.

A smile slipped through my lips once I was out of his view. I was sure all warriors often changed in front of each other without a second thought, but the princess in me was still a little coy.

I did have on the usual under-clothes that came with my warrior gear, fighting some of the chill of the night. I dropped my tattered dress to the ground before I carefully slung an arm into the vest, babying my injured forearm as much as I could.

The metal was cold against my skin, but once the vest slipped on, it felt heavy and solid and *incredible*. It felt so protective and powerful, like the history of all warriors before me linked each chain together. The shoulders of the vest hung loose but sat surprisingly comfortably.

"Done?"

His voice broke the silence, head tilting halfway toward me.

My fingers caressed the smooth metal hanging over my torso before I wiped away my smile. "Yes."

He turned, his eyes scanning me with an intensity that lingered longer than it should have. He studied me in the silence, his gaze remained unreadable, until he finally coughed out, "Almost there."

Before I could respond, he leaned over to untie, then pulled off his boots, tossing them at my feet.

"Let's go," he muttered gruffly, unimpressed by the little sense of awe that lingered off of me.

I almost objected, but I couldn't feel my toes anymore. The vest may have warmed my upper body, but my feet were on the verge of freezing to the ground.

There wasn't much time to object anyway. He was already several paces ahead of me, moving without a care in the world.

"Wait. Did you hunt enough?" I'd almost forgotten.

"Plenty," he replied over his shoulder. "Can you walk?"

I rolled my eyes. "An arm injury doesn't affect my

legs...I'm not completely helpless." My voice trailed off as I strode past him, determined to prove my point—even though I had no idea where we were going or what the rest of the night would bring.

SEVEN

My request to carry the makeshift sack of clothes was, unfortunately, granted. I needed something to cover my face with in case the dark of the night didn't hide my identity well enough.

It was easier to disguise myself in winter, but hopefully if anyone looked too closely at us, their attention would settle on the tall, barefoot figure walking ahead of me instead.

The sack hung comfortably over my sling-less shoulder. Thankfully, most of the citizens were asleep by the hour we arrived in the town.

Despite my dark, wavy hair–a disheveled mess over my face, I didn't expect to be that noticeable–especially in this attire.

No one ever expected royalty in the middle of town, especially at night. I'd learned that sometimes hiding in plain sight was the easiest disguise.

A few stragglers dotted the cool, mucky streets of

Capital Town, which was made up of narrow buildings with little to no lighting on the streets.

Frost from what was left over after the winter lingered in patches, slicking the ground, but hopefully not making it too unbearably cold, for Kallias's sake.

Those who were out were mainly workers leaving for work or coming back from. Men, women, some children even.

Sullen faces, dirtied by their labor drifted past us silently. The heavy clangs of blacksmiths were sporadic, booming in the distance, past the low whispers of couples tucked away in shadowed alleyways.

A light fog tickled at our feet like dust as we wound through alleys I didn't recognize.

Once we reached a halt, Kallias knocked weakly on a thin door, where an older lady with a wooden stump for one leg led us into her skinny, tall home plastered with wooden slabs and two small windows on each of its four floors.

"Price is double if you bring guests."

The older woman spoke in her shaky voice, not bothering to look our way as she stuck out a hand, waiting for her payment before moving out of our way.

Kallias guided me up a swirl of steep wooden stairs that creaked with every step and whistled with the gentle wind seeping through the cracks. The building inside was a poor type of craftsmanship that was an unfortunate mixture with age. It was barely held together. Each creak of the stairs made them appear to be slanted.

At the top of the stairs, we stopped before a narrow door that barely seemed wide enough for one of me to squeeze through. I dropped the sack at the top of the stairs with a sigh, releasing all my spent energy I'd use to carry it up.

"What could possibly fit in here?" I muttered as Kallias pushed the little door open and crouched to walk in.

The room was oddly spacious compared to the house's exterior. It held only the barest of things: a couple stools in the corner of the room, a bed shoved against the wall, two small bookshelves that only held several books that looked abandoned.

Light wood-paneled walls and half-burned candles scattered sporadically, illuminating the room well enough, giving an odd warmth through the night's chill.

I shifted uncomfortably, attempting to scratch my shoulder under the coverings, but unable to find the right spot. "Do you get itchy under all this metal, or is that just me?"

I lingered awkwardly in the middle of the quaint room while Kallias moved around me, arranging the small stools and candles near the window. The potential of fatigue weighed on me, my eyelids growing heavier with each passing moment.

"Take it off," he commanded again, tossing a thick, long–sleeved shirt on a stool for me. My eyes narrowed at the sound of his serious tone, but I began shimmying beneath the chained vest.

He had the sense to turn away this time, using the time to put away his sack of clothes while I changed, painfully shrugging off all of the gear I had and slipping the shirt over what was left of my underclothes. The shirt was warm and hung past my hips.

As comfortable as it was, my attention quickly shifted back to my arm as I pushed up the cream sleeve to reveal my blood-soaked wrap that clung to my arm.

The bleeding seized, but when I unwrapped the fabric, it fell to the floor in a wet slap.

Kallias halted mid-step when his eyes locked on my gash, his expression tightening briefly before walking right at me.

Without a word, his hand clasped onto my wrist, twisting it slightly for better inspection of the wound.

The sharp sting dulled, but seeing the raw, jagged edges of my skin pinched something at my stomach. In response, I shoved my strained gaze upward, fixing on the small candle chandelier hanging low from the ceiling.

His other hand rested on my shoulder, guiding me gently yet firmly to sit on one of the small stools he pulled up for me by the window. I complied, though part of me bristled at his presumption.

He hadn't asked for permission to touch me—though, at this point, it felt like we were well past those royal formalities. Still, I couldn't help but notice how every uninvited touch sent a new type of sensation through me, one I couldn't quite place.

"Wait," he commanded with a rough sincerity, like the

calm, yet lethal wolf that stared me in the face.

A wet rag lined his hand as he carefully wiped the dried blood crusting over my wrist. He wiped around the wound, working silently, carefully cleaning each smudge of red until the rag was almost completely pink.

He cleaned it with an intimate type of precision as streaks of red disappeared into the rag. He worked upward, all the way up to the few lines up my shoulder, tucking the rag under the sleeve to reach all of my arm.

I didn't look at the wound he tended, though I already knew it had clotted well enough. I expected it to leave a very threatening scar. The type of scar someone would see on a warrior.

It was pertinent to my hazy state to shift my attention and think about anything else but the stinging in my forearm. Instead, I let my gaze settle on him.

I shifted to watch the crease of his brow, the occasional twitch of his chin, the faint tension in his jaw. His lip twitched, just barely, before he spoke again.

"I don't know any healers in this area. Would you know any that you could trust to help?"

My face tried to still as I thought of the type of warrior he must have been to know healers by name, potentially in different kingdoms too.

I didn't know a single healer by name. I hardly knew where our medical centers were located. I wouldn't even know where to find them.

I wasn't allowed to wander anywhere on my own. Even to explore my own kingdom. I had only seen one or two medical centers before Mother died.

After that, nurses or doctors would have been summoned to the palace instead. Or I was left to care for it myself. I'd become a master at wrapping my scraped knees and bruised ankles.

"We don't have many—that I know of. I wouldn't know where to find them." I straightened up. "But, I don't need one. It doesn't hurt anymore."

He hesitated, eyeing my heating face.

"Yes it does. I know how painful a cut this deep is."

He was right, but I still didn't want to admit it.

The fist I kept clenched beneath the cloak on my lap probably had more blood from my nails digging into it than my actual wound did.

"Don't hold it in."

Kallias stood up. "It's not good for you."

I rolled my eyes again before watching him disappear into the bathing chambers.

"You don't have to keep telling me what to do," I muttered from where I sat in the room.

The sound of a weak stream of water trickled from the little room by the stairs. I took the opportunity of solitude to relieve myself of the pent up pain.

I winced and grabbed my arm, desperately searching for reprieve. I blew on the crimson gash, despite knowing nothing would come from it.

I fanned it for a moment and looked at my other hand, just as bloodied from the night. I looked up again and blinked any idea of tears out of my head when the faucet turned off. My expression relaxed after a few deep breaths before he returned.

Once again, those surprisingly gentle hands took mine and I tried not to make my change in breathing noticeable.

He stuck his hand out to me, reaching for mine, but I pulled away.

"What?" I asked.

"I wasn't done," he answered, grabbing my dirtied hand.

"Well, you have a rude way of asking for a lady's hand."

"I wasn't asking."

His hand wrapped around my wrist. He began cleaning it further, pushing past my initial protest.

"I don't know how the South works, but up here— touching a royal without her permission could really get you in some trouble."

His shoulders jerked in a tiny laugh.

"Shall I alert the guards?"

I snickered. "*Ha. Ha,*" I said humorlessly after an eye roll, but I peeked at his smile that caused one of my own to slip out.

His grip on me was the perfect balance of force, without being harsh. It was something I wasn't used to from a man. The surprising gentleness in his touch wasn't anything I'd ever expect to experience from a warrior.

He wrung out the rag one more time and returned with a salve in a small jar that must have only contained a dollop of cream.

"This will fight off infection. But it stings," he said while applying the burning solution right in the center of the slit.

Both of my arms jerked at the touch, but he didn't let go of my wrist. He did, however, lean in and began to blow a gentle puff over the sting. It was careful and deliberate and was helping more than I expected.

I tried not to think too much about our close quarters. I should have been more wary from the beginning, but if he was so careful in keeping me alive, and relatively unharmed, it was probably safe to assume he wouldn't try to kill me anytime soon. Not after showing this much care—more care than I'd experienced from any man the past few years.

At least these injuries were accidental.

EIGHT

Kallias finished wiping my hand clean, moving carefully as he twisted my entire arm to inspect the scab.

I watched him in silence, my eyes lingering on his untethered concentration that creased a line between his brows. Once he seemed satisfied by the lack of blood smear, he rose from his stool.

"You're welcome," he tried to tease.

"For shooting me?" I shot back, arching a brow up at him.

His almost-smile slipped into a sigh, the sound weighing with enough regret to drop his large shoulders.

"Don't worry," I added to ease his tension, offering a smile. "I've had far worse injuries than this. Most of this was my fault anyways."

He ignored my attempt at reassurance as he fetched a towel from the chamber, intending to wrap my arm in. This I fought him on, promising him it would scab better when exposed to the air.

Reluctantly, he gave in, tossing the towel over his shoulder.

"How does it feel now?" he asked, his tone softer.

I shrugged. "Fine."

The knowing edge to his tired smirk was as annoying as it was luring. Though it did little to distract from the pain.

"Liar," he accused, amusement growing in his smile, hidden under his growing scruff.

It was somewhat...adorable.

He reminded me of a tired bear, rugged and straight out of the woods, but with an air of sleepiness that made him seem the most approachable he'd looked since I first laid eyes on him.

As crazy as I was for trusting a man that shot me, accidentally or not, I couldn't help but let my gaze drift to the strong, meticulously muscled back whenever he turned away.

It looked like the back of a victor with a history of countless battles and a lifetime of hard work. I wondered what scars lay beneath the knitted fabric.

The thick knit sweater clung perfectly to his broad frame. As if it was tailored to him. I forced my eyes not to continue tracing the line of his neck and shoulders, where a peek of his collar was visible.

It was merely a brief distraction from the evening.
Short-lived.
When he turned back to face me, he sat on the small

stool across from mine. A stool he barely fit onto.

He leaned forward slightly, one arm resting on the windowsill. Only a small, wax candle sat between us, its faint glow casting the smallest tint of orange light across his face.

"Tell me about your evening," he asked, his tone steady and sure.

I blinked at his determination.

"Straight to business," I mumbled under my breath, leaning on the windowsill too, looking out into the cold, void narrow streets below, their emptiness echoing my thoughts.

It was probably safe to discuss now. I didn't think I had any tears left. If I did, I could blame it on the gash.

My hesitation was unintentional, but he seemed to have caught on as he quickly added,

"If you're all right discussing it." His voice dipped, genuine sincerity intertwining in between his words. It provided some ease—the illusion that I had a choice.

I took a deep breath, trying to ground myself before giving as detailed a description as I could to him in the most matter-of-fact tone that my tongue could manage.

Halfway through the explanation, my tone shifted and I spoke to him how I used to speak to Libby—comfortably and descriptively.

I complained to him as I stared off into the night, letting my words settle into the quiet.

It felt strange, opening up to someone I barely knew or trusted. But since he had helped me—and didn't kidnap me for ransom yet, I'd say I had to trust him.

Still, I avoided certain truths from the night–mainly about my father, how he used his powers to stop me.

I wasn't prepared to relive that. I only said enough to paint him the outline of the picture, leaving him to fill in the painful parts however he wanted to.

The night was too dark, the single streetlight at the far end of the street seemed too lazy to pierce any shadows.

Though the shadows were oddly comforting. I felt wrapped in their embrace. Hidden. If anything, I felt safe knowing nobody knew where I was.

From the window, I could watch the few figures that walked on the street below. The dark separated me from the world I wanted no part in. The world I never had a choice but to be a part of.

Kallias leaned forward even more, resting his elbows on his knees while he listened, flashing those silver eyes straight through my anger and into the softer part of me–the part I barely acknowledged existed.

His knees were so close to mine that for a second, I thought he'd reach out a hand of comfort.

But of course he didn't. He wouldn't. That would have been quite inappropriate on his part. And I didn't want that–at least I thought I didn't.

"...But enough about that," I said, forcing a steadying tone to my voice. "I can find a way to handle my family. I'd rather resume your discussion of the attacks. Do you have any new information?"

He waited patiently, giving me space to steady my breathing. His gaze never wavered, his expression carved with patient intensity.

Every word I spoke seemed to matter, as though he weighed every single thing I said. His unwavering attention disarmed my armored wall, loosening the tightness in my chest. I relaxed at his gaze and unclenched the coiled muscles in my shoulders that I didn't realize were pushing me shut.

The dark, the candle, his eyes, I couldn't help but sense some peace through it all.

"Thank you for telling me," he said, his voice crisp but soft with sincerity. "I respect your honesty."

He sat straighter on the stool, adding too much space between us. But not in his eyes. His eyes remained steady on mine.

I masked my shock at how sincere his tone was. It was suitable for the night, like soft music in the back of my mind.

I'd never been thanked for complaining before. It was an odd sensation. Maybe I wished I had a friend like him sooner. If I could call him a friend. He was probably the closest thing to it.

"I followed that carriage," he said, his voice drawing me out of my thoughts.

I blinked, startled by the shift in topic. I'd almost forgotten. My curiosity stirred, and I leaned forward instinctively.

"And?" I whispered, the word slipping out like a secret between the two of us.

"It confirmed my suspicions. They didn't even try to cross the boundary line. It stopped in a forest I couldn't get into. An empty forest, free of animals and living, breathing things."

The crease between his thick brows returned. "It stayed there for nearly an hour. No noise, no exit on the other side. It was like it disappeared during that time. I almost left, but then heard it leave through the opening it came in through."

"Where was this?"

"Closer to the center of the borderlands."

"What? That's hours away by carriage! Did you walk there and back?" My voice shot up accidentally.

The sudden outburst startled him, but I kept my eyes widened, waiting for an explanation. He merely shrugged. "Yes. It wasn't much."

I blinked at him, incredulous. I would die if I ever walked that much.

"Anyways," he continued, shaking his dark, shiny curls out of his face. "The carriage returned back to the palace, but I couldn't tell if there was anything left in it or not. It looked like a small supply buggy, but depending on its contents, it still would have benefited my kingdom. Spices, yeast, herbs, plants, medicine. Anything could have been in there and it was lost in the middle of the forest, then the buggy returned. Whatever was in there must have been taken since the time passed by quicker when it returned." He rubbed his scruffy chin, slow and thoughtful.

I watched his look grow more concerned. The tension between his brows aging him slightly. "The King didn't speak much about the issue to me at the Biannual but..."

My head tilted at his words. I didn't suppose he would speak of it to any common warrior. Perhaps a general, but Kallias seemed too young to hold the title.

Then again, my only experience with generals was with the older, retired men who spent their days loitering around Father's court once they passed their prime.

"Are you a general?" I asked, leaning on the windowsill.

He straightened at the question, his postures somehow becoming even sharper.

"In a way. I'm more...an advisor to the general."

"Is that a thing? What do they call you? Advisor General?" I arched a brow, analyzing his face, trying to learn something from it that I hadn't learned yet.

He paused to think, his head giving the slightest tilt.

"No...They don't call me anything in particular. *Warrior* is honorable enough of a title."

"How noble," I said pointedly before I crossed my arms. "I can't believe my father didn't speak to you about the problems in your kingdom—a kingdom my mother once loved. I thought he loved it there too."

Kallias's eyebrow lifted at my words, his amusement, or perhaps disbelief in my words evident.

"What?" I questioned his doubt. "I know my father?"

"Have *you* ever been to my kingdom?" he asked.

I stayed silent.

I hardly ever went to other kingdoms, save for the occasional Biannual, wedding, or party. Even then, we rarely ventured beyond the North.

"It's fine if you haven't. It's been years since the King visited anyone in the South," he bit out.

However...Father just told me he was there months ago. Why?

"I have some...*theories*, but I would never accept one as fact until there was more evidence. That is why I planned to approach someone at the Biannual."

He appeared to swallow back a thought, hesitation flickering over his face, along with the candlelight.

I supposed he would have settled for anyone willing to listen. Perhaps he wished it was Libby, but was stuck with me instead. Me, with my stubbornness, complaints, and clumsiness, sitting as the injured inconvenience before him. That was who he had to rely on.

"I see," I murmured, my shoulders dropping under the weight of the silence that followed.

It became silent. The clicks from the burning wick of the candle was the only noise louder than my breathing.

"Although..."

He straightened again, his expression shifting. "Although I'm..." His gaze lingered on the skinny window before returning to me. "...glad it was you."

I pursed my lips, meeting his silver-lined blue eyes. "Really? Why?" I huffed softly, the questions escaping before I could stop it.

He cleared his throat, his eyes darting around the room like the right answer might be hidden there. "It seems we might have more in common than I thought," he admitted at last, his voice steady. "Perhaps."

I nodded before echoing back. "Perhaps."

I appreciated his honesty. He was almost too honest.

Maybe warriors were naturally more trusting of other warriors—or potential ones. Or perhaps there was some other reason he found me trustworthy.

I hoped there was.

I wasn't exactly known for my honesty—not in a way that inspired respect, at least. But a part of me wanted that. I wanted my honesty to be something good, maybe even honorable.

The singe from the dying candle filled the silence. The room was so quiet it almost felt suspended in time. Even the street was now void of sounds and souls. The town was more lifeless, especially when it grew colder.

"What is your end goal here, Warrior?" I finally asked, breaking the stillness of the moment.

"Well, tonight, I'm hoping to monitor your wound so there's no festering infection. Then I'll get you to a *real* medical professional."

"Good. You've done a terrible job," I jested, smirking at his arched brow.

He narrowed his eyes playfully, blinking into the silence as he seemed to carefully choose his next words.

The intentionality of his tone only made me listen more intently to the man.

"I need allies in the northern kingdoms to help bring supplies to my Kingdom and its surroundings. We could also use more warriors. Numbers are lessening and I don't think we can go much longer with only eastern and southern soldiers towards the creatures. I fear we might need a continent-wide call to serve."

I nodded, somewhat familiar with the system. Warriors were trained within their sector of the continent based on where they were born. However, once they graduated, they stayed in the groups assigned to wherever their kingdom believed the need was greatest.

I always thought the structure was odd. I wasn't sure if warriors themselves agreed with it or if they simply followed the orders.

Some kingdoms kept the best warriors within their land, then sent the lesser ones to poorer kingdoms—as was required. It was a common practice, more common in the North than anything, but I assumed it would come back to bite them one day.

"And what about the creatures?" I asked. "What's your plan for them? Will you simply keep killing?"

He shook his head slightly. "We've been trying that. It hasn't gotten far. We need more strategies, but to plan and strategize, we'd need greater opportunities for academics and warriors all over the continent to study and understand the creatures to better eliminate them. I think we need to stop killing them and try capturing them. Or at least immobilize them for a certain amount of time."

I let my confusion evidently form across my face. "I'm sorry, I just don't understand—have you told my father this? It makes sense to me, I can't imagine he'd turn his back on your reasoning."

The question earned another odd reaction from him.

"I told you I had...theories," he replied, his voice more cautious.

"Like what?"

His tone shifted again—rougher but fragile, as if anything more he said could snuff out the candle between us and leave us in the dark.

"I don't care to solely rely on rumors—and I wouldn't want you to think I believe this...necessarily"

A cautionary lump formed in my stomach, but I remained silent, letting him go on.

"I don't know if you've heard the rumor that..." He paused to clear his throat, his gaze darting momentarily away. "Perhaps the King could have benefitted from the death of..."

Something in my mind snapped into place, but I hesitated, waiting for him to say what I thought he might before my reaction got too out of hand.

I had enjoyed our conversation for too long, and I had a feeling all of that was about to change. I shouldn't have let myself enjoy it–the first real warrior-to-warrior exchange I'd had where someone didn't brush me off, demean me, or censor me.

Now that seemed to be washing away.

Now, I was getting angry.

I was so sick of being angry.

"Yes. I've heard," I said through gritted teeth "—and is that what you think?" I inquired too quickly.

"Not entirely." He remained soft-spoken. "However, I have heard theories that might make sense as to why."

"Like what? Tell me—now."

He paused for only a breath, but it was a breath too much.

"*Tell me*. Right. Now."

He sighed, a quiet exhale that only further fueled the anger inside. "As you wish, Princess."

He straightened himself, taking a few deliberate breaths. I nearly commanded him again, wondering if I–as a royal–could pull rank on him, but he began to speak before I could.

"Your mother was quite powerful. My kingdom knew this, though no one fully understood how she used her powers–or if she ever did in the North. I know your Kingdom— the King—" he corrected, "doesn't encourage them that much, save for the King's and his court's abilities. Most Northern Courts are so. Some theories speculate that if anybody, including the wife of a King, became more powerful than him, that might have a reason for...elimination."

I shot up from my seat, dumbfounded, furious, and utterly dazed. "How can you say that?"

The disbelief in my voice cut through the room like a blade. I scoffed, clenching my fists, ignoring how the movement tugged at the scar warming my arm.

"Take me back to the palace immediately."

I turned toward the door, spinning with the rest of the words in my head.

A gentle sigh stopped me in my tracks.

"If that is what you wish."

His soft voice carried through the room, steady and unwavering. "I'll do whatever you command me, but...you wanted to hear this. Perhaps you'd be willing to fight past your feelings and try to listen."

I spun back to him, ready for another round of dagger practice, but his next words caught me off guard and I froze.

"If I'm so incorrect, then prove me wrong. What are your powers?" he challenged.

More silence.

"Does the King permit your powers? Tell me that much, at least."

Powers? Me? The words rattled in my mind like loose gravel. Why would I have powers?

"I don't possess any," I stammered out.

Out of pure bewilderment, I relaxed from my fit. He flinched at my confusion, posture relaxing, head tilting as he studied me.

"Your sister then?" he asked, more curiously.

I shook my head.

The speed at which he rose to his feet alarmed me enough to take a step back. I had let my guard down during our conversation, and I'd forgotten how tall he was. Only a few inches taller than me, but it felt like so much more in the small space.

"You don't need to lie to me," he added urgently. "You can tell me. I thought you could trust me by now. I trust you—"

I straightened my posture swiftly, meeting his gaze head-on.

"Who are you to call me a liar?"

My voice clipped. "I believe I would know if my sister or I possessed any powers."

Many royals were known to have powers—at least someone in each bloodline did, and it was typically exposed once royals entered an elder age. It was why they preferred to marry fellow royalty.

The Fates only blessed a select few outside of the bloodline, even then, only those destined for great wars, world-changing events, or some pertinence to the future of our world.

That was what I was taught.

My Father didn't speak of his powers often, but I knew

them well enough to not question their impact. I'd only seen them several times and I'd never seen the extent of them.

But he was Father.

He was the King.

He was meant to be powerful.

We weren't.

Libby and I were simply daughters, only eligible to the throne through marriage. Our lives weren't as impactful as kings. As Generals. As Queens.

Perhaps Libby had the potential of powers, lying dormant, awaiting to awaken with time? I didn't know how any of it worked. The more I tried to piece it together, the deeper the headache pulsed in my temples.

"Father says only true Kings are blessed with real powers," I muttered numbly, trying to make sense of it all. "Other powers are vague and unyielding. Simply luck. Powers are meant for ruling, and winning wars. Only few can possess them."

Kallias's stern look stayed unreadable, his silver eyes narrowed. "You *are* your mother's daughter, are you not?"

He watched for a reaction, or maybe looked to detect a lie before turning slightly, mumbling under his breath. "Of course you are...you look just like her."

He began to pace in quick movements. I narrowed my eyes on him, doubt creeping over the hair on the back of my neck.

I had my mother's eyes—my favorite part of her, the

only token of her that I felt eternally grateful to carry with me. But that was where the comparison ended.

"I don't understand," Kallias spoke in disbelief again, his voice tightening. "How could he do that? How could he suppress your powers?"

I couldn't take it anymore.

"*Stop*." My voice wavered. "Stop saying these things— you don't know what you're talking about."

I steadied myself and sat back down on the stool. My sharp breaths nearly blew out the candles as my fingers swirled the pain in the temples.

"Princess," he said softly, back to the tone he had earlier in the night. "Any descendant of two power-yielders means they possess powers too. It can't be denied, even by Fate."

I didn't know what to think. What to feel. What to say.

I just stared at him.

I had never possessed any powers.

Though I had wished, like anyone would. I wished— many, many times. Life would have been way easier if I had something more than my mindless, good-for-nothing tongue that consistently got me in trouble.

I rubbed my forehead harder as my head spun, trailing my hands down to scratch at my chest when I struggled to catch my breath.

He couldn't be serious. There was no way. If I had powers, I would have known.

"What does your Academy teach you about powers?" His measured voice was careful.

I stuttered, trying to gather my thoughts. "J—Just that the Fates bestow them upon certain royalty o—or sometimes warriors deemed worthy. Only those pure of heart...so their powers will be respected, protected."

He sighed, the sound heavy with something I couldn't decipher.

"All right. That's one way of viewing it."

He turned from me to face the dimly lit room. "There are many ways to develop powers...and not all of them are... honorable."

Something in his tone shuddered something like fear in me again.

"Maybe...it's different in other kingdoms?" I offered weakly.

He tilted his head, considering it. But his answer came quickly. "I don't believe so. Powers belong to the person, not to the location."

Of course. How could I suggest otherwise? I wasn't thinking straight. My chest tightened further as my chest tightened.

"Breathe, Princess."

My eyes snapped up to his.

Two words. And yet, they distracted me enough. More than I expected them to.

"Fia—" I still scolded, shaking my head. "And I'm all

right...you can keep talking." I forced my hands to rest on my knees.

I felt him keeping his eyes on me a little longer before continuing.

"However," he mused, "perhaps a power was placed within your kingdom to keep other powers at bay. I've heard that theory too."

He pointed at me, as if I was the one that came to the conclusion myself. "Good observation."

Instead I was just sitting there—useless—on a fragile stool while my world crumbled around me. And yet...despite everything, I hated how good I felt at the acknowledgement. Maybe coming here wasn't a complete waste of time.

I exhaled, resting my elbow on the warm wooden ledge of the window, letting myself lean back into the draft of air seeping through. It was warmed by the candlelight, but it was air nonetheless. A small relief.

"Have you ever noticed anything different about yourself—about your body—when you leave your kingdom?"

The question lingered in the air, heavier than the silence that followed.

I was rarely permitted to leave my kingdom.

Maybe that was that on purpose.

The realization hit me faster than the arrow—one I would have preferred at this point. My face fell into my hand.

I'd never left my palace grounds. Even Academy was right on the border of our town and the one nearby. Many students in the North were boarded in Academy and went home for the weekends.

We had that choice, but unless we were snowed in, we never spent more time at Academy than we needed to because home was so close by. We went home. We were always home.

All I knew was home.

I shook my head frantically. "I can't believe this. I—I don't know. I don't know what to think."

Kallias sat back down across from me, his hand naturally pressed on my knee in a gesture of silent comfort.

"Fia, please don't fret. Strengthen your mind to try to understand this. You can do it. The first step to becoming a great warrior is controlling your mind—learning to process what is around you and react appropriately."

I could have cried—from confusion, fear, anger, frustration, all of it—but I forced myself to look past my hand and into his encouraging eyes. Something in those crystal pools tugged at my vulnerability.

"Tell me what's around you," He commanded silently.

"What?"

My breaths were shakier than they should have been, but I couldn't find it in myself to be embarrassed.

"Point out a few things you see around you."

He steadied his voice, patient. I almost didn't take him seriously, but he waited for me to indulge this odd request. I welcomed the distraction.

"The window?" I breathed out.

He nodded, waiting for more.

"Fire." I glanced at the candle.

"And the wax."

I watched the smallest droplet of wax slide down the side of the candle. I removed my hand from my forehead and touched the little rusted tray the candle was melting over.

"Silver," I finished, running my fingers over the rusted metal before looking into his eyes and feeling the regulated breaths returning to my lungs. Those eyes would have talked me off the ledge just fine on their own, but...this was nice.

"Yes. Now tell me what you're really thinking."

"I'm scared I'll never become a warrior."

The words escaped me like a tear would have in any other circumstance.

His grip tightened on my leg. "Fia." His voice carried the weight of a command, the kind that made it clear how he became a general.

Advisor general.

Whatever.

My eyes widened slightly at his tone, bracing myself for what he would say next, but his hand relaxed, his eyes shifted over my eye and something tipped a scale in between us and he no longer looked at me like I was a immature warrior, or a princess, or whatever he saw when looked at me before.

Then his voice slowed, speaking more intentionally, more...meaningfully. "I don't think you should let anything, or anyone, prevent your true self from becoming."

I leaned into his encouragement, but hopelessness remained a gnawing animal at my side.

"You can fight for this," he continued, though it felt like he was speaking to both of us. "There is always another way," he whispered.

Silence.

His eyes danced between mine again.

His solemnity carried into his words and requests. He spoke to me as if he needed something from me as much as I did him.

"I will help you find a way if that's what you command of me."

My eyes narrowed at his words.

Who was this man to fight for a stranger? To help someone from another kingdom? He had no real loyalty to my kingdom. To the continent, perhaps, but nothing forcing him to desire my command. And yet, I believed him when he said he could help me.

"Help me."

The words unbound themselves from my chains and flew away. I couldn't stop them. I needed someone on my side–anyone. I needed someone besides myself to believe in me, because minute by minute, I knew my faith in myself wouldn't be enough. I knew I would give up if every option was taken from me. I'd have no choice. It wouldn't be in my control.

We sat in silence until I felt the warmth of his hand and

looked down at it. My hands were on my lap too. Our fingers were grazing each other as my hands overlapped his.

We were touching.

We quickly retreated and leaned away from each other. I swallowed the nervous lump choking me and lowered my head slightly.

"But I don't know how you can help me."

He cleared his throat. "I'm not too sure either, I'll be honest." Running a hand through his shoulder-length hair, he added, "But I will find some way—any way to help you."

I didn't wait to question him this time

"Why?"

He paused. One moment. Two. Three. Several. Too many.

"I feel as though we are more alike than we realize."

A vague answer, yes, but somehow, all I needed. I simply nodded.

I had to stop looking at those eyes. I was starting to trust them too much. And yet, I could almost feel the pain and sympathy radiating from them.

"So—the creatures. What do they look like?" I crossed my arms again and quickly shifted my seat a few inches away from his.

His countenance altered, thankfully. Pulling us back to reality. I shook the thought away. It was just the candlelight—everyone looked good in dimmed candlelight.

Kallias spoke of the grotesque details of the creatures–how many of them looked like deformed, giant animals. Rats that were wolf sized, worms as long as horses, bats bigger than dragons. Others were a mixture of odd animals. A thin squirrel with talons, or a rat with the teeth of a wolf.

I wanted to hear more, but the sorrow in his voice unsettled me in ways I didn't expect. He glanced at my arm only once before inviting me to sit on the bed, where he propped my arm up on a pillow. I was too tired to fight him on it.

Night deepened beyond our conversation.

I wanted to know about my mother's powers and her kingdom–but more importantly, I wanted to know how loved she was, by whom, and why. I wanted to know more about his kingdom, his and Costan and the entire south. I wanted to know too much.

I didn't know where to start.

"What else do you do in your kingdom? Besides being a warrior."

I sat up in the small bed as he pulled the stool closer, to sit near my bare feet.

"I advise and lead warrior groups–one of the youngest to do so."

As impressed as I might have been, I didn't show it.

He grabbed the edge of the thin blanket and tugged it

over my feet, while I asked my questions. "Do you like your kingdom?"

I wondered what it was like to enjoy the kingdom one lived in. What was it like to belong to a kingdom—to truly be a part of it?

"I love my kingdom. I've visited most kingdoms in my time, but I still find our scenery magnificent. Every kingdom has its charm, but there is nowhere as perfect as home."

He spoke of the greenery, the food, and the beach not far from the capital city.

I'd always wanted to see the ocean. We had many lakes, but every depiction, poem, and painting I'd studied in Academy convinced me I couldn't die before seeing the ocean and its vastness.

He spoke so eloquently—educated. Not that I didn't expect it, but warriors, especially young ones, weren't known for their refinement.

He painted beautifully simple images, his voice sure and still whenever he mentioned his home.

It made me want to visit his kingdom—visit anywhere but here. I wished I could speak of a home like that. I wasn't sure how much I would miss it when—if—I ever become a warrior.

I knew I'd miss Libby and Taroh, but beyond them? I wasn't so sure what else there was for me to long for. I cared for others, but everything always seemed temporary. Like one foot was always at the edge of a doorway, waiting to step through the second it opened.

The later the night settled, the lower and raspier his voice became.

He discussed the smaller size of his kingdom, how well the people and royals mingled.

He spoke of its parties, events, and holidays–celebrations the entire realm shared as one. I envied how close the people were.

Mother was loved, at least by those in the palace. Not that I ever saw otherwise. She was one of the few royals that always spoke with servants like they were friends. Father was like that once. Mother made him a better person. That became more evident after she was gone.

Libby and I strove to be like our mother. We tried to befriend the staff, and we might have succeeded–had Father not fired over half of them over the years.

Sleep came out of nowhere. I drifted into a dreamless, cozy rest on the tiny bed, forgetting the horrors of the night I'd left behind. Kallias' voice lingered in the background as I let myself slip away.

NINE

A muffled shriek jerked my entire body awake.

My eyes flew wide open, frantically searching the unknown space around me until they caught Kallias. He was slumped against the weak bookshelf, his brow twitched as he began to stir.

Booming thuds echoed through the house, sending a tsunami of adrenaline through me.

Kallias' eyes flickered open. I watched the realization seep into him. The moment he registered the present, his body tensed.

Without hesitation, he reached for his sword and jumped to his feet.

"Wait—please don't kill anyone first thing in the morning," I managed to rasp out as I swung the blanket off my legs.

The skinny door burst open in a thunderous slam before I could move any further.

Northern guards filed into the little room in groups of two, per usual formation. Thankfully, Kallias didn't lunge at anybody.

Instead he placed his body between me and the door, blade raised and ready.

"Wait. Stop!" I scrambled over the bed as my heart just about fell out of my ribs.

I grabbed Kallias' shoulder, trying to turn him away from the guards. He held his ground, sword unwavering, prepared to take down the six guards. Some I knew by name. Not that that meant they wouldn't kill him if I asked.

"Don't hurt him," I pleaded to the guards, nearly tripping over the floor to step between them.

Two guards flanked Kallias, completely ignoring me as they seized his arms. He only fought for a moment–but they were well-trained, and in the second he hesitated, they forced him to his knees.

"Stop! No. He didn't do anything–he's..."

"State your name and purpose," one of the guards barked down at him.

Kallias didn't speak.

"Last chance. State. Your. Name."

He slightly groaned.

My eyes were so wide at his silence.

"Kallias." I told them, looking at him, pleading for him to say something. "His name is Kallias–"

He still didn't say anything, and I swore I might have

163

seen his jaw tighten, as if this was some intentional act of defiance.

"Wait—" I stepped forward, but before I could reach him, the guards were moving.

Kallias was quickly shoved face-down onto the floor, his arm wrenched behind him. I would have frozen in shock at the sight, but a sharp *crack* splintered through the air, followed by a barely restrained scream.

"STOP!"

My voice was a shrill scratch, but the guards didn't flinch.

Kallias' head pressed into the splintered, wooden planks of the floor, his breath ragged. I spun, shoving at one of the soldiers.

My arm held onto his, earning me a glance from him. Only a glance from his dead, hazel eyes at my arm before a new wave of force rolled through him. The guard raised his sword.

"The harming of a royal is punishable by death—"

The blade glinted in the room, preparing to be brought down and ending the only ally I'd ever had.

My knees hit the ground immediately, falling over Kallias, shooting my other arm up at the guard.

"Stop! Please. You don't understand. He—" I swallowed my dry mouth. "—he saved my life."

My heart beat so wildly, I couldn't decipher which was louder, my shouts or its beating.

"I—I—"

164

I lied.

"I was in the forest," I punched the words out of my gut. "I was lost and injured. He—he found me and sheltered me. I would have died without this man. You *will not* hurt him..."

I glanced at where his forehead was buried into the splintered wood. "Anymore," I added in a cringe.

It was the only thing I could think of to spare Kallias from execution.

I raised both hands, palms open in a truce and a silent plea. Kallias' breaths were even deeper than mine, rough, uneven, and with the occasional shudder that I felt as much as I heard. My own arms felt tight in pain.

My eyes pleaded to the guards like they never had before.

The guards exchanged looks as I held my pleading gaze. Desperation clawed at my throat as I felt their hesitation slipping away.

"See?" I stuck out my injured arm. "He even tended to my wound."

Come on...

The guard with the pointed sword relaxed its position in the smallest motion before grunting in irritation and lowering it.

"Then the King would like for you both to be returned to the palace immediately."

I nodded quickly, forcing my expression to remain

composed. "Yes—yes. Take us both back then."

They hesitated, but within moments, we were thrown into a carriage after filing out of the tiny house one by one.

As soon as the door to the carriage shut, I lunged to Kallias' side, gripping his uninjured arm.

"*Heavens.* I'm so sorry. I didn't think they were—I mean—I—"

Apologies tumbled in my mind, but I couldn't get a single one past my lips.

He groaned a bit then shot up his hand at me. "It's all right, Princess."

I gaped at him, unsure as to how he was speaking. He turned his face away, but I caught the wince he tried to hide. I watched helplessly as he groaned again, struggling to properly sit up. I tried to help.

Then, without hesitation, I yanked the fabric of my pants at the knee, slicing a clean line with my dagger. My whole outfit was already destroyed, so marring it any further didn't seem to make much of a difference.

I knelt before him, pressing a gentle hand against his leg.

"Kallias?" I whispered. I wasn't sure if he was ignoring me or was too focused on not being in pain that he didn't hear me.

I tried for his attention again.

"Look at me," I whispered.

His eyes carefully blinked open and held my gaze. I had

fashioned some shorts for myself from the fabric and carefully wrapped the extra fabric strips around his neck and under his arm for a makeshift sling.

I'd only dislocated my shoulder once in my life, but falling out of that tree had been enough of a lesson to make me empathize with him.

His jaw tensed like carved stone, his teeth locked as I adjusted the sling around his neck. His breathing was slow but measured—controlled. When I finished tying the cloth securely, he gave me a curt nod, avoiding my gaze.

"Lay down."

I shifted to the other side of the carriage, waiting for him to comply.

His eyes flicked up to me, hesitant. "I'm fine. It's not as bad as it looked."

I narrowed my eyes at him. "Liar," I mocked. "I know how much a dislocated shoulder can hurt."

A ghost of a smirk, laced with pain, pleasantly appeared on his strained face.

He exhaled, relenting, and carefully eased himself onto his uninjured side. The cramped space barely accommodated his frame, and by how tightly he shut his eyes, I doubted he would rest well.

The carriage rattled and swayed around me. I watched him despite myself. The ride stretched on, feeling like days instead of hours. At some point, he must have drifted into a light sleep. I might have too.

His face remained surprisingly calm.

At first, I thought it devoid of emotion, but looking closer, I realized it wasn't emptiness—it was mastery. He had perfected the art of hiding, stilling his emotions, a noble kind of restraint. The kind I'd only seen on royals.

Not all royals.

I could only wish for that kind of control.

Libby always laughed at how my expressions gave me away, saying I was incapable of subtlety. Either too animated or too severe—never in between.

It was the dark eyebrows on my slightly tanned skin I was born with; even in my most neutral state, I always looked a little irritated. I didn't mind. It kept unwanted advances to a minimum.

My gaze lingered on Kallias, and a thought sparked from nowhere. Kallias and Libby would make an incredible pair. Her effortless elegance and his reserved countenance—the epitome of a perfect couple. I was almost jealous of the thought.

As much as I dreaded returning home under these circumstances, perhaps it would give them a chance to meet.

Perhaps *that* could become the solution.

If he and Libby married, maybe Father would restore relations with the kingdoms. And if she was already wed, maybe—just maybe—Father would stop caring so much about my status.

Maybe...

I could think of a plan—to introduce them, to convince him, and her. The proposal matches were only months away.

I could refuse him. Then he could fight for Libby's hand instead of mine.

She was always impossibly particular when it came to men, but Kallias was different. A warrior, yes, but an honorable one. Strong. Disciplined. Loyal. Any woman would be lucky to wed someone like him.

The idea settled in my mind, neat and logical, a present falling perfectly into my lap.

And yet, as I glanced at him—his face still drawn in restless sleep, his injured arm held close—a sharp, unspoken uncertainty buried into my chest. I ignored it.

This was the solution. The only solution.

Wasn't it?

TEN

The dais of the palace was a cold, white expanse of marble and limestone with polished floors stretching beneath towering columns framing shadowing hallways, some blocked off by iron doors. The domed ceiling bathed us in enough light but didn't shield us from the cold air wafting in from every opening.

Despite the brightness of the stone, the palace was as dark and cold as could be. Above us, the windows in the dome loomed–a vast pane of thick glass like an eye of some unseen Fate shining down on me, watching, judging.

Some believed Fates would bless royals like us if they looked down on our lives.

But nobeing with a view this close to the palace of Sevaire would look at our people and ever choose to bless us for anything.

Father stormed in. My heart instantly froze. Any pleasant feeling seeped out of me as dread drenched over me.

His presence was a mighty blade slicing in a scream through the bitter silence. As expected.

He came to a halt at the very center of the family crest painted in the middle of the marble beneath our feet.

"*Your* guards—" I scolded, not wanting to wait for him to speak, despite being expected to. "Nearly murdered my savior."

Beside me, Kallias shifted his weight, his arm hanging stiffly at his side as he began to slowly lower himself onto one knee before the King. Father had to see the pain in the rigid line of his jaw. Yet he didn't tell him to rise.

"Explain," Father commanded, his voice crackling through the room. But his eyes didn't stray to Kallias, left kneeling beside me.

He was speaking to *me*.

Right.

Because this was my mess to explain.

Through his brooding, judgmental eyes, his presence demanded answers. It made me want to faint so he couldn't possibly have more opportunities to scream at me.

But I had expected this.

I lifted my chin and met his gaze.

I proceeded to give him the lie about an animal nearly mauling me to death and what it led to.

"...and then your careless guards decided to act like animals nearly killing him—"

"*Do not* raise your voice at me," Father boomed. "Or I

will happily allow my guards to resume."

My jaw clicked shut, but I kept my chin up. Kallias remained unmoved, still on one knee.

I swiftly became aware of how awful I felt with Kallias at our feet and folded my arms in front of me. I let my head dip down an inch to my Father.

"Yes, *your Majesty*," I said, addressing him the way I only did when I truly didn't see him as my father, but as the King—A reminder I often needed. A reminder my father enjoyed enforcing.

He shot his gaze to Kallias. His soulless eyes darted at the figure kneeling before him.

"Don't humor me, Prince Kallias. Stand up."

I froze.

Prince?

The word swung through the air like the cataclysmic explosion it was.

A prince? As in *the* Prince–*the* Prince of Lyen?

Kallias flinched, barely perceptible at the title as he pushed himself to his feet, transforming his kneel into a brief, stiff bow.

I stared at him standing fully erect and my mind shattered. The image I had of him fractured into thousands of unrecognizable shards.

The quiet, noble grace. The eloquence.

The lying.

The way he carried himself–not just as a warrior, but as

someone backed by some power. The way he had spoken to me without hesitation. The way he had touched me, like he had that right. Which, I supposed...he did.

I scrutinized him through a whole new lens. It explained so much—too much.

My head spun.

A prince.

I wanted to demand an explanation, wanting to rip the truth from him with my own bare hands—but I couldn't, not in the middle of my father's judgment.
"Prince?" The word slipped from me in a pointed whisper. It was all I could manage to say.

I let my anger cloud me, but when the guards bowed to Kallias—*Prince Kallias*—I turned to him, mirroring their required movements in a slight one of my own. An instinct drilled into me that I used right now, partially to hide my perplexity.

Perplexity and anger.

Anger from how easily he had hidden his real self with an ease that was unnerving.

I was putty in his hand, trusting a man who spoke to me as an equal, all while hiding his true identity. If he could lie so easily about this, what else could he have been lying about?

I couldn't wait for this stand-off to end so I could break his other arm.

Kallias dipped his head away from me for a fleeting moment, then turned back to the King, avoiding my gaze.

Coward.

"You have recently finished your decade as a warrior, have you not?" Father's voice rang through the hall, a bell warning that the worst was yet to come.

He didn't even glance at Kallias' bound arm–typical. He ignored my injury too.

"Yes, Your Majesty."

Kallias' rasp had not subsided.

"Child?" Father directed at me.

The word cracked like a whip. The word I'd grown to revile over the years. If I offended Father by calling him *Your Majesty,* then *child* was his equivalent payback.

I nearly jumped back at his glare. My body stiffened, pulse stammering in my throat. If my eyes shot daggers, then his released cannonballs. Giant ice-cold, indestructible cannonballs.

"Consider yourself lucky to have only escaped with a wound. Have you learned your lesson, or must I have a guard to supervise you day and night?"

We had tried that before.

The memory cried into my mind, coming alive too quickly–locked doors, silent nights, a shadow trailing my every step, someone predicting my next steps better than I could.

I wouldn't dream of subjecting any guard to that... again.

"No, Your Majesty," I said, my voice as controlled as I would allow it.

"I hope you bid your farewells to that dresser that was against your door. It has been destroyed."

His tone was a measured calculation. A test. Everything was a test or game or power move.

I knew he was holding back–for now. He would get to the actual yelling at me later.

I met his gaze, silently glaring back.

"As for that tree outside the window—"

My breath hitched.

"It will be chopped down today."

My lips parted, armed, and ready to protest. He knew it too–the smallest tilt of his head was warning enough. But I wouldn't let myself lose this round. I wouldn't let myself lose control. Not in front of Kallias.

Prince Kallias.

I bit my tongue, forced my fists to open, and unlocked my jaw. Every muscle in my body tensed as I willed myself to be still and nodded at my father.

"Find your chambers and stay there until dinner."

Another nod out of me, then I turned to Kallias, unsure whether I wanted to say goodbye, or thank you, or a *how dare you.*

I didn't have time to decide, not as Father's voice cut me off.

"He is to stay here the remainder of that day," Father commanded.

I swallowed my irritation. "A healer should be brought

too," I added before losing my momentum. I prayed to Heavens he didn't have my head for cutting in at his command.

Father straightened, causing me to still. I cleared my throat in an attempt to sound a little more pleasant to my father. It wasn't my best strategy, but occasionally I would let him believe that he actually knocked me down a notch.

"It's the least we could offer to...*the prince*," I trailed off, throwing in the last bitter emphasis before I disappeared. I backed away a few steps, waiting for my father to turn his back to me first.

"Thank you, but—" Kallias began.

I shot him a glare, cutting him off, then took another step towards my getaway: the stairs.

As infuriating as his deception was, maybe it was a blessing in disguise.

He was a prince.

Another reason he and Libby should marry.

She would handle this royal better—calm, level-headed. Meanwhile, all I wanted to do was strangle my father with the few shreds of fabric left on my skirt.

"The Prince will stay until he gets treated," Father declared to the guard. Then his gaze snapped back to me, freezing me mid-step.

"Now *leave* before you try any more of the limited patience I have reserved for you." He turned his back, permitting me to leave. "You will be seeing me momentarily," he added over his shoulder.

A private screaming-session with my father.

Great.

I'd rather slice my other arm.

I sprinted away with the guards trailing behind. Thankfully, they weren't too much of a nuisance. I should have seen it coming—the increase in babysitters—but I still shot them a glare before slamming my door shut.

If I was going to be treated like a child, I had no reason not to act like one as well.

It wasn't their fault, but I hoped they knew me well enough to not take it personally.

I turned to lock the door.

The entire door knob was gone.

Nothing but an empty hole left in its stead.

It wasn't just a lack of a lock, or privacy, or secrecy. It was my father making sure I knew that I had nowhere to hide.

That no matter what, as long as I was in this palace, no one would ever have more power than my father. Especially me. No power, no freedom, no choice.

But that was all about to change.

ELEVEN

I spent hours sitting on my windowsill, staring out my window.

I'd miss that tree.

I hoped the birds would somehow sense their home would be taken away and would move out before then. I felt ridiculous caring about a bunch of birds more than Kallias. But he didn't deserve my sympathy right now.

"*Lying bastard,*" I mumbled to myself.

I kept my window wide open, offering refuge to the birds if needed. Only one flew in—the one I'd assumed was the mother bird. I welcomed her in—this one time. At this point she could have it. It was my fault her home would be taken away from her and her family.

She hopped around the ground. I would have shared some food with her too if I had any, but I accepted Father's decision to starve me again—a punishment he often used. I should be thinner than a bird with how often I was starved.

As much as I hated its effectiveness, I still sneaked through servant passages for midnight snacks–or meals–whenever I could.

Libby had taught me the servant passageways after I was locked in the butcher's closet for two days for beating up Ptolem and starting a food fight at one of their Biannuals.

There were a few little passageways in odd areas of the palace. Some from the kitchen to outside. Some from their quarters to the stables. But I learned a little too late.

That memory was still too fresh–thrown into a butcher's closet, full of suspended, dead pigs. I was stuck in the dark until I threw up, then starved in my room days after. Not that I could have eaten anything anyways. I blamed Jayce for that one too–the weasel got away with everything. I hadn't eaten pork since.

Even now I couldn't say I regretted it.

Father stormed in right before dinner and didn't hesitate to scream at me for my incorrigible *something* and reckless *something else*.

He just screamed and screamed and screamed.

I nodded along, playing the role of regretful girl. He screamed more while I pretended to listen.

I wanted to scream right back at him. I wanted to ask about everything I'd learned, but whenever I *thought* about speaking over his yelling, he doubled my detentions. And after last night, I wasn't going to risk getting myself killed.

So I bore the names he called me, the threats he made, the projectile spit that threatened to sprinkle on my face. I distracted myself with the idea of pushing Libby and the Prince together.

Prince.

I thought about how Kallias might have known Mother.

He had said I looked like her. He wasn't related to us—I knew that much.

So *how*—

My eyes blinked at another speck of spit flying at me.

"You try *anything* like this one more time and I *will* leave you to the wolves. And even if you manage to make it back, I will be sure the word *Warrior* never leaves your lips again." He jabbed his long, crooked finger at me. "Heed my warning, child. It will be the *last* one."

He stormed out without any reaction from me. His word was law, after all.

I waited until his footsteps faded before I dared near my door.

A minute later, Libby burst in.

We embraced immediately. I held my sister tightly—she was my only comfort after my father's screaming matches.

"Fia, I was sick with worry—"

I stiffened at her words and pushed her away as the memories of last night shooting into my mind.

I took a step away from her. "You shouldn't have been."

I folded my arms over my chest, as if to shield my heart.

"Fia, how could you run away like that? I almost went to find you myself."

My eyes rolled.

She sighed at the expression, trying to paint on an angry face. Even then, her beauty didn't falter.

"They said you were hurt?"

She reached for my arm, but I pulled it back, remembering how literally everyone I'd encountered the last twenty-four hours had lied to me and apparently I was the last transparent person on this damned continent.

"I'm sure you're very concerned. Since you clearly don't think I can fend for myself."

Maybe she wouldn't be completely wrong.

"I'm sure you assume I'm just some helpless little girl who could never become a warrior. Right?"

I couldn't force the words out to be as painful as I desired them to be. No matter what, I could never try hard enough to hurt my sister, even if she had hurt me.

"Fia. Stop." Her eyes narrowed in concern. "You *know* how much I look up to you. You know I believe you can do anything you set your mind to."

She moved to sit on my bed, motioning for me to join her. "Let me explain."

I sat next to her and let her grab my hand, but

remained stiff.

"I will always support your endeavors. I'm proud of how far you've come since choosing your specialty. But I've been hearing talk about the creatures at the borders, and—"

"You have?" I cut in. "What have you heard?"

How could she know more than me?

I studied these things whenever I had a free moment.

I asked about this often. She knew that, yet she didn't inform me about something she learned regarding this?

"How long have you known—"

"It's not much, but I hear the guards speak. You know they never take me seriously, so they talk around me like I'm not even there."

That was true.

I hated that she noticed the way men ignored her.

Most women in our kingdom were easily overlooked. Our society made it seem that the more beautiful a woman was, the less she was regarded as anything more than breeding lineage. They spoke over her as if she were nothing more than a beautiful sculpture embedded into the palace walls.

Sadly, she didn't have any information Kallias hadn't already told me.

"Perhaps...Fia..."

She held my hand in her small, pale ones. "Something so brutal wouldn't be the best for a princess."

Her hand gripped mine gingerly.

I sighed at her careful words.

"Libby, warriors aren't meant to be safely stuck in a room. *I* know this. *You* know this. I'm not an idiot–I knew what I was getting myself into–"

"Fia, think about it. If you get into the hands of an enemy kingdom, you wouldn't be just a faceless warrior, you'd be a political risk. You could start a potential war."

I glanced at her worried expression. She looked more concerned than I'd seen her in awhile. I could tell she had thought a lot about this. I almost considered her point. However, there had to be a way around it.

"Libby, my plans were to stay in the North–inland–you know my dreams. We've talked about this all my life. If I don't do this–what are my options? I'm not suited to marry, I have no other talents to provide, we don't have family to allow me to become a co-ruler. If I don't do this, I'm more useless than a blind carriage driver."

Her sad look brought little comfort, leaving a sinking feeling in my chest.

"Fia, you are so much more than that. You have so much to offer just as yourself. There is always the Quintennial–you could pick up a sport? Or you could co-rule, we could find someone–I'm not sure–I don't have a perfect answer...You may be my little sister Fia, but I've always found you so–"

"Libby, I appreciate your concern. I do." I turned to face her. "But you have to see this realistically. I don't have that many options if I can't become a warrior. This conversation is five years too late. Even if it wasn't, it's not that this is my dream. It's now my only option. I made sure of that when I changed my classes at Academy."

I crossed my legs on the bed to face her.

"You know Father won't care if I'm ever captured and used as blackmail."

I watched her beautiful eyes round in worry.

"And if you're that concerned...then maybe you could help me out with an idea I had."

She squinted, like she somehow already knew this was a bad idea.

"I think I have a solution for me to still become a warrior—potentially."

She drew a breath to protest, but I spoke up first.

"Hear me out—I want you to meet this...prince."

"What are you talking about? Where did you meet a prince? You—" Her eyes widened. "Prince? You spent the night with a *prince?*"

My hand smacked over her mouth, but she simply laughed into it. "Tell the whole palace, why don't you?"

I waited until she was still.

"It wasn't like that," I whispered. "I was hurt, and he found me. He was the warrior from the party."

I let her go.

"I didn't know he was a prince."

"My Heavens," she gasped. "You run away, you meet your suitor—who turns out to be a prince—then you sleep with him." She crossed her arms. "I didn't think you could amaze me any more."

I nudged her shoulder.

"I'm not a harlot. I didn't *sleep* sleep with him. We slept in the same building." I shook my head. "Forget about that. I want you to meet him—officially. I think he would make a great suitor for you."

"What are you talking about?" she retorted.

"Libby, he's a noble, handsome warrior prince. Imagine how this could unite the kingdoms. You've spoken before how you want to be closer to Mother—we both have. This might be the way to do so. He's from the South, like she is and they've had some unrest the past several years."

"But he was *your* suitor. He asked for *your* hand. You marry him," she scolded.

I sighed.

"Stop it, Libby. You know that's not happening. End of discussion. But *you*—"

"No. You're being insane. I don't want your suitor."

I scoffed at her dismissal.

"Listen...This could potentially be beneficial to everyone involved. I doubt Father would care about my position if two kingdoms grow from such a union. I'm actually surprised he hasn't thought of it already."

"Stop it, Fia." She stood up. "I do not wish to marry some stranger you—"

"Then don't! Just...meet him and see if he could be a

good companion, if you hit it off. It can't hurt."

"Stop this, Fia. This isn't you. If you like the idea that much then you should do it. I'm not going to marry a man just because you don't want him."

"I didn't say I didn't want—"

"Ha!"

Her little finger pointed to me. "Then marry him. You two will make a great warrior couple. I have my own suitors to worry about."

"But you always believed that the best marriages start from friendships and kinship and respect. You would respect this man, I'm sure he'd be easy to love."

She narrowed her eyes on me. Then she directed a question to me. "Could you marry someone solely out of respect? That would be all it took?"

"Sure—" my voice lilted skeptically "In theory. This is one of the most respectable men I've ever met."

"Then tell me again why you can't marry him?" she nearly sang.

I rolled my eyes.

"How can you even ask that? I've never been suited for marriage. Even if I were, I doubt Father would help another kingdom *I* married into."

I slid my hands over her arms.

"All I'm asking is for you to speak to the man at dinner and tell me what you think." I tried to sound as sweet as possible.

She huffed.

"Oh, I will definitely tell you what I think." She uncrossed her arms. "Have you learned much about him?"

I shrugged. "A little. Not much, but from what I can sense from him, he seems to be a decent man—despite the whole lying-about-being-a-prince thing. It suits the role, though. Just talk to him about his kingdom. I'm sure it'll help keep the conversation alive."

"With you back, I doubt that will be much of an issue."

TWELVE

After getting dressed for dinner, I frantically penned a letter to slip to Kallias later tonight.

I didn't expect I'd get a moment alone with him ever again, so I had to hand off some form of communication, and I wasn't completely fond of the idea of talking to him right now. Now that I knew he was a royal. A lying royal.

I told Libby I'd meet her downstairs, and luckily, she didn't fight me on not helping me get ready. She waited at the bottom of the stairs in a simple blush gown, perfectly paired with her rose gold jewelry.

I joined her in a pale gray dress that was growing too tight around the corset.

"Are you ready?" She asked, linking arms with me.

"No."

I was seated across from Kallias.

I still hadn't forgiven him, which he knew, as he ignored my many harsh glances and instead fixated on his food, playing with it more than eating it.

Royal guests were always required to join us for dinner. It was one of our worst customs—not just because of today but because of all the dinners I'd been forced to sit through with the many bland faces I'd forgotten the second they stood up from the table.

I still hoped Father wouldn't say anything too despicable to Kallias. Though I doubted it.

I always received the worst of his wrath, and I didn't mind it being that way. I always hoped he'd never transfer that to Taroh. I'd truly kill him if he did.

Father sat as stoic as ever, more stone than man. The clash of forks on plates filled the entire dining room, seemingly the entire kingdom.

I wasn't sure how I'd get my letter to Kallias. I wouldn't be able to sneak out of my room anytime soon with my increased security.

Perhaps I could ask one of the servants to slip it to him. A few of them owed me favors from secrets I'd kept for them, but I doubted I'd find a moment to escape and track one of them down either.

"Fiadh..." Erie began, likely irritated by the silence or the constant bouncing of Taroh's leg under the giant table. "... has anyone brought you your delivery yet?" She tucked a strand of her straight, auburn hair behind her ear.

My face scrunched in confusion at her as I shook my head. She patted her thin lips with her red napkin, her manicured, jeweled fingers resting lightly on the table.

"Prince Jayce has sent you some sort of...*gift*."

I pushed out a scoff. "I'll get it later."

Her voice turned teasing, and I wasn't sure if it was due to the lack of conversation or some odd fascination of marrying me off just to be rid of me. "You and Prince Jayce always seem to enjoy each other's company at these events."

I tried to hide my annoyance at the topic, knowing exactly where it was going, and knowing exactly how much I did not want to discuss it. Still, I supposed I should have been grateful that, for once, the focus of the conversation wasn't about my mishaps.

Yet.

Still, my lips stretched into an exaggerated smile as I spoke to her. "Trust me, that overgrown weasel is nothing but a child. Taroh's more mature than he is. Don't consider him anything but a nuisance."

I sipped the spicy potato soup, anticipating dessert. "Do not be so rude, Fiadh," Erie grit out, forcing a faux, pleasant tone.

No one spoke after that. The silence grew so thick, if I shut my eyes, I would almost believe I was alone in my room. I wished I were.

I turned, summoning a servant. She approached me promptly. Grasping her pale arm, I whispered, "Please tell me Matty's back making those little lavender pastries?"

I thought I was starved for any food, but the moment I

caught the faintest whiff of vanilla and lavender, it redefined the entire concept of hunger.

Father's glare snapped to the servant, sending her scurrying back to her post.

"Is dessert really your main concern at the moment?" He spoke with assertion.

My chin dipped as I resisted the urge to roll my eyes. His voice remained as calm and assertive as usual. Though he probably ran out of energy from screaming at me.

"Forgive me, your Majesty. *I'm...a little hungry*," I mumbled with a tasteless smile.

"Then think before you act next time you want to escape these grounds."

My nails dug into my knees as I forced my smile wider. "Yes, Your Majesty."

Libby slipped me a sweet smile before clearing her throat—a silent reminder to keep myself in check.

We dove back into the silence. Libby blinked harshly at me until I met her gaze. My brows furrowed when I did.

Her head tilted towards Kallias, motioning for me to talk to him. I checked the table, certain no one else was watching.

You talk to him, I glanced back at her, shaking my head.

Come on, her widened eyes said.

I rolled my eyes as I shook my head briefly.

"What–" Taroh asked slowly, his gaze darting between

the two of us.

Libby jumped in before Taroh pointed anything else out. "So...Prince Kallias, what made you ask for my sister's hand at the Biannual?" she asked tenderly.

I shot her the most obvious glare I could muster. *Really?* My eyes demanded. She ignored me, slurping her soup.

Despite myself, I felt Kallias's gaze settle on me from the corner of my eye.

He swallowed his food before answering Libby. "I found her...easy to talk to," he said flatly before returning to his plate.

Your turn, her eyes challenged.

I sipped my soup loudly, glaring at Libby before finally giving into her coercion. "Your arm looks better." My voice remained low enough for only him to hear. "Did a healer come?"

There was no real reason to be so quiet, besides the embarrassing show it would be for my family to see me interact with a man.

Kallias looked up at me, his gaze bringing an unexpected warmth to the otherwise frigid spring evening. My hands no longer felt cold under the touch of his soft expression.

He nodded a short bob, his eyes lingering on mine. I returned the gesture before we both fell back into the silence of dinner.

Everyone ate.

I stole another glance at Libby then Taroh, making sure he wasn't letting his curiosity get the better of him. I would make sure he never would–he wouldn't be too much like me. Not in this palace.

I looked back at Libby, who continued motioning her head at Kallias.

What else am I supposed to say? I shrugged.

I don't know, anything! She leered back.

Why don't you *talk to him?* I bobbed back, ending the movement by miming a ring sliding onto my finger and pointing at the two of them.

He likes you, she mouthed after rolling her eyes.

No he doesn't. I shook back.

Just. Talk. To. Him. She ended our silent battle with a sharp look before looking away from me, enabling me from responding unless I wanted to speak.

I cleared my throat a few times, earning concerned looks from Erie and Taroh. "Why don't you drink more water?" Erie said pointedly.

I nodded at her sarcastically, grabbing my glass of water and taking a sip. When Libby finally looked back at me I tilted my head to Father. *I can't talk in front of him.*

Fine. She sneered, offering a reluctant truce.

The endless, silent dinner only possessed a little bit of chatter, mainly from me to Taroh since no one else knew what to say and I would only talk to someone who hadn't infuriated me the past couple days. Not that his limited language skills offered much conversation.

The dinner did end with the pastries I'd been waiting all evening for. I was ecstatic for Mattok to be back from the cooking courses he was enrolled in at Academy. I had to endure weeks of disappointing desserts in his absence.

I devoured the entire cakelet in one bite, moaning in pure delight as I ignored Libby's judgmental glare.

"When do you depart back to Lyen, Prince Kallias?" Father asked in a levelled voice.

Prince.

Was I supposed to call him that, too? I usually called people whatever they introduced themselves as formality annoyed me. As did my full name, which was why I never introduced myself with it.

Princess Fiadh Alepha Dagny, *Jewel of the North.*

I did not miss writing that out at the top of every Academy assignment.

"Tomorrow morning, Your Majesty. Thank you for your hospitality, I wouldn't wish to overstay my welcome."

Erie chimed in, all too eager.

"Nonsense! You are welcome anytime. Perhaps under *better* circumstances next time."

I ignored her pointed glance as I chewed another mouthful of cake.

"I'm honored," Kallias responded in a practiced, royal tone. "You have a lovely home. Thank you for your kindness on my intrusion." He spoke the phrase like it was rehearsed.

"Oh never an intrusion!"

My stepmother softened, turning into her friendly self again. "Come back any time."

Her oddly flirtatious tone earned her a look from my father. She ignored him, sipping her cider—probably drinking more than she should.

I did love when she ignored him.

Dinner ended, and Father asked for a private word with Kallias. Even though I wanted to speak with him too, I didn't attempt to intervene with my father's command, knowing how that would end.

Instead, I bowed goodnight to my father and then to the prince, offering my hand for him to kiss.

He didn't hesitate to take it.

"Thank you for your company and all you've done to ensure my safety." I spoke as awkwardly as I expected to in front of my family. "I am in your debt." I said with just enough facetiousness.

More importantly he picked up the little folded note in the hand he kissed and subtly pocketed it. I gave him the faintest satisfied smile before Father excused me to my chambers.

After my shower, I dressed in my warmest pajamas and climbed down my window, slipping into the small servant's door hidden in the corner wall, tucked away safely in the shadow of my tree. My time with this tree was running out, and I intended to use every moment I had left.

The little door, barely half the size of a normal one, had once been used for garbage disposal before renovations turned it into just another drainage port for the rainy season. But it held more value than that—it connected to a few interconnected tunnels leading to a couple different sectors of the palace's main floor.

It also doubled as a romantic meeting corner for the servants, thanks to the deep shade beneath the tree. Which was precisely how I'd built up so many favors. Little did the servants know I wasn't the gossiper most Northerners my age were.

Fraternizing amongst servants wasn't strictly forbidden, but Father searched for any excuse to expel "useless staff," as he so charmingly referred to them.

Slipping through the door, I moved past the kitchen staff barracks and into the butcher quarters. The stench was as awful as ever, dredging up memories I'd rather not revisit, but it provided a clear path to the back of the kitchen.

I glanced around for my baker boy, but it seemed they'd released him early tonight.

Three large coolers lined one of the walls in the kitchen. I opened the one that usually held desserts and grinned when I noticed more of those pastries.

I inhaled three or four more pastries before grabbing a wrap to stuff some more food into. I noticed Kallias had barely touched his soup, so I took a few extra pastries for him as well—along with a pre-made sandwich someone must have saved for tomorrow.

"Sorry," I mumbled to the essence of whoever left their sandwich behind.

A flash of sandy brown hair and light brown eyes peeked out from behind the freezer box. I jumped before realizing who it was.

"Matty!"

If my arms weren't full, and if it wasn't completely inappropriate, I would have hugged him.

"How have you been, Princess?" His boyish smile made me feel truly at home now.

"Hungry."

He chuckled at my full hands of food. "Tell me you're back for good, Matty."

He nodded. "Studies are finished. I'm back as an official baker."

My cheeky smile spread across my face. "Well, I am beyond glad. No offense to the rest of the staff, but no one bakes as well as you."

He gave another soft smile.

"I will come back tomorrow, perhaps, to catch up, but I have to run back now."

He nodded, ever understanding. Matty had always been a better friend than baker, and honestly, he was one of the few friends I had left in my life after Academy.

By the time I maneuvered my way back through the

maze of tunnels, I spotted Kallias. He stood beneath the tree outside my window, concealed by the thick shadows of its branches.

My greeting came out as more of a grunt.

"Good. You got away from my father."

"Yes. He's quite...protective. He probably wouldn't be so fond of you out here, alone. Unsecure. "

He sounded more relaxed than he did at dinner—no more choppy, curt phrases or silent glances.

I rolled my eyes. "It's secure enough. And—I assume I can trust you. You haven't proven me wrong—Well, except the whole prince thing. Thank you very much for *that* surprise."

The moonlight caught in his eyes before he averted them in an admission of guilt.

I tried not to stare.

Instead, I held out the bag of food. "You didn't eat much today."

He hesitated for a second before cautiously taking the bag and taking a seat by the tree. "Thank you."

He exhaled in relief as he dug inside, immediately reaching for the dessert.

A man after my own heart.

I didn't ask about his silence during dinner—I didn't have the time to ask. "We don't have much—"

"These carvings..." he interrupted, his gaze fixing on the trunk of the tree. His eyes glazed over the scattered etching—random cuts at various angles, some resembling birds, some various letters, others sad attempts at flowers. I had even tried to carve one of my daggers too, but was not as artistic as I wished I were.

"Did you do them?"

He pointed to one of the flowers that I carved to look like it was a separate piece blooming from the tree. It was probably the only decent one, though still jagged around the edges.

"Yes, but you don't get to judge me. I was very young when I did most of those." Which was probably evident as they didn't go higher than shoulder-length.

I followed his gaze, the sight of my old carvings stirring an ache in my chest. This tree had grown up with me. Losing it would feel like losing a piece of myself.

"No, they're...nice."

Hunger must have had a weird effect on him, softening him. I almost smiled.

"But you shouldn't cut into trees. It could damage them."

My smile morphed into a scoff.

"Don't tell me what to do with my trees."

I crossed my arms and glanced back at the carvings.

Focus.

"We have to be quick." I threw a glance at my window. "My sister will probably look for me soon, but I wanted to let you know my plan."

He leaned against the trunk of my tree, speaking

through a mouthful of pastry. "Plan?"

"Yes. I think I've found a way for us all to get what we want."

I stood before him, hands raised—prepped to explain my idea.

"Hear me out—"

He took another bite, watching as I paced.

"Obviously you already asked for my hand. However, Libby's proposal matches always come first, since she's older. So—you could show up to hers when they ask if anyone was missed during the Biannuals. I will get her to agree to accept. Then you can compete for her hand instead of mine. If you make it to the end, there's no way they'd make you compete for my hand too. There would be no point to. Not as long as there is someone else there. As far as I know that one boy is still coming—I don't really know. Either way,"

I shook away the unnecessary details.

"The point is—you should fight for her hand—I already started trying to convince her to marry you, and I think if we work on your people skills a little more we could convince her together. Then you two can unite the continent, and hopefully it will be easier to convince my father to get off my back."

He listened thoroughly, chewing each bite carefully with those dark, furrowed brows. He waited too long to answer.

I quit my pacing, narrowing my eyes at him. "If you don't like it, I'd love to hear whatever recommendations you have.”

He swallowed his last bite, then leaned forward, forearms resting on his knees. His silver-rimmed blue eyes met mine, cutting straight through me.

“No.”

I blinked at him.

“No? What do you mean.”

“I mean, no. If I marry anyone, it will be you.”

THIRTEEN

Once again, this man had me at a loss for words. I didn't care for the feeling. It took me a moment to recover, shock lingering on my tongue before I forced some words out.

"I'm not meant to marry."

I spilled out each syllable carefully.

"Why not? Because you want to be a warrior?"

He wiped his mouth from the crumbs speckled on his lips as he watched me. "I would let you become a warrior if you married me. You'd be free to train as you see fit."

A sigh escaped me. "As romantic as that sounds..." I said dripping in sarcasm. "It's my sister's dream. Not mine. And she's perfect for it."

I was still shocked he didn't jump at the opportunity. I remembered boys in Academy offering a ridiculous amount of riches for my assistance in winning favors with my sister. I humored them, of course, lying to them about all the things she liked.

It was a fun time, until it grew too disgusting and men of all ages began offering me the world to convince my sister to give them a chance. Not that I blamed them.

Not only did Libby look like she would be the perfect wife, she was the oldest, she would inherit the North anyways and that was worth more than my life to many.

He wiped his mouth again with the back of his hand before dusting them off.

"I need allies from different kingdoms, and you want to fight for the future of our continent. Unless your father suddenly develops a change of heart—which I don't see happening—he will just expect you to marry someone anyways. If that's what you want, then that's your prerogative, but if that's your only option, I don't mind saving you...again." His smirk was as annoying and rugged as it was charming.

But I sneered at him. "I don't need you saving me, *jerk*."

The little smirk he gave me was subtle, barely there, but it irritated me more than a slap to the face.

Still, he didn't stop.

"Maybe not, but I need you."

His soft voice carried in the breeze. I searched his eyes for any hint of a joke, or some deception.

"I'm never going to force you into anything," he said with a gentle tilt of his head. "It's an option. As for your plan—I'm sure your Biannual will be remembered. I did ask for your hand after all, and I meant it. The people expect me to fight for

203

you anyways."

I rolled my eyes, ignoring the sensations tangling in my stomach—anger, maybe something else I didn't care to name. "That can be undone."

I could always say no.

"I carry through on my promises. I will keep my honor."

I scoffed. "Your honor as a warrior, or as a prince?" I shot back, crossing my arms as a shield from him and the gentle wind of the night. He fell quiet. "Why in all Heavens didn't you tell me?"

Finally, he sighed. "I just don't see myself that way. I'm only royal through marriage, not blood."

"That's still significant—"

"Not to me."

His voice was a firm reflex. "I am a Warrior who's father happened to marry a royal. That's all."

I breathed in the cool air before I lowered myself to join him on the ground.

"That's how I feel sometimes." I tucked damp strands of hair behind my ear.

"Why?" he asked.

The question caught me off guard.

I couldn't remember the last time someone asked me that kind of question, actually wanting to know the answer.

I shrugged.

I couldn't manage any other reaction. It was too sudden

of a question. But I thought about it. I really thought about what it was that made me feel so alone in my family.

Yes, I always had Libby. My best friend. I would have been impeccably lost without her, but...

"I think a part of me has always wanted something... other than this–this life–this family." I paused, instinctively picking at my nails as I stared at the cold, limestone wall before me. "And I don't mean that solely to complain about the hand I was dealt but...I don't know...it feels like everyone in this family has a place and future that makes sense for them. It suits them. But I–I never thought this was it for me.

"The parties, the events, the politics of it all–it feels... hopeless. And I don't care for that feeling. Not where there's an entire world out there with, full of so much that I never experienced."

I sighed, letting the words drift with the breeze.

"Maybe it's the fear of missing an opportunity to discover who I'm supposed to be, or the fear of going down in history as nothing but a powerful king's daughter that ran around her palace dreaming for more, and never finding it.

"Or...maybe I can't stand the thought of knowing there are hundreds of people dying for something real, something bigger than me, something I don't fully understand, but am supposed to nod along and accept." I exhaled. "Take your pick. Any or all of those reasons."

Silence replaced the breeze in a rare kind of quiet.

When was the last time I had told someone this?

When was the last time I felt someone had listened?

"You speak like a warrior, Princess."

I glanced at him. His blue eyes were steady, serious. Maybe it was the color—deceptively light, adding a softness to his face despite the overgrown, dark hair, the untrimmed brow.

He looked nothing like a prince. Everything like a man with his own scars, his own secrets, stripped of his title and slipped into armor.

For once, my heart rested in the moment. I leaned into the vulnerability, though I didn't know how to put it into words.

"You can call me Fia. Just Fia."

He shifted his weight, leaning back against the tree trunk. Arms folded, ankles crossed. A casual shake of his head to clear stray hair from his face.

"Fia. The Warrior Princess." He smirked, looking up into the night. "Rolls off the tongue."

I didn't hide my smile. "And what do they call you? Warrior Prince?" I arched a teasing brow.

He smirked "Most just call me Lias. Or General."

The smallest laugh escaped me. "Lias? No way. That is way too cute of a name for you. I am not going to call you that." My head shook at his look of disbelief.

"I take it back—no one calls me that," he said, trying not to smile behind those flickering eyes. "You, on the other hand, can simply call me *husband*, once you make up your mind."

My smile fell as my elbow made contact with his shoulder. "Stop it. It's not a good solution. Trust me. I'd be an awful wife."

I actually had no idea how to be a wife, now that I thought about it. It was drilled into me—what an honor and great responsibility it was, but it was the last thing I wanted, next to being a stable girl the rest of my life.

He feigned pain with a dramatic wince at where I elbowed him. "I never said I wanted a wife. I told you, I need an ally."

Even though it wasn't so cold anymore. I tucked my legs below me and huffed a laugh at the idea. "Can you imagine? Two married, royal warriors." I echoed Libby's phrase with the shake of my head.

It sounded like something out of a fairytale. "A death sentence for any kingdom," I mused.

His lovely eyes met mine again. "Or an asset beyond all imagination."

Something in his voice made me look at him again. He made it sound more like a prophecy.

My eyes met his again.

"How so?" I asked with the tilt of my head.

"Two warriors, side by side in battle. Celebrated when they return home from yet *another* victory. It would be... historical."

I chuckled. "You paint a pretty picture. It's hard to believe you weren't born a prince, with the art of persuasion you seem to have mastered."

Turning away, I lifted a hand, tracing a thumb over one of my oldest carvings, a single flower I carved. Never a bouquet, or a pair. Always one. "But sadly, I work better alone."

He stood before offering me a hand. "Me too."

We shared a glance. I bit my lips inwardly before standing on my own, brushing the grass off my pajamas.

His scruffy chin lifted as his lips quirked to the side. "However, I could learn to be less selfish and share the limelight."

I narrowed my eyes at him, disbelieving he was the type of man to actually remain in the light. He definitely wasn't one to stay in the center of attention.

I looked away from his grin, stepping away from the warmth of his presence.

"What time do you leave tomorrow?"

My gaze remained at the bare feet I seemed to constantly sport. He sighed a hum that sounded almost like disappointment.

Perhaps I was the one disappointed at the thought of him leaving. Although I shouldn't have been. Either way, there was nothing wrong with missing my little information-bird who would fly away tomorrow.

"First thing in the morning. As soon as a carriage is ready for me."

I ignored the twisting in my stomach. "When will I see

you next? How should we communicate?"

He stepped closer to me, erasing the bit of space I had carefully created. "I will find a way. If there's a chance I can send you information, I will—but I won't risk it if it's not safe."

His fingers brushed over the scruff on his chin. "Otherwise, I will see you at the matches."

I pulled his hand from his face. "You're not fighting for my hand—" irritation bled into my voice, but he matched it when he cut my words off.

"I'm a man of my word—And if it's the only time I'll see you, then I have to do it."

A blink of his silver eyes later made me acutely aware of how close we were standing.

"Will you still promise me you'll try for my sister's hand first?"

His eyes turned to slits for a split second as he pretended to think about it. "Hm—no." He turned to walk, but I grabbed his solid, thick arm again.

"Why not? It's still a decent plan—"

"Princess, I said what I said."
His matter-of-factness was unnerving. "But I just said—"

He stopped abruptly, pulling his arm away from my grasp with effortless ease before his hands—strong, steady, unfairly large—gripped my shoulders.

"Princess you can say no to whoever you'd like. I'm trying for your hand. I'm not guaranteeing it."

I blinked.

His tone, the weight behind his words, sent something sharp through me. I didn't linger long enough to figure out what it was before I wrenched myself from his hold, straightening my spine as I placed my hands on my hips.

"Yes. You're right." I huffed. "Plus, you might fail the matches."

He flinched with a scoff. "I won't fail."

A smirk crept onto my lips. "You're that confident?"

He stepped closer, arms folded across his chest in the most insufferable male way possible. "I know my abilities and limitations."

"I see. I suppose that should be expected from a prince?"

His smirk deepened.

He looked good when he smiled like that.

Charming even.

Stop it—

"Don't call me a prince."

My smile deviated as I faced him.

My head tilted up at him innocently. "I'll call you whatever I want...*Prince Kallias*." I sang with the royal bow of my head, biting back a grin when his face darkened from his exasperation.

By the time my eyes darted back up to his, I was smiling again, growing used to the feeling.

But the serious look filling the eyes looking down at me spurred a feeling I definitely wasn't used to. My throat cleared as I looked away from that weighted gaze.

"Anything you want me to look out for while you're gone?" I asked before eyeing the branch I needed to jump to to climb back into my room.

"Just listen. See if your father says anything at all. Servants too—they know more than anyone what happens around the continent."

"Understood."

I took another step towards the tree.

"And what do *you* want from me?"

His voice became tender.

His eyes caught the moonlight, reflecting it back to me. I sunk into the look, watching the moon and stars twinkling inside them.

"Just keep your word. Help me become a warrior, and..."

And what?

What was it I wanted to say?

What did I really want from him?

My eyes danced over his. My fingers curled at my sides. I swallowed whatever built in my throat.

"...don't die anytime soon."

FOURTEEN

The birds outside my window sang until I bothered to wake up.

Today, I pitied them too much to shush them or throw a pillow at them in hopes of five more minutes of sleep.

Instead, I forced myself to walk to my desk and write another letter to Kallias, detailing my observations from the carriages—what they were believed to be carrying.

I filled the paper with anything that might be useful and signed it with another *don't get yourself killed* farewell.

I forgot to ask Kallias what room he was staying in. A mistake that cost me half an hour of wandering through empty corridors, peering into unoccupied chambers along the east wing of the palace.

Waking up before the servants wasn't always ideal, except for those mornings I slipped into the town before the rest of the kingdom awoke.

I barely ever made it back in time—the town was

almost a two hour walk—but it was worth the risk. Worth ridding myself of the palace, even for half an hour of freedom.

Kallias and I parted too quickly last night. I wasn't even sure if he had made it back to his room alive.

The halls were void of any souls besides a few scarce early-rising servants. But I forced myself to find him before he got to his carriage. I greeted the servants in passing, my hand faithfully clenched around the letter inside my dress pocket.

Another set of servants followed, but none seemed to know where the guest prince was staying—if they even knew there was a prince here at all.

I even braved asking a few guards near the dais.

Nothing.

By the time I turned into the south wing, my gaze flicked over every empty space. Every doorway. Every shadow. I barely glanced at the next servant that was passing me as I asked them too.

"Excuse me, do you know where our guest is staying?"

My focus lingered on the corridor, searching for a sign of luggage or fussing or groups of servants, or for Kallias himself.

A group of guards at the end of the hall was all I saw besides the servant next to me. I turned once more, feeling as if I had missed something.

The man next to me didn't answer. Annoyance prickled. I sighed, finally glancing at him—

And then I froze.

My breath caught as I stumbled back a step, words tumbling out without thought. "Kal—I—"

The warrior prince stood before me. At least, who I thought the Warrior Prince was. I didn't recognize him. I wouldn't have, if it wasn't for those eyes.

His face was smooth. Clean-shaven. His wild, tangled waves of hair were gone, shortened to a neat cut that only hinted at their former shape. But it was his *eyes* that caught me—

Without the scruff, without the curtain of dark hair, their brightness was striking.

Too bright. Too sharp. Too—

A smirk tugged at his lips, slicing across his now-exposed features.

And that wasn't even the most shocking part.

The smirk he wore revealed the faintest, slightest hint of dimples.

Dimples?

"Kal?" He questioned, way too amused at my reaction to him. "I guess that's better than *Prince*."

Truth be told, I couldn't remember what, if anything, I said. My widened eyes scanned the figure before me, my mind struggling to reconcile this man with the Kallias I had grown to know.

"You're...so...*clean*."

His dark brows lifted, arms crossing over his chest—the movement only emphasizing the smooth, strong forearms that somehow looked even more powerful in the pastel gray shirt. He was freshly washed, his scent crisp, his entire being transformed into something polished and princely.

"Why does that surprise you so much?"

I studied his face, head tilting again. He really did look like a prince now. Younger, somehow. The lack of scruff and untamed curls blurred his age, making him appear just a few years older than me.

"I don't know. I didn't recognize you. You look like...a prince."

And then he smiled again.

And again I flinched at the sight of them.

Dimples...

"I guess that's kind of the point," he said, amused. "Going back home usually requires me to revert back to my royal self." His eyes flickered over me and the wandering eyes I couldn't seem to control right now. "I see you like the short hair."

I didn't think before my mouth responded. "Actually, I liked it slightly longer."

The words escaped before I could stop them. I *humphed*, barely holding back the grimace at my own ridiculous observation.

His eyebrows lifted, a slow, teasing smirk curving his lips. "Is that so? I suppose I'll keep that in mind for when I see you next." He paused, eyes glinting cocky in their state. "Luckily, your hair is perfect, so you have nothing to worry about on my end."

As soon as the words left his mouth, he bit his lip. I didn't hold back the toothy grin I tossed back at him.

"*Perfect?*"

"No. I meant—"

"I've never heard anybody call my hair *perfect* before."

I flipped back the few waves of hair that rested on my shoulder, my grin only widening.

"Listen...I only meant—"

He gestured vaguely, as if trying to wave the moment away.

I bathed in his embarrassment and the power I now felt over him.

"It all makes sense now."

I dramatically lifted my hands. "That's the *real* reason you asked for my hand. How could you not, when you think my hair is just—*per*—"

"*Fia.*" His voice came out firm. Low. Very low.

The teasing laughter in my throat paused at the look on his face. I bit back any further reaction.

"Sorry, I couldn't hear you past my first hair," I teased more carefully.

He stepped back.

"You just don't know when to stop talking, do you?"

I released my breathy chuckle. "No, I don't. Is that going to be a deal breaker? Does my hair not make up for that?"

He restrained a smile, but one dimple teased an appearance. "Perhaps," he teased back.

I nodded, echoing back to mock him. "*Perhaps.*"

He slid his hands into his pockets, eyes basking in this moment we shared. Until a servant scurried in the distance, breaking whatever connected our eyes.

"I think I am to depart soon."

"Right."

I straightened at the reminder. "I assumed as much. I just wanted to bring you this—"

I handed him the letter, my fingers brushing his for only a second, "—and wish you farewell before my father throws you out."

I turned to leave, but before I took my first step, I glanced back.

"Kallias?"

He had already been looking at me. His clean face—so unfamiliar, yet still so *him*-tilted slightly as he held the letter in his hand.

"I look forward to seeing you. Soon."

My eyes traced over his features one last time, memorizing this version of him before I turned and walked away.

Another dimple.

My family stood beneath a sky heavy with gray clouds, watching the carriage disappear down the white, rocky road.

Kallias and I exchanged bows. That was the extent of our farewell. I had said enough of a goodbye in the letter—anything more in front of my father would have been pushing it.

Libby shot me a sideways glance, clearly pleased at Kallias's new appearance. I maintained my facade of not noticing him, or her, as he stepped into the wooden carriage from his kingdom. Smaller than our royal carriages, yet elegant in the details of its dark-carved panels, it carried him away beyond the limestone wall and the iron gates.

Father was cordial enough as the gates closed behind Kallias. But the moment the iron met stone, his hand clamped around my arm, yanking me toward him with enough force to twist me around.

"You are *not* to marry that man."

My eyes shot open.

Not at his anger—that was always expected—but at the certainty in his words.

I couldn't speak. There was no way to decipher why on earth my father didn't want me to marry Kallias.

Unfortunately, anything my father forbade this fiercely only made me want to do it more.

"I thought you *wanted* me to marry. I assumed you'd be the biggest supporter of this ridiculous idea."

I tried yanking my arm away, but his grip only

tightened. Anytime I pushed Father's physical limits, I was quickly met with the reality of his strength that unnervingly seemed to increase with age.

With a forceful pull, he dragged me towards the dais. I stumbled, catching myself just before hitting the marbled ground. I didn't hesitate to find my footing again. I wouldn't give him the satisfaction of keeping me down.

"You *will* marry somebody—but *not* him."

The thundering of his voice wasn't foreign to my ears as it boomed through the hall. The timbre with which he screamed at me almost became a normal decibel to my ears.

Still, I couldn't help but wince at that sting beneath his tone. There was something different about the way he yelled at me today. A new crack beneath the fury.

If I didn't know the man, I would assume something similar to worry crossed his expression for a brief, imaginary moment.

If it was worry, it was worry for the future that wasn't playing out how he intended. Or it was worry that his careless daughter would ruin whatever plans he had set in motion.

"Why?" I breathed. "Father, what base is there to your insanity? Give me some details of your grand designs for my life or free me to live as I please."

His shoulders lifted with an infuriatingly slow breath. Then, with a trembling hand, he thrust that annoying, shaking finger in my face. Another action I was used to, but for once in my life realized how old that hand was that trembled before me.

I saw the subtle lines on his face, deepened with time. The veins in his hands, no longer hidden by youth.

I couldn't remember the last time I really looked at my father and realized how aged he became—how human he was. How mortal.

Mortal like the rest of us.

Mortal like me.

One day, he would die. One day, his rotting body will be returned to the ground. If I had no other hope for my life, I could hope for *that*.

Maybe I didn't need to live out all of my days in the North. Maybe I just needed to outlive him.

He was barely in his fifties. Not near death—but neither was Mother when she died. The Fates were cruel. The Fates were unpredictable.

"Spoiled girl," he barked. "You think you have the right to make demands? Clearly, I have let you remain a child for too long. That ends today."

He took another step toward me. From the corner of my eye I could make out Libby's small frame shift forward in hesitation.

"If you'd like to have an opinion—if you'd like to be an adult—*fine*, I will treat you as an adult."

The same fear I carried lined the delicate features of her face. I flicked my gaze toward her. Because as used to my father's wrath I was, whenever Libby was at risk of feeling the same wrath, the panic flooded in.

I gave her a quick shake of my head. A silent warning that told her to stay back and let me handle him.

"An adult is tied to their duties and responsibilities," Father declared. "Tonight, I will bring you your long, extensive list of responsibilities from here on out. Kiss your Warriorship goodbye and start accepting your life here–forever–as a princess. If you refuse to marry. Die alone in this castle if you so desire, but know that you will *not* be marrying that man, or any Southerner."

My eyes widened. Was that really what this was about? Someone with my title demeaning myself down to a Southerner?

The scoff that escaped me was a reflex.

If it was a fight my father wanted, I was more than happy to oblige. If he wanted to have it out here, we could have it out here.

This time, the rising, simmering rage twisted my lips in a snarl that I couldn't restrain. This time, I welcomed his powers. I hoped they would reach up and freeze me. I hoped that my face would forever be preserved in this scowl, a bitter reminder to him that I, his spiteful daughter, was the one being that could not be tamed by him.

"Why don't you say what you really want, Father? Why don't you cut the shit for once and say what it is you want for my life–since we both know I've clearly never had a say in the matter."

His hazel eyes widened, flashing a ring of white around them.

The second they narrowed back at me, the back of his hand met my cheek, silencing the dais even further after the sharp slap.

The burn was nothing compared to my anger. It didn't even warrant any other response from me but a blink.

"You *dare* raise your voice at me, *girl...*"

A sharp inhale of the cold air between us was all the armor I needed. I let it steel me against the man who caged me my entire life.

Then I laughed.

The smallest huff of amusement escaped me. I couldn't hold it back. I wouldn't have wanted to. It was as cold and bitter and loud as he was.

"I see it now," I rasped between my laughter. "I know exactly what you want."

Whatever spark of civility I had disappeared like the last sizzle on a flaming wick. A candle that had been burning for ages, finally having ended, never to be re-lit.

"You want me to die here like Mother. Is that it?" The bitterness on my tongue was becoming quite delicious right now.

I stepped closer to Father, unafraid of invading his space. Unafraid of too much right now.

"Did you even *care* when she died? Or was she just as much of an *inconvenience* to you?"

My voice dropped as I chose every word with immense intentionality. "Maybe I remind you too much of her. Maybe that's why you feel the need to push me and release your endless anger on *me*—because she's gone."

The smallest gasp escaped Libby in the background. She was right to be surprised. We knew—*knew* the love my father had for her.

But the father we watched love my mother was not the man before me now.

Now, I couldn't stop telling this man exactly what I needed to say. Even if I wanted to. The words had been buried in my chest far too long.

And now, they were spreading their wings, finally free.

I was amazed that, despite the burning rage in my heart, my words poured out smoothly—a clean, slicing blade, piercing straight through him.

"Should I expect to be killed if I continue to disagree with your demands?"

I scoffed at him, looking at him the way I always wanted to. "Because if I have to spend the rest of my life in your palace, you may as well kill me now and save me whatever horror Mother suffered at your hand. Thank the Heavens that death relieved her of a life with you."

Silence would have been too loud of a word to describe the weight of the air around us.

The look on his face was one I'd never seen before. It was worse than cold. Worse than blank. There was no way to describe the look carved into his expression.

I waited for him to smite me here and now. Or maybe for the Fate's to punish me for saying something so terrible. I almost wanted them too.

I had pushed the needle just far enough to draw blood, deep enough to pierce bone, and now I couldn't stop the fountain of blood leaking all over the white floor of the dais.

He stayed still for an amount of time no number could measure while fury boiled beneath his skin. Fury and... something else.

I waited for the snap of his anger, for the powers to strangle me.

But he just stood there.

Maybe my cause of death wouldn't be his rage. Maybe it would be this. This unbearable, suffocating silence.

How long could this man be silent? Not a breath or a blink. I almost said something just to confirm time itself hadn't frozen us in this terrible moment.

A silent wind whistled into the courtyard.

No other noise dared to make an appearance, lest it be choked by the growing void between us.

Then—

"*Go.*"

The word was soft.

Barely an order. Barely a whisper.

An inquiry.

It almost felt like a plea.

For a fraction of a second I almost believed an emotion such as fear could inhabit a creature like my father.

But then, as if my thoughts were voiced—as if the very idea of humanity disgusted him—he blinked the emotion away.

His voice came back at full force. Louder than usual. Thunderous. A volume louder than I'd heard him use on me.

"Go to your chambers and *do not* leave until I *personally* retrieve you."

His voice struck the air like a world-ending siren. His venomous spit spewed past me, sizzling like acid. "I don't care if that is days, weeks, or a whole *damned year*!"

My breath caught.

"What's that supposed to mean?"

His glare sliced me in half.

"*Libra.* If I see you near her room you will be subject to an even worse punishment."

Libby and I exchanged a single glance.

Just a glance.

Shutting me away was nothing new. The sooner he locked me out of sight, the longer he had to think of a way to deal with me.

But *weeks*?

The longest I'd ever been shut in my room was several days. Never weeks or...months.

"*NOW!*"

His voice brought the palace to a tremble.

I took a step back.

Then another.

Not chasing the emptiness, but running away from the frost that crept up towards me, quickly curling over the ground, licking at the walls. Blue ice crackled in my wake, closing around me, above me.

The vibrations of his voice still rattling in my bones.

I wasn't sure if my feet were moving out of fear of the ice splintering while chasing me, or the desperation to escape my father.

Either way, I ran—chilling air nipping at my heels. I bolted up the stairs until the sweet release of my slamming door almost convinced me I was safe.

Almost.

The moment my hand left the door, a cold mist curled from the void the lack of handle left behind.

I stumbled back, falling onto the ground, watching as thin lines of ice crept across the floor in jagged lines, stretching toward me like hands preparing to drag me to my true punishment.

A scream from the hallway shattered the lump of ice lodged in my throat. I feared for whatever poor servant got in the way of my father's wrath. What poor soul was suffering the punishment I was meant to receive?

My feet didn't stop pushing me until my back hit the little bit of brick below my window.

The contrast burned—ice before me, warmth behind. I winced at the feeling and began rubbing my neck, then my arms for warmth as ice spread into the walls of my room, crackling up to the ceiling. It even slithered towards my window.

Cool mist coiled through my room, wafting around me until my own breath puffed out in clouds.

The threat of angered tears burned my eyes when I heard a sound I was hoping was anything but what it was.

I braved standing and gripping the icy windowsill and stared through the frosted glass, down at the group of men below.

Axes had already begun swinging, chopping down my tree. The men swung with all their might to strip away my last piece of freedom.

The ice bit my toes and I pranced over the ice floor, my flesh sticking to each step until I leaped onto my bed, the only un-frozen sector of my room.

I curled onto my blanket at the foot of my bed and listened to them hammer away. Each strike echoing, loud, final, like a gong.

My cold feet buried under my blanket. My hands pressed over my ears, trying to block out the screeching of the birds that joined in with the axes.

I couldn't stand hearing their cries, though I couldn't deny the prickle of companionship they brought me. They were the only ones who understood.

I had no one else.

Nothing else.

A perfect punishment.

Locked away where I couldn't ask any questions. Couldn't make any more messes. Couldn't eat. Couldn't fight.

I sat at the foot of my bed for hours, shivering as ice claimed my room. I didn't care to bring myself more warmth or relief.

Maybe I did deserve it.

Or maybe the fire in my body was the only heat I needed to keep me alive.

White tulle curtains wafted around the room, their pale color matching my now paler, bloodless fingers. I shivered in anger, indifferent to the stinging pain in my extremities.

I could only hope Kallias was safe, far from the wrath my father reserved for me.

But I had no time to think about him.

Not when there was only one thing left for me to focus on: getting me out of this kingdom.

Not just for tonight.

Forever.

Father wouldn't be letting me out soon. That much was certain.

If I was lucky, I'd only be stuck a week.

Muffled shuffling of metal, guards boots sounded at my door.

I turned my head against my knees, watching as Father's power retreated slightly, starting to slowly thaw on the walls and dripping onto my floor.

It wouldn't all thaw. At least, not anytime soon.

My door remained sealed–frozen in a thick, unyielding block of ice. Frozen in every crack.

Curling, teasing, mocking mist eliminated off the frame.

Fine.

I would accept my punishment.

I *needed* to accept this punishment, however long it was, because it would be the last punishment he'd ever give me.

Part 2
The Room

FIFTEEN

Droplets of water trickled down the icicles pipping my door frame.

My room had thawed throughout the sleepless night. There was no more ice throughout my room—except for the ice sealing my door shut. Even the gap around the handle was frozen over. Had I no window, I would have blissfully suffocated to death.

My first day locked up in my room went as any other punishment did. I paced through my wet room in punitive asperity, forcing myself to acknowledge that, at the very least, I was alive.

I made no attempt to leave my room the first couple days.

I didn't even think to try.

I had no desire to eat—I could feed off of my anger a little longer. I didn't care to fight for a chance to see Libby or Taroh if it put them at risk.

I craved this loneliness. I craved the anger it stirred within me. I wanted to use that to ignite the flame that would light my next steps. I wanted to *plot*.

So I wove through ideas—where to go, who to trust.

I had no answers, and I wouldn't get them anytime soon. But I knew one thing: when the chance came, I would run.

I would escape this palace until my legs gave out, or until I stumbled upon a town where I could live the rest of my life in secrecy.

Perhaps I'd flee to one of the islands, or search for the worlds beyond ours, if such a thing existed.

By the third day, I still hadn't slept, forcing myself to endure the exhaustion. It was easier to maliciously deteriorate than to weep over the present.

Each day my room seemed to close in on me, smaller and smaller. My dreams felt more like nightmares—visions of ice creeping up the walls, layer after layer, closing in until I was trapped in my bed. A box of ice for a coffin.

The nightmares would rip me awake, pulling me to my window, where I needed to gasp at the open air and empty space. But the relief was always short-lived.

My gaze would inevitably land on the guard stationed beneath my window. After flashing him a particular finger, I'd crawl back to my suffocating bed.

By the fifth day, I discovered my blanket was long enough to loop over the beam that suspended in the center of my ceiling. It took several tries to throw it over, and after tying a chair to the end, I succeeded, then used the blanket to pull myself up onto the beam.

I sat on the beam for hours, climbing it again and again, bringing different carving tools, and even pillows to make the wide block of wood more bearable. It became my only form of entertainment since I had countless whittling knives and no excess wood.

I should have worried more about falling from the beam and breaking my neck than dying of boredom.

But neither was a great alternative.

A week of starvation and false hope passed before I finally had no choice but to wash myself—unless I wanted to smell so awful the guards would check if it was me or my decaying corpse.

The smells of the vanilla and orange soap on my skin nearly made me lick my own flesh for a taste of something sweet. But I wasn't *that* desperate.

Not yet.

Day nine was a different type of breaking point.

I barely had the strength to pull myself up my beam.

Yesterday, I ran out of food—the secret stashes hidden

throughout my room, now either gone or spoiled.

I stayed on the beam most of the day, thinking, maybe hoping, it would be my last day.

Father's punishments rarely lasted more than a week. Yet even with the ice nearly thawed from my door, I feared that freedom wouldn't follow.

Climbing the beam had become so routine that a few birds had started building a nest at the other end.

I swung down, landing on my bed with a dull *thump*. The sheets hadn't been washed since before my confinement, but I settled in anyway, bracing for another day of this wretched waiting.

On day ten, my body was weaker than it had ever been, but I still forced myself up the beam.

The wood was now riddled with little carvings— expletives, rough sketches, anything to pass the time.

The nest at the end of the beam held seven small, blue eggs. They looked more and more edible by the day. My self-control slipped by the minute.

The hour.

The day.

Day eleven left me with no strength left to climb. And I missed Libby and Taroh almost as much as I missed food.

I kept telling myself the end was near, but the light at the end of a tunnel had shrunk to a speck.

The silence outside my door was suffocating. No hums from Libby. No giggles from Taroh.

The one time I pushed against the door, a guard's metal gauntlet knocked against it, reminding me that even if I could thaw out the door, I would never get out.

Surely, Father wouldn't keep me locked up for Libby's birthday in a couple weeks. I knew not to take his threats lightly, but even this felt excessive.

I was starving. Weak. Tired.

It had been a week since I'd had a real bite of food and I was tired of drinking the water from the sink and I was sick of my harrowing thoughts being my only company.

SIXTEEN

Two weeks.

It had been two weeks since I had been thrown in this room.

I sat up to stare at the sun outside, slowly setting beyond the stone fence. The only way I knew time was passing was the tally I kept on my ruined headboard.

It was day fourteen. Or fifteen.

I'd been sleeping and waking at such erratic hours that a part of me wondered if I had gone mad—if I had unknowingly slept through entire days and nights. Maybe it had been months.

Or maybe this was how I died. Maybe father's theatrics were just a cruel way to stretch my suffering, to let me waste away in slow agony.

Each passing hour strangled what little hope I had left.

This was getting ridiculous.

I threw off the cloak I had been using as a blanket and

stood beneath the beam. It felt so far away now. But the birds'
nest was just within reach. The nest that had eggs, last I
checked. Eggs that probably weren't near hatching.

There was no more reason left in me. Not when my
stomach twisted in unbearable emptiness.

My paled hands reached the blanket. After a small
jump, my fingers caught hold. My wrists—thinner, weakened—
trembled from hunger, fueling my rage. I managed to lift
myself a foot, reaching for another grip, but my arms quivered
under the strain.

My grip faltered.

I tried to kick myself up, but the blanket slipped
through my fingers.

I jerked too quickly. Then I fell straight on my right
foot. My ankle rolled sharply. A strangled scream tore from my
throat as I collapsed onto the floor, clutching my foot. It was
the loudest, maybe the only, sound I had made since being
locked up.

The only time I opened my mouth was to speak to the
birds on my beam.

I knew how insane it was, but sometimes, it felt like the
only thing keeping my head on straight.

I rocked back and forth on the ground, moaning at the
relentless shock pulsing through my ankle. *Three feet*. That
was all I had fallen—three feet—and yet my body had failed
me.

Father had already won.

If he got what he wanted, why was I still here?

Why was I still in this room?

I couldn't call it a room anymore.

It was a coffin, and it closed in on me, day by day.
I tried to stand, but my leg gave out beneath me, the pain
jolting through every nerve.

I hated how weak this confinement had made me.

I hated my father.

I hated this room.

I hated this palace.

I needed to get out.

I limped to the door, desperate for some help–some
human contact, for *someone*.

I winced past the pain as I reached the door. Pressing
against it, I pushed with the little strength I had left, but the ice
was still too thick. I was still firmly trapped. It was still solid,
save for the gap where the handle was thawed a little. If
anything, it only ensured that no sound could escape.

My hands slapped the door in frustration.

Without hesitation, I fished a small whittling tool from
my packet. Carefully kneeling before the door, I jammed it into
the lock, flinching as shards of ice flew around my fist. I
stabbed again.

And again.

And again.

A crack splintered through the ice inside the keyhole.
After several more jabs, the blockage finally shattered free.

"Hello?" My voice came out hoarse, barely above a whisper.

No response or movement or sign of any life on the other side of the door.

"I'm hurt," I tried again, louder this time. "Let me out."

The silence swallowed my words.

"I order you–"

I clenched my fists and pounded against the thick wood.

"LET ME OUT!" I tried again.

I hit the door until my hands were numb, until my voice cracked under the weight of my screams. A string of curses and pleas tumbled from my lips.

I screamed. "Open the door!"

I kept banging until my knuckles throbbed, until the stiffness in my fingers begged for reprieve. Still, I struck the door, slamming it with everything I had left. My starving body ached, my hollow stomach gnawed at itself, but the rage burned hotter.

I pulled myself up to scream into the hollow space where the handle had once been.

My angered pummels unraveled into sobs.

"Let me out."

My voice broke as I slapped the door one last time. Weakly. "Just–once. I...I'm sorry..."

My hands slid down the wood as my body collapsed to the floor, surrendering to the weight of exhaustion.

I didn't know where the tears came from. I didn't know how I still had the strength to cry.

It ached.

I couldn't stand.

I couldn't move.

My puffy eyes blurred as my mind slipped into depths of a darkness I had once feared. Somewhere I had fought to avoid. A place I was terrified I couldn't come back from.

But I was already drowning in it.

I sobbed harder.

"Please…" I called out to nothing but the empty air.

Like a tide dragging me under, my sanity began to slip alongside my consciousness, pulling me deeper into the one place I never wanted to be lost in. The place where only memories survived.

I gasped through my cries, chest caving in on itself, my voice barely above a breath as I called out to the only person I actually wanted to be here,

"Mom…"

SEVENTEEN

It was Libby's birthday today.

Day seventeen of my isolation was also Libby's twenty-second birthday. It was the first day I realized I really had no hope left in me. I hadn't moved from my spot on the ground in two days.

At least, I thought it was two.

I stopped keeping track once I realized nobody was coming. Nobody would visit, or check in on me, or even confirm I was alive.

I didn't care to count down the days to my death. Not when it would happen here—on the cold floor of my room, alone and rotting. With one swollen ankle and no heart.

Father doubled the amount of guards outside my door, and when I finally forced myself to limp over to my window to test how useless my foot truly was, I counted four visible guards stationed on the ground.

I wasn't getting out of the room at all to see Libby today, or maybe ever.

I wasn't even going to try.

Even if I already had her present hidden away in my bathing chambers.

Libby threw the best birthday parties. Once she was old enough to plan her own events, she stepped effortlessly into her role as the woman of the house. She and Erie butted heads at first, but soon enough, even Erie let Libby take control of events that were deemed beneath Erie.

But her birthdays were something else entirely. They were uniquely Libby-*esque*, beautiful in both style and decor. There was always a performance, someone she had personally vetted and scouted.

And very *very* rarely, some common folk would be allowed to attend. She used to invite the few friends I had at Academy—until Father forbade anyone but royals to attend any palace events they weren't working in.

Once, she was adamant for fighting for the common folk and royals to attend the same parties and gatherings. Then, suddenly, she stopped bringing it up. Stopped fighting.

One day I thought she would be a perfect symbol for change, the next she acted like she'd forgotten what she once believed in.

Maybe it was the whisperings of rebellion amongst the poor or the threat of war overseas, but she gave it all up so easily.

I knew a lot changed after the love of her life—an orphan boy—died. Though Libby and I knew just about everything there was to know about each other, she didn't talk about the boy much to me. Or anyone.

Would losing me change her, too?

Would she feel alone, with no one to bring her comfort?

Or maybe she would be better off. Without me dragging her down, she could rule divinely.

Still, the thought of being away from Libby made me want to cry. Being apart from her—knowing I wouldn't be by her side—was the worst part of all of this.

My still—throbbing right leg hung out my window as I sat on the windowsill, watching royal carriage after royal roll down the entry road, sickening me even further.

I could already picture it—Northern youths dressed in the shiniest and finest, feigning concern over my absence, offering Libby empty compliments, and perking up at every whisper of gossip. Their bedazzled faces and jeweled hands all sly, all uncaring.

But as much as I hated these events—every part of this, I couldn't stand being here.

The faint strain of string instruments carried through my open window, blending with the birds' evening song. The world outside was moving on just fine without me while I remained trapped and alone and sad.

Captive in my own home.

Away from my sister.

I let myself sob to sleep.

Again.

EIGHTEEN

I was sick of seeing nothing but the same four walls. The same two curtains. The way they danced through the room would have been beautiful once, but I had no capacity to find them anything but unbearable.

"Fia?"

The faint sound slipped through the haze of my mind.

I sat up slowly, certain it was a delusion—my mind, desperate for company, conjuring someone to talk to.

My eyes skimmed over the wrecked room, ignoring the sharp ache in my stomach—pain from hunger, pain from sobbing, pain from everything.

The foot of my bed was littered with wooden specks from whittling the beam above me.

"Fia?"

The voice whispered again and I almost teared up at how similarly it sounded like Libby's.

I blinked tightly before whipping my head toward the

door—toward the small gap where the handle used to be, the only part of the door not frozen over. The ice around the door had thinned, but not enough to open the door.

It took all the strength I had left to hoist myself up and narrow in my sight on my door.

A small flickering of light slipped through. Then the outline of an eye came into view of the little gap.

"Libby?" I rasped out.

My body barely functioned, but I forced myself forward, crawling to the door until I was kneeling before it, pressing my face to the gap.

Relief crashed over me like an earth-shattering wave.

I couldn't suppress my breath when I saw her face.

She looked so beautiful. Well-fed, well-rested, and more alive than ever. Her pink cheeks and pinned up hair sparkled in the candlelight flickering through the hall.

"You have two minutes," a guard to her right called out.

Libby nodded sharply before turning back to me. We stared at each other, and for a moment, I thought I was dreaming. Then, she lifted her hand, pressing her fingers to the door.

I mirrored the gesture.

Her smile—Mother's smile—was soft, warm, and real. She pressed her fingertips against mine, and I never thought I'd miss her touch so much. A living, human touch.

"I didn't have time to give you your birthday present," I croaked.

She blinked a moment before her faint smile faltered, and she rolled her eyes in disbelief.

"How–" I started.

"We don't have much time–" she cut in. "I spent almost all my birthday money to talk to you."

Before I could protest her waste of money, she dug into the pockets of her burgundy dress and began pulling out various bundles and dropping them to the floor.

My eyes widened at a line of three bratwursts still linked together.

"Here."

She shoved one end through the gap, and I grabbed it with trembling hands. The scent alone sent a jolt through me— spiced peppers, garlic, rich, savory meat.

My senses roared to life for the first time in forever.

She didn't stop as she dumped a small bag of hard candies in her hand and pressed them through, followed by a block of cheese she began tearing into pieces to fit through. She did the same with a loaf of bread, shredding it apart. The icing on the cake was a tiny jar of jam that was just small enough to fit through the hole.

I smiled at the sight.

The jar was one of the trinkets I'd won from a Pasirfi royal—once filled with rouge or some other makeup before I gave it to Libby last year.

"It's not much, I know, but I did what I could. What else do you need? I can't promise I'll be able to get back in, but

I promise I'll try."

Her gaze flicked over my face, her expression twisting into something worse than pity—something sadder than disgust.

"Fia…" her voice broke. "I'm so sorry."

I shook my head. "It's fine. Just try to bring me food when you can–but don't risk Father finding out."

I forced a smile at her before whispering, "And a carving knife would be good, if you *happen* to come across one."

She rolled her eyes, and I nearly cried at how much I missed that expression.

I shrugged at her. "Apparently, they don't last long when you spend all day stabbing wood over and over again," I added lightly.

I left out the real reason my carving tools were now useless—the way I'd gnawed on them, how the wood dust and splinters on my floor had looked too appetizing at one desperate point.

Hunger did strange things to the mind.

I regretted it instantly, but chewing on wood kept my mouth occupied, kept my thoughts from drifting toward the bird's nest.

I shifted, giving her a clearer view of the room—wood shavings scattered across the floor, the blanket hanging from the beam.

She flinched at the wreckage.

"Wrap it up," the guard barked.

Despite their disregard for her, Libby always answered them with a soft smile.

It was not enough time.

I wouldn't get to ask her anything–about her birthday, about Taroh, about anything going on in the world.

"I almost forgot–" Libby reached behind her, revealing papers tucked into the waistband of her skirt "Here–in case you get bored."

She folded the envelopes into a suitable size. "I would have brought you some books, but I know you won't read them. And they wouldn't fit."

A bundle of letters were dropped through the hole. The last thing she gave me before she stood to leave.

"You'll get out soon, Fia. I'm sure of it."

I tried to force a smile, shoving down my disbelief.

"Goodbye, Libby."

I swallowed hard. "I love you."

She smiled before turning to leave. "I love you, too. I'll find a way to see you soon, Fia. Stay strong."

Then she disappeared, like she was never here.

If not for the scattered food around me, I might have believed she'd never been here at all.

I missed her dearly. But I couldn't wait a second longer before sinking my teeth into the bratwurst.

A moan tore from my throat at the taste of real food. Nothing had ever been as perfect as this cold, day-old sausage.

I inhaled every bite. Unmoved from my icy door, I devoured every morsel of food around me.

I should have spaced out my consumption. I knew that.

But bite after bite, the feel of food in my mouth—I was powerless against it. Even as each swallow made my stomach ache worse, I couldn't stop until I was a bloated heap on the floor.

The pain in my swollen ankle pulsed, but I forced myself up. The little energy that remained was needed to be spent on a shower.

When I limped into the shower and caught a glimpse of myself, I understood why Libby looked at me the way she did.

My hair wasn't simply a mess—it was a tangled nest of oil and wood shavings. My lips were scabbed from the wood splinters I gnawed on. My face was grimy from sweat, tears, and dirt from the floor.

As pointless as it felt, I stepped into the shower anyway.

The food left me as quickly as it entered.

The next day was spent curled in pain. But the aching was a little better than hunger.

I licked the last piece of food I had left—the jar of jam—clean and tried to ignore the fact that I still didn't know when I would get out of here.

If I'd get out of here.

NINETEEN

My ankle had improved, barely. The food Libby gave me felt like a distant dream, its taste completely lost to time.

The shower I took last night was another low to add to my every-growing list. I bit into the bar of vanilla-cinnamon soap. I chewed longer than I should have until I threw up to the point of dry heaving over the drain.

At least, I thought that was my lowest point.

Standing on my windowsill before the night, endless and cold before me. The guards stationed below were practically asleep, oblivious to my open window and the thoughts flying through my mind. The thoughts of the inviting darkness and its call for me to jump.

I wouldn't, though.

Obviously.

Even if it had been a month that I'd been locked up.

The past two days I didn't jump. I only stood here, staring for hours, willing myself to sprout wings and fly away.

Willing something—anything—to come pull me out of this life.

Tonight was no different. The temptation grew stronger each night I stood up here.

It was more than just gravity pulling me down.

I stared at the ground, calculating.

I wouldn't do it.

I *probably* wouldn't do it.

I didn't today.

Tomorrow would be harder.

Hope felt like a rotting corpse stinking up my room. Even if I was freed from this room, what then? Would I bow to Father's will? Would I try to kill him?

Every night, I asked myself these questions. Every night, I planted my feet on this ledge, staring into the abyss one step away.

I didn't just look down.

I looked back. At the blanket draped from my beam. If I really wanted to end everything, I would make it a spectacle for a high family.

A princess found hanging from her own window—now that would be a tragedy to remember.

Plays would be written. Ballads composed.

I could even dress up—paint myself in our usual shimmering paint, wear my golden bangles and cuffs and earrings and hair pieces. I'd make it theatrical.

My eyes alternated between the two. The ground or the noose.

I probably wouldn't do it...but if I did, I'd make it worthwhile.

It would be so easy, swift. One step, one blink, and one breath.

One second and I would be free of my cage. I'd be free to fly.

The night was tempting.

Like it needed something to happen. As if it welcomed the madness creeping from every corner of my thought, whispering, taunting me to do it, to lean forward, to hear the whispers in the wind.

As easy as it would be...I couldn't.

I sighed, taking in the night air I'd gotten so used to.

I didn't want to be remembered as a coward.

As poetic as this revenge might be, I refused to let anger make the decision for me. I didn't want the easy way out.

Maybe.

Maybe I could still find a way out.

Not like this. Not in surrender. It was in me to fight. I couldn't lose—not to my father.

The anger rooted me in place, keeping me from moving forward. But the temptation...it swayed me, back and forth.

Back and forth.

A fleeting shadow caught my eyes, stopping me from my swaying. A silhouette that moved along the palace wall, slow and deliberate, stepping carefully around the sleeping guards.

I eased down from where I stood, kneeling instead of standing on the windowsill, babying my right foot the entire time. My eyes narrowed to make out the first. Small and careful.

The moment it stepped over a slumped soldier, the flicker of light from my window shone on the sandy brown hair.

"Matty?" I whispered.

His head snapped up. Then he stepped closer, right beneath my window.

That familiar, lopsided smile was an indescribable form of relief.

Even if I was dreaming, it was a relief from the nightmares.

He waved at me with one arm, gripping a large bag sack in the other hand.

"Princess Libra sent me as a reinforcement!" he called out.

I frantically waved for him to quiet down. I would have to risk jumping to save him if one of the guards woke and caught hold of him.

"Don't worry they'll be asleep for a while. Their food might've had a little extra surprise in them tonight."

My jaw dropped.

"Matty, why would you do that? You could get fired."

After everything he'd done to secure his position, it still didn't guarantee he wouldn't be thrown out of his role at first sign of defiance. Especially if it involved me.

"For someone who hasn't eaten in weeks, you worry a little too much about others."

I scoffed. "Matty, I'm serious! You need to be careful. I don't worry about others. Just you."

I shot a glance back to my door, making sure the guards couldn't hear us over the thawing ice.

Matty stepped closer, nearly pressing against the wall, and for the first time I saw his face clearly.

The same Matty. The same grin. But it felt like too much time had passed. We both felt so old now, no longer kids sneaking out of the palace for a night out on the town together.

Realizing the cruelty of time brought a slow, aching panic tightening my chest.

"I brought you food! I'll throw it up!" Matty tilted his lips into a grin.

I leaned further out the window.

"No, don't throw it, it won't make it–"

I hesitated, glancing back at my room, then over to him.

"One second."

My steady feet found the floor and I limped a step over to my curtain and ripped it with all my might–which wasn't much–until the rod at the top of my window fell. I was able to stop it before it hit the ground and made any real noise.

"You have little faith in my strengths, Princess Fia," Matty teased from outside.

I ignored him as I tied the two curtains together and threw one end out the window and wrapped the other around my arm.

"Tie it to the end!" I called down carefully.

The two curtains were a weak fabric, but they were just long enough to reach low enough for Matty to only need to rise to his toes to secure it.

I would have climbed down, but I had no confidence in my strength, and it would look even worse if I died here, with Matty and a handful of unconscious guards around me.

He tied the bag securely. The moment he gave the all-clear, I hauled the bag up.

It was either way too heavy, or I'd lost every bit of strength I had worked years to compile.

I was out of breath by the time I hauled the little bag into my room.

I unwrapped the sack, my breath taken away when I saw an entire roasted chicken wrapped in wax paper.

"Matty!" I leaned back over the window. "This is too much! I—I can't thank you enough," I said, my voice choking at the end.

I looked down at him, one of my only friends in the palace, whom I didn't see often but I had grown up with ever since his grandmother began working with us six years ago.

He grinned, folding his arms against the night's chill. The guards snored from their slumped positions.

"Do you know when you'll get out?" He asked

hopefully.

"No," I faintly admitted.

He only nodded, as if he expected the answer.

I swallowed and forced out the question I'd been avoiding. "How was Libby's birthday?"

Matty's smile softened—sad, but still more comforting than in the cold indifference I'd grown used to.

"Fine," he said. "Fine from the kitchen's end. Libby said she missed you."

I perched on the windowsill, careful not to lean too close to the edge this time. "I'm sure she had enough fun with her friends."

Matty shrugged. "Maybe. But she didn't look as happy as she does when she's with you."

I wasn't sure if that was supposed to make me feel better or worse. Still, I offered a smile.

"I made her a bigger version of that blueberry lavender cake. I guess you're not it's only fan."

My eyebrows shot up.

"No way! Lucky..." I sighed dramatically, securing a laugh from Matty.

"Maybe you should keep digging in that bag of yours."

My smile stretched so much, the unfamiliar feeling was almost painful.

I fell to the floor, rummaging through the sack until I unwrapped a small cloth-wrapped bundle. Carefully, I unwrapped it—revealing a slightly squashed, yet unmistakable slice of purple cake.

My stomach twisted with something other than hunger.

I rushed back to the window, clutching the napkin like it was the most precious thing in the world.

"Matty, I love you! Thank you!"

I took a bite, the familiar taste hitting me like a punch to the chest. I should have savored it. But I knew there was no chance I'd make it through the night without finishing every last crumb.

Matty watched me happily, maybe a little nervously, but content despite the distance between us.

I would have given anything to wrap my arms around him. I'd give my entire foot to feel the embrace of another person. But this—this moment—was enough.

"Thank you, Matty," I murmured, my voice quieter. "But you shouldn't do this again."

His cheeky smile faltered as he shifted on his feet, tightening his jaw. "I'm not going to let you die in there, Fia."

I blinked, realizing that might have been the first time since we were kids when he had called me my name without my title. It felt...friendly.

I sighed, licking vanilla and lavender frosting off my dry lips. I couldn't give into his concern. I couldn't accept his worry for me.

So I wiped the crumbs and solemness off my face, painting on a smirk instead. "If you promise to make me this cake when I'm out, I promise I won't die."

TWENTY

I didn't track the days anymore. But it had to have been six weeks.

I was out of food again.

I had been for a couple days.

No Libby or Matty appeared, as much as I willed them to. I spent the days dreaming of any other place than here.

Vanda, with its cherry blossoms and the best seafood on the continent.

Or the mysterious islands our Academies know little about, dangerous and forbidden.

My main choice would probably be Pentago—the only ruling Queendom and a city by one of our major ports. I could work there, have first access to the finest clothes, spices, and books.

Its history was brutal.

The former queen, jealous of any male who wasn't her son, purged male firstborns. After that, most children born were girls. And with Pentago hosting the Quintennial Courts—the continent's sports competitions—the men rarely stuck around long enough to make a home in the queendom.

Desica, on the other hand, with its marshes and treehouse villages, might have been perfect. But I couldn't live in the same kingdom as Jayce. But I could find an abandoned treehouse to live out my days.

But I couldn't.

Running away from one prison to another wasn't a fate I'd accept.

Then there were the Southern Kingdoms. Kingdoms I knew little to nothing about—except what Kallias had told me. I wondered if I really could be a warrior under his command? Or would I just be trading one ruler for another?

Was that my only option? If I didn't leave my kingdom through marriage or for a life on the run, I'd never leave.

I swung my legs out of my window, staring into the dusk laden void. My mind drifted to the night Kallias and I had spent together. The night Libby thought we actually slept together.

Maybe I should have.

That might have been my only chance.

I'd never given much thought to losing my virginity, but I never expected to die at nineteen either. If it had to be anyone, it might as well have been him.

He was a stunning specimen of a man. And those eyes... I would have loved to find out how those eyes would look in a different light, hovering on top of me, similarly to how they did after I was attacked by those warriors.

I looked at my hands, pale, skinny, and scabbed. I recalled what he said about the powers he claimed I had.

He'd been rough, insistent. Annoying at the time—but thinking back, his voice was intoxicating. I should have enjoyed it more, knowing I might never hear it again.

I still didn't believe I possessed any powers. If I did, they were quite useless now.

I knew little about powers beyond what I'd seen from my father and a couple distant relatives. Powers in general were rare, especially in the North, where many were married into royalty, not born into it, and they almost never had powers.

Academy taught us nothing.

Well, not *nothing*, but nothing memorable. I wouldn't even know how to check if I had any.

However, from the little I knew, my father was a young teenager when he first showed signs of his powers.

It wasn't until the mandatory three years of warriorship all men used to be required to attend that his powers strengthened beyond comparison.

I'd never shown any signs and most were told once they surpassed their teen years, there was no point in waiting around for them to show up.

So I never waited for them, not once Libby showed no signs of any either. But now—now would be a great time for some magical intervention.

Yet the hands before me were nothing more but just flesh and blood.

Probably.

It might have felt ridiculous, but there was no pride in this forsaken place. Not for me, at least.

I shut my eyes and clenched my fists, racking my brain for an idea on what it felt like to *reach* for something unseen.

But despite my hopelessness, I reached. I tried to find any part of me that felt powerful. Magical. I focused on what I wanted to feel—what I needed to feel. The only thing I felt was the need to pass gas from clenching so hard.

I must have tried for hours. Searching the darkness behind my eyelids like a map.

I tried and tried, feeling up from my toes to the top of my head. I even gritted my teeth and forced out a command into the air—to the wind—the Fates—whatever.

For a moment, I almost thought I felt something— something tiny ripple over my skin. But when my eyes opened and my fists released, I figured the tingling was just from the lack of blood in my hands.

It was probably for the best. If there was one power I'd rather die than inherit, it was my father's.

I looked back at my hands, listening, waiting for something to feel different. Besides the faint whistle of wind and a few distant chirps from the birds, there was nothing.

I glanced at the drop below my swinging feet.

Maybe if I jumped, some power would emerge to save me. And if not...then maybe I wasn't meant to have powers. Or life.

Maybe a quick shuffle forward would give me an answer.

Maybe I'd finally know.

Maybe Libby and Kallias and everyone else would be better off.

I didn't have much to show for my life now, but maybe it was better to finish something before it ever truly began. Maybe.

Maybe...

Maybe the fall would be easy. Maybe the wind would sweep me away–

A cracking sound from my door turned me away from my thoughts. I carefully twisted then climbed down, taking a wobbly, cautious step towards the door.

I didn't need to look up to know who was about to enter once a chill brushed against my feet, stealing my breath. I blinked up slowly, like a cat staying perfectly still—afraid that one wrong move would make the big bad wolf pounce.

Then, finally, I slid my eyes upward.

My father stood at the door.

TWENTY-ONE

The blood in my veins solidified, turning me to stone—a statue in his presence. Maybe he had the power to do that.

Nothing in my body moved.

His commanding presence made my room feel so minuscule I didn't know how both of us fit.

Even the baby birds that had begun chirping last week, now silent in his presence.

My feet stayed rooted as our eyes locked. Eyes I no longer felt anything for gave me no indication of what to do.

My hands at my sides gripped the skirt of my dress—the dress that draped over me two sizes too big. My face had lost its youthfulness. My eyes were as soulless as his were now.

But I wouldn't fall before him.

My thinned, sleek chin would stay high.

I wouldn't say a single word.

I didn't need to.

He tossed a small cloth sack onto the ground between

us. Some raw vegetables rolled out, but neither of us looked at anything but each other.

"Eat up. You and your sister are to attend the Biannual in Kivo next week. She will get you ready tomorrow. Stay in your room until then."

He disappeared faster than he arrived.

I waited for what felt like an hour before I fell to the ground, sobbing—pure joy and relief flooding my lungs, my slightly swollen ankle, every inch of me.

I sobbed as I bit through crunchy carrots and raw potatoes. I sobbed as I clutched my chest—the chest that had lost its volume and pride. My protruding sternum was accompanied by decaying breasts atop a hollowed stomach.

For the first time, I didn't recognize my body.

The sight and feel of myself only made me cry harder. My tears filled the space of what I had lost.

I ate my weight back in vegetables, but it was all for nothing.

Emotions overwhelmed me so much I needed to run to my chambers and throw it all up minutes after consuming it.

I stared at the chunks of food that left me, my throat burning from their return. But even through the pain, it didn't stop the hope permeating through all of my senses.

The hope of seeing my family again.

The hope of being free.

TWENTY-TWO

Libby and I were required to attend two Biannuals a year in other kingdoms, in addition to our own. Years ago, they were nearly every other month, but had since dwindled the older we got.

Father also limited the locations we could visit.

I assumed he either wanted to avoid certain political ties, or he was too cheap to fund travel to distant kingdoms.

I had no choice in which Biannuals I attended or who would be there, but I wondered if Kallias would be at this one.

I was ready to see him. Frankly, I was ready to see anyone that wasn't my own reflection.

That alone was enough motivation to prepare. Letting Libby make me a dress was necessary—I'd lost too much weight to wear anything I owned.

I avoided mirrors more and more, as if the less I saw myself, the less tangible my frailty became.

Some part of me had hoped that once I was free, I'd return to my old self, my old life. But every time a mirror found me, I wanted to cry at the weak girl staring back at me.

Father commanded Libby to inform me of the list of rules I was to follow while at the Biannual.

I was to be painfully polite, ensure the palace sent him a good report, and give my new babysitters–guards–nothing but great things to say about my accommodations.

My dreams of running away wouldn't be fulfilled since walking down the stairs was a feat in itself.

Libby was excited–to go, and to see me. I was ecstatic too–to be out of my room and with Libby again.

We held hands in the carriage as she told me all about her birthday party I missed. Hearing about it reminded me of the most painful part of being locked up–not being able to see Libby on her birthday.

The letter she had slipped me had been detailed, listing every guest, every performance, every moment. But it wasn't enough.

I still handed her the small gift I had made her–a sloppy, stemmed flower I spent weeks making for her. Libby still accepted it gracefully, tracing its details as she spoke.

I didn't want to hear her words–I just wanted to listen to her sweet voice, her gentle falsetto, music like no other.

We still had half a day to reach Kivo, and Libby filled every moment.

I had little to say, so I let her chatter about her suitors and whatever else she felt like updating me on.

Other kingdoms could search for suitors here, but

formal proposals had to be made at the Biannual of the lady being courted—unless, of course, a suitor arrived unannounced on the day of proposal matches, though that rarely occurred.

This was the last Biannual before our matches, which always made Libby nervous.

Every time they drew near, Libby became a wreck for the entire month leading up to them.

For Libby, Biannuals were about reuniting with friends, flirting with gentlemen, and dancing until dawn.

For me, they were simply an escape from home.

Especially now.

I debated stealing the carriage and making a run for it, but the two extra guards we were assigned would make that intentionally difficult.

I used to like dressing up with Libby for events. Before she made so many friends, the evenings would be ours to dress up and dance together.

Now, I preferred sitting in the corner all evening, watching the world move around me. I had to admit, it was always beautiful to watch, before someone would ruin it all by doing something annoying, like talking to me.

Traveling was another perk of these long journeys— exploring new places, trying different foods.

However, in my current state, I would drink boiled potato water and savor it like it was my last meal. The only dinner I was permitted to attend was last night, and it was as horribly silent.

Today I was ready to make up for my months away from good food.

Libby designed her own dress. The seamstress perfectly replicated the scooped-neckline, lined with studded pearls. The dusty pink corset bodice, made of simple silk, contrasted beautifully with the full skirt gathered at her waist to reveal a cream underskirt. It made her look like a blooming lily in a way only Libby could look beautiful in.

The pearl pins that held up her curls were a shame. I loved when she wore her locks down.

Despite her elaborate get-up–the glitter on her chest, the string pearl earrings, the studs of jewels along her eyelids, it was her radiant smile that never failed to capture every gaze as we were announced into the ballroom.

The older we got, the better Libby perfected her eye for design, and tonight, she didn't disappoint.

This might have been one of my favorite dresses she'd ever created for me.

Though I found the square neckline and thin straps uncomfortable, the navy sequins tracing the collar were as dazzling as they were itchy. I tried not to make that too obvious. But what truly made the dress was the skirt—layered fabric draped in soft scoops, mimicking the delicate wings of a butterfly. The navy sequins lined each layer, shimmering with every step.

It was breathtaking.

And I felt utterly unworthy of wearing it.

The heels, however, were not my favorite. Though maybe that was my fault.

I hadn't told her about my ankle. I hadn't told her much about my time away. I didn't want to relive it, and I didn't want her to see just how horrible it had been.

It was in the past now, and I was fine forcing myself to forget all about it, even if that meant getting no help on my ankle and living on the hope that time would heal it.

The designers had their work cut out for them when they saw my sunken figure. They layered on blush to restore some color to my pallid skin. A part of me hated that it worked—that I looked so weak. The truth buried beneath a fresh coat of makeup.

I looked nothing like how I felt.

But I would endure any facade if it meant getting me out of the palace.

Despite the differences in our dresses, Libby and I somehow perfectly matched. I was the butterfly fluttering around the flower.

The layers of my dress fluttered softly as I walked. I tried to keep my focus ahead, or on Libby, but I kept sneaking glances at the skirt.

"I can't believe you designed this, Libby. It's so perfect," I murmured as we stepped into the palace.

Made of a dusty red stone, it stretched longer than it did taller, flanked by scattered cherry trees, in the beginning of their bloom and countless fountains.

The largest fountain centered between two towering white columns behind it, leading to the grand entrance

A herald announced our arrival in a typical Kivoan accent of rolled *r's* and held out *s's*.

I kept my gaze on the polished, wooden floor, avoiding the inevitable stares of royals around us.

We walked arm in arm toward the front of the ballroom, where our designated table awaited.

It was the same routine at every event. Princesses of the largest kingdoms, put on display like prized artifacts.

We were always seated at the front, near the thrones, as if our placement could win someone favor.

Little did they know.

Our guards took position against the wall near us, near two other Kivoan guards that exchanged subtle, but familiar pleasantries.

I turned to Libby, pulling her attention from the flood of smiles and waves tossed her way. "If I ever do have a wedding, you're designing my dress."

"I *better* be the designer," she sang, flashing a wide grin, "Otherwise I won't come."

I giggled at her, but schooled my expression whenever I caught another gaze, determined to avoid any unwanted invitations to dance.

"Oh. I see some friends! And Rosette," she sneered in the nicest way possible, "I have to say a quick hello and come back," she said, squeezing the hand I had on her arm.

"Wait—don't leave me!" I whispered, but she simply patted my hand with a playful slap.

"Would you like to come then?"

I sighed, flopping back into my chair with a scowl as she waltzed away.

A few others joined our round table. Not only was it positioned at the front, it was tucked away from any windows, robbing me of the simple pleasure of gazing at the night sky all evening.

Instead, I had a prime view of the three buffoon brothers from Zapadt, seated directly across from me.

I eyed each one before rolling my eyes, sighing in irritation as I searched to find where Libby had run off to.

The boys fidgeted in their seats, their previous confidence shrinking as they turned among themselves—like timid mice cowering beneath the glare of the big, bad cat.

Libby had been gone so long they had already announced the prince and started the first song.

A line of about fifteen people had formed, waiting their turn to meet the prince.

The women had little pressure in Biannual encounters —just a polite greeting and an invitation to dance. That was all. But I still found it painfully embarrassing.

I had only done it once. And that was only as a joke to Jayce.

He had bet me a brand new carving knife that I wouldn't twirl and blow him a kiss at the end of my request to him. That carving knife had been my favorite for the longest time.

I would do a lot of embarrassing things for the right trinket. I wasn't particularly prideful at fourteen. Even now, a good bet was a good bet.

Was Jayce here?

It was a long way from his kingdom, so I doubted it, but either way, I was determined to find the dessert table—Jayce or no Jayce.

The palace of Desica, where Jayce was from, was known for its sugar-dough crunch balls filled with cherry jam, which were their own kind of magic.

I stood, scanning the room. I should have found the desserts as soon as I had walked in, but they had rearranged the tables since my last visit. Had it really been years since I had last been here.

"Excuse us for a moment, boys."

The deep, smoky voice pulled my attention sharply back to the table.

I turned, my body swiveling against my still-tender ankle only to be met with Kallias's gaze.

For a moment, we simply held each other's stare—just a beat too long.

Then he raised his brows at me—once he let his eyes fall to take in all of me. The new me.

He didn't say anything once his initial reaction faded and his brows now knit together.

"Prince Kallias," I stuttered in greeting, forcing myself to sound indifferent before offering a polite nod.

I cleared my throat, attempting to mask the flicker of warmth in my voice, and dipped into the barest curtsy.

From the corner of my eye, I caught the three princes scrambling to their feet, bowing one by one with ridiculous urgency.

Buffoons.

Kallias offered each prince a slight nod before he met my eyes again, letting them linger. With the same measured nod, he dismissed the boys.

The three exchanged awkward glances before their eyes darted back to the two of us.

I leveled them with an agitated glare.

"Bye—" I spat at them.

They nearly tripped over each other in their scramble to leave, scattering every which way like frantic birds.

"Hello, Fia."

His voice wove through the ballroom like a smooth, husky cloud, wrapping around me until the hum of conversation muffled behind me. I debated smiling at the sight of him, after spending months uncertain on whether I'd see him again. But I caught my lip between my teeth, waiting.

He stepped closer, grasping my gloved hand—navy silk stretching up to my bicep—and lifted it to his lips.

A kiss.

The customary greeting in Eastern Kingdoms, but rare

enough to me that it sent a ripple through my body.

The surprising action spurred me to swallow, pressing my lips into a thin line.

His hand lingered a moment, as if feeling the bones in my hand.

His eyes glanced down at where he held it. His analyzing made me pull it away faster, because the way he held it would have made its weakness more obvious.

Yet, he still scanned me head to toe before meeting my eyes again.

"You look–" He paused. "...different."

He kept my gaze as he returned to his tall stature. Then, with a barely perceptible glance at my guards, he took a step closer, voice dropping to an unrecognizable tone.

"Why do you look like that? What's wrong?"

I arched my brow, tempted to brush it off. I was almost surprised at how quickly he cut to the inevitable.

"You're not the only one who knows how to clean up," I smirked, opting for a lighter tone.

He didn't bite.

Whatever hard expression painted his features didn't shift–not even a flicker of amusement.

"Who did this to you? Did your father do something?"

His voice hardened, the soft husk sharpening into something pointed and commanding. The voice of a general demanding an answer.

Any excitement at seeing him drained from my blood at

the mention of my father.

I glanced over my shoulder at the guards, making sure they were truly out of hearing range.

"Nothing out of the ordinary," I murmured, my voice trailing off as I twisted to find my seat.

Kallias followed immediately, pulling out my chair for me and pushing it in as I sat. He took the seat beside me, angling himself toward me.

I felt the shift in the room. The way my guards stiffened against the wall, their unease curling around the edges of the space.

His eyes raked over me again at a much closer vicinity.

There might have been a time when I would have almost blushed to catch his eyes on me. But this wasn't one of those times.

This wasn't mysterious or unnerving. It was scrutiny. And it was humiliating.

I knew that the fragile, painted version of me sitting here—this careful illusion—was more uncomfortable than any dress that had ever scratched my skin. I felt naked before him, before everyone here.

"Tell me what happened."

His command was so quiet, but it carried a weight that settled deep in my chest. I barely heard it. But I felt it.

Concern might have been present, but something deeper, something heavier flamed beneath it. I wasn't used to whatever this was. And despite how weak I wouldn't let him see me any more broken than I already was.

So, I rolled my eyes to lighten the situation.

"Just a few missed meals, nothing new when it comes to my fathers punishments," I lied, ignoring the layers of makeup masking the shadows beneath my eyes, ignoring the constant tenderness in my ankle.

I cleared my throat away from his analyzing eyes and sat on my hands.

"I didn't know you'd be here."

I struggled keeping my chin up in front of his overbearing stature. But I was determined to steer the conversation elsewhere.

Even with the small gap between us, I felt small. Fragile.

And the look on his freshly shaven face—what could have been mistaken for anger—did nothing to help.

Whatever it was, it didn't change the way he acted. His posture was calm, his voice measured. But his hands betrayed him, the tension clear even as he kept them still.

As much as I wanted to deny it, I couldn't ignore the relief curling inside me from being in his presence.

Kallias wore a dark navy tunic, so dark it was almost black. Subtle gold threaded the lines of the coat in intricate swirls, reminiscent of leafy branches. Every bit the prince he was when he had left my palace. As if no time had passed since I last saw him. Not on his end.

But despite his royal look, his eyes—they still carried

the fire of a warrior. That untamed glimmer, fleeting but there.

I forced my eyes away, refusing to keep drinking him in.

I was weak.

Mentally. Physically. The last thing I needed was to be weak before him too.

"I read your letter."

His voice lowered, but sounded pained. As if he didn't want to change the subject, but was forced too.

I lowered my voice too, wary of wandering ears.

Kallias leaned forward on the table. I mirrored while taking the lead in the conversation.

"Good. Sadly, I have only a few things to update on since the letter," I murmured. "I've been a little...preoccupied. And I don't feel as though I know anything you don't."

I updated him on the patterns I'd tracked from the carriages—departures, arrivals, durations. What little I could see from my window. I had written down and memorized everything I thought could be useful.

Kallias listened carefully, waiting for more.

My words faltered when I caught how intently his eyes stayed on me. I stumbled before straightening, pushing forward.

"In other news—Libby is too indecisive about marrying you. Don't be offended, though. She can never make a decision when it comes to men. Not a good one at least."

I finally caught sight of her on the dance floor, twirling

with a friend's brother from Daerom. I scoffed. Another terrible choice. He wasn't the worst-looking man out there, but his reputation of chasing girls a little too young for him ruined my image of him.

I'd always been a better judge of the character of men than Libby. I knew there was something off about him because every time he smiled, I had this incessant need to want to slap him.

Kallias leaned back, the movement irking me for some reason. He grabbed a flute of golden liquid, lingering at the rim before sighing.

"I don't want to marry her."

He downed the drink in one gulp.

I squinted. "It might be your only option."

"There's always another option."

"I'm guessing you're still stuck on–" He fixed a glare on me that made me pause.

"You."

The word was a fleeting bite, his tone almost dangerous. Had he spoken to me this way when we were alone in the forest, I might have run from the promise in it.

I rolled my eyes as I swallowed my own drink.

"How many times are we going to go through this?"

His eyebrow arched. "A few more, apparently." The soft irritation in his voice nearly made me smile. My gaze caught on a scar just below his left brow, thin but noticeable. Healed over but recent, maybe. I hadn't seen it before.

"Unless you found a better way to become a warrior?"

He got me there.

I grabbed another drink.

"I thought so."

His winning smirk suited his princely attire, infuriatingly so. He turned his attention to the dancers, and I followed, watching people drift across the ballroom in flowing silks of deep blues, reds, and browns—matching the kingdom's colors.

Still, I felt isolated. In my mind. In my life. In general.

Perhaps I was never meant to be a warrior. Perhaps I *was* meant to be like them.

But I had always wanted more. I wanted to help people, not be among the ignorant. To protect the ones I loved. Was I to give that up because of one man's command? Even if he was the most powerful man on the continent?

My gaze slid back to Kallias—his jaw smooth, his neck long and elegant, nothing like when we first met.

An entirely different man. A strong man. A real prince.

A decent husband? Perhaps.

Maybe this was my only option to consider.

Perhaps...if he passed the matches—if we tested at the Well, maybe I could consider whether this was all fated. There were worse men to be bound to.

Many, actually.

He seemed patient enough. No one was ever so patient with me. Plus he was a warrior. He told me he'd let me become one.

I still couldn't really believe it, but maybe I needed to accept the fact that I needed a man to *let* me be anything.

That, I couldn't change. The only control I had over my life was choosing between these few limited, menial options.

"I can feel how hard you're thinking. Care to let me in?"

His voice startled me out of my thoughts. I forced myself to relax the tension in my forehead.

I exhaled, leaning forward again, resting my chin on my gloved hand.

"You must think highly of yourself if you think you can handle me as a wife."

He paused for a moment, then smoothly leaned onto his arm, closing more of the space between us. The scent of drink lingered on his breath.

"I can handle more than you think."

I huffed a small laugh and broke our stare first. His smirk only grew.

"Have you always been this confident?" I squinted, crossing my arms to suppress the smile threatening my lips.

I searched his face, but could only do so for so long. For some reason I couldn't look at this man for too long. It was maddening. I never cowered from men. Well, no other men but my father.

But there was just something about Kallias that could make anyone cower. I tilted my chin up to mask my unease.

"I would need a lot of guarantees before I even think

about agreeing to be your wife."

His eyes flickered, glinting more silver in the dimmed light. His lips tightened into an understanding line.

"I expect nothing less."

He crossed his arms, mirroring mine.

"Tell me these guarantees you need."

My lips pursed in delight.

"Well...."

I shifted my chair closer to him, our knees nearly touching.

"This doesn't mean I've agreed yet–but if I do, first thing's first—Obviously you have to help me become a warrior. By any means necessary."

"*Obviously*," he mocked in a shrug.

I shushed him. "We also need separate rooms–that's a given. Also access to the kitchen. At all hours," I said quickly, hoping to avoid questions. "And you have to promise me you will give me free rein on my off time. I'm sure I'll have responsibilities, being married to a prince—as we all do—but my free time is *my* free time."

He nodded in thought. "All right. As long as that free time doesn't disturb my free time, that shouldn't be a problem."

"It shouldn't." I wasn't about to tell him that my free time consisted purely of napping, eating, carving, and riding horses.

Horses—

"And I want more horses. I've only ever had one, and I love him, but the older he gets the worse I feel about pushing him by riding him too much." Not that I'd ridden him much this past year. "Father says I don't need a younger horse, but he's wrong."

Kallias smirked along to my banter.

I continued. "You can bring all the horses you want to the palace too. I'll make sure Father lets us have the country house. It has more stables."

His chin twitched as he gave me an unsteady look. "What do you mean?"

I blinked. "I mean—our palace."

"In the North?"

I nodded.

"Princess, I can't leave my kingdom. With my warrior duties, and family–" He shrugged his broad shoulders, drawing them in tightly. "I can't afford such a luxury."

"Luxury? Your alternative is asking me to leave my sister and the only home I've ever had–I wouldn't consider that a luxury."

He scanned my eyes further. "I thought that's what you wanted," he said softly.

My mouth opened a moment to object, but I froze. I had no idea what to say.

He was right. I did want to leave my kingdom. Well, the palace at least.

I had assumed marriage would mean moving to

another palace in the North. That's what Northern Royals always did—the one with less power relocated to where the one with more power lived, or they chose an already existing palace. It was routine. Expected. I must have assumed that was what all royals wanted.

But he loved his home.

This marriage wasn't an escape for him. It was for me...

I frowned, picking at the tips of my gloves. *Of course* he couldn't leave his kingdom. It made sense that I'd be the one to leave. I was the woman, after all.

I looked away for a moment to steady my breath.

I caught Libby elegantly twirling nearby with another gentleman now.

She danced. Careless and free. I couldn't help but want that for her.

She deserved it after all she's done for me. This wasn't how I wanted to do it...but perhaps this was a way I could protect her.

If I left, Father wouldn't pressure her to marry for anything other than love.

I hoped.

She was one of the few people that believed marriage should be for love. Albeit a foolish belief for a northern princess, I still wanted her to have it.

But this marriage–warriorship or not–meant I couldn't be the Queen's Guard. Never be assigned to protect her for the rest of our lives. I couldn't have that and be married to a southern prince.

I'd have to give up my dream.

In exchange for my freedom.

I swallowed down the lump in my throat. I'd shed too many tears the past few months.

Kallias met my gaze. His blue eyes were unreadable, neutral. This wasn't in his control. I wanted to snap at him, to tell him how stupid his assumptions were—but he wasn't wrong.

"Right. Well...I better get all the horses I want then." I crossed my arms like the act was the sign off on the agreement.

Kallias studied my shift of expression, rightfully wary.

"And," I added in a careful tone. "If possible, I would like to arrange to see my sister once a month, at least."

I tried to sound unbothered—strong, but a grief began to pierce a hole in my chest. I was getting too worked up over something that wasn't even decided yet.

Kallias scanned my face a bit more before a faint smile tugged at his lips. He leaned in slightly, inches away from my face.

"Anything else, Princess?"

The ease in his voice lightened my mood far too quickly. I smirked, shifting in my seat, raising a finger to point at him.

"Oh. I'm only getting started..."

TWENTY-THREE

Halfway through my extensive list of unreasonable demands to Kallias, the Palace Announcer appeared at the other side of our table. Dressed in his white and brown kingdom attire, he looked oddly foolish, like a misplaced chess piece.

Any amusement wiped off my face, the room growing louder by the second.

"The prince asks for a dance with the princess."

"Who?" I sneered as roughly as I could.

"You, Princess of Sevaire."

After a quick roll of my eyes, I turned to face the man. "That would be my sister. Her dance card is probably full by now, sorry."

I waved my hand and turned back to Kallias.

But his gaze fixed on the announcer.

Confused, I looked back to the skinny, pale man awkwardly towering over our table.

"What?" I scoffed, thoroughly annoyed that the only decent conversation I held tonight was being interrupted.

"My apologies, but I'm certain it was you he requested a dance with."

He motioned behind him to the prince standing in front of his throne, staring at us.

The boy stood with his hands tucked behind his back, his pointed chin held too high as he looked over the ballroom.

I'd met him a few times. He was a boring boy. Nothing special. I barely knew him.

His older brother was the handsome one and received all the attention at Biannuals. But this prince, Lorik, at least had grown into his height.

I exhaled sharply, giving the announcer a look that screamed, *Do I have to?*

After a short-lived stare-off, I steadily rose to my feet and offered Kallias a quick, brusque bow.

"I'll be *right* back."

I scowled when I noticed him biting back a laugh.

Flattening my skirt with choppy movements, I stepped to the announcer's side and followed him toward the prince.

I doubted my dress was comfortable enough to dance in. The prince had likely asked me only because Libby was unavailable. Parents often forced their children to maintain relations with my father's kingdom, even if that meant suffering through a dance with me.

I reached the prince just as he strode down the steps.

Before I could open my mouth to ask if he'd like to reconsider, he bowed and extended his hand.

I hesitated, purely out of irritation, but placed mine in his. He kissed it. My curtsy was brief.

"Prince Lorik," I greeted flatly.

Before I could withdraw my hand, he jerked me toward him, shifting us into the first position of a waltz.

Though I preferred the ease of a waltz to any other dance.

His hand greedily slid to the lowest part of my back, and before I could spit out a remark, we were already in motion with the next song.

Our strides were long and fluid as we moved toward the center of the dance floor, the cello's deep resonance rising above the rest of the orchestra.

The sound reminded me of Jayce.

He had played a similar piece at his last Biannual—his viola mastery so breathtaking it could bring an entire palace to tears. His performances had always been the highlight of the night, the only reason I had ever looked forward to attending.

I forced my irritation back into place and leveled Lorik with a dry look.

"All right, Lorik, let's keep this quick. I'm sorry my sister was too busy to dance with you—"

"Your sister?" he interrupted, far too comfortably. His grip didn't loosen. "I never wanted to dance with your sister."

I reached behind me and shoved his hand higher up on

my back, shooting him a warning glance.

"*Sure*," I muttered.

The symphony twisted the dance floor into a spin. I twirled out of his grasp. He pulled me back in—too forcefully, as if he wasn't used to handling someone who pushed back.

The dress fluttered as I spun, a shimmer of movement so fluid it almost felt magical.

I buried my brief fascination since there was no way I'd give him a reason to ask for a second dance.

His grin was sharp, amused—far from the dull, harmless boy I remembered. He must have grown into a jerk over the year I hadn't seen him. I'd heard enough rumors about his brother that it wouldn't surprise me if the same idiocy had infected Lorik once he came of age.

"I just *had* to dance with the most beautiful woman here," he murmured prickishly.

I closed my eyes to keep them from rolling straight out of my skull.

He smiled a pig-like smile. "One dance is all you're getting," I whispered.

"Why so quick to dismiss, Fiadh?"

Our arms extended and retracted in another sweeping motion.

I flicked my gaze to where he went—to our table.

"Isn't that your one and only suitor waiting for you at your table? Looking oh-so-impatient?" His smirk sharpened. "What a good guard dog you've let in from the streets."

Kallias was, in fact, glued to our dance.

"Are you referring to the Prince of Lyen?"

I smirked.

Lorik did a double take. Word must not have gotten around that a southern prince had cared to show up to a Northern Biannual, let alone to ask for a Northerners hand.

Why wouldn't that become the main gossip—that the lesser sister actually caught the attention of a decent suitor for once. Well, decent to those who didn't look down at Southerners too much.

"Not that it's any of your concern."

I flashed a vicious smile.

"*I see*—well, I'm surprised you don't have more suitors, now that everyone knows you're on the market," he winked. "Maybe you shouldn't dismiss the short roster of men willing to dance with you."

His comment might have accidentally made my foot slip. Right on top of his. Pity.

"Maybe you should learn to bite your tongue before you lose a toe," I grit out with a fake smile.

He seemed a little too pleased by the quip.

"You aren't too bad at playing with gentlemen either, are you Princess Fiadh?"

His not-so-subtle gaze swept over too much of me as he spun me once more. "I see age has been your friend."

Of course my loss of my strength was some sort of beacon to weak men, wanting someone just as weak as them to push around.

"I wish I could say the same to you," I teased, looking over him with disgust.

Lorik's smirk deepened. "Still *Feisty Fiadh*. Your reputation precedes you."

I wasn't trying to be flirty, but men like Lorik had a way of twisting rejection into some sort of invitation.

"How much longer is this song?" I muttered.

"Careful, Princess. You might just make me want another."

I let my eyes keep their rolling momentum. "Careful before you make me give you an ankle injury."

He laughed a little too loudly, flushing me with instant regret.

The song ended us in a dip and I turned my head as far away as possible from his, but he didn't hold back from bringing his face so close to my neck that I felt a small exhale of air escape.

I refused to shudder in disgust. Instead I stood and dropped into a brisk curtsy.

"Thanks, Lorik. Let's never do this again."

I squinted and quickly stomped away, despite his hand lingering its grasp on mine. Only when my irritation ebbed slightly did I notice that the ache in my ankle grew too much from the one dance.

I reached the table—only to find Kallias' seat empty. The three brothers were back in their places. My pace slowed as I scanned the nearby tables, searching for any sign of him.

"May I…"

The low, measured voice sent the smallest spark of a thrill down my spine as I twisted to find it.

Kallias with a bare, outstretched hand hovering between us. "…have a dance?"

It was a lifeline I didn't realize I needed.

Still lingering in my previous annoyance, I turned fully to face him. "And why would I do that?" I teased.

He lowered his hand, but instead of stepping back, he leaned in, his breath warm against my ear.

"Because we should practice for the many dances in our future—once we wed."

My lungs forgot how to work for a moment.

I rolled my eyes to mask it.

Before I could pull away, his fingers curled gently around my wrist. Hesitant. Testing. Then, as if deciding for himself, he slid his hand into mine. But he remained still, not taking full control.

So, I grabbed his other hand and placed it on my waist. "This doesn't mean I've agreed to anything yet."

His grip stiffened—only slightly—but his gaze never wavered.

I stepped into his embrace.

For a breath, he just stood there, looking down at me. I tilted my chin up, meeting his eyes from this new, oddly enchanting angle. A soft flush dusted his cheekbones.

I swallowed and forced my expression into something unreadable, though I couldn't quite smother the feeling.

He was warm.

I glanced at his wanting expression.

"Did you want me to lead, or—"

His head gave the faintest shake, like he was waking from a daydream.

"Sorry."

His voice came in rougher.

He cleared his throat, then stepped forward, guiding us into motion.

His hand pulled gently on my waist—so light I might have thought he'd let go.

Unlike handy Lorik, Kallias didn't press too deeply into my back. In fact, he placed his hand higher when I pressed into him.

Despite his towering frame, he moved with the grace of a prince.

It was good for show—if we did end up marrying.

I wouldn't admit how much I was enjoying it. He was effortless to dance with.

We flew through the crowd in a movement that felt so freeing, my heart lunged into the desire to make it last forever. For the first time since I had left my room, I didn't care if this ruined my ankle. This was, dare I say...fun.

We were one of the taller pairs on the dance floor. He was definitely one of the tallest men in attendance, though this kingdom wasn't lacking in height.

Strength-wise, he was built like a palace guard—lean muscle, controlled power—but his formal wear made him appear more refined.

"What are you thinking through that serious face?" His voice was a low hum, smoothing over any residual tension.

I blinked my furrowed brows away.

"That you're a better dancer than I thought," I said quieter than I intended.

A flicker of something crossed his face—amusement, maybe. "Is that so surprising?"

The corners of my lips twitched upward. It was... nice, seeing him like this. Loose. Almost teasing.

"Your palace doesn't host any Biannuals," I noted inquisitively.

"There's no need for them," his tone was factual. "My brother won't marry, and neither will I. There is no other kingdom around willing to host them until our little cousin gets older, so we don't waste our time to find women there is no future with."

He spun me then softly pulled me back into his embrace. His grip eased, settling more firmly against me.

"Before I met you, that is."

His words were a whisper, brushing against my ear just before he pushed me into another spin.

I schooled my expression.

I had never felt anything while dancing before—

nothing but annoyance. But the way he spoke, the way his hands moved, the way he held me...it was new.

The song ended too soon.

I curtsied quickly before returning to our emptied table.

I sat down, exhaling—trying to rid myself of whatever unnamable feeling was settling in my stomach.

Lifting a hand, I fanned myself, only for Kallias to return and sit close beside me to watch.

"Sorry." I blurted out.

His gaze flickered over me in assessment. I prayed my cheeks didn't reveal anything. "It's too hot out there..." I fanned myself. "*Temperature-wise,*" I mumbled on.

I didn't look at him right away. Instead, I grasped another flute and made it disappear. I could already feel the warmth furling around my mind.

I was too thin to handle my drinks the way I used to. Smacking my lips, I surveyed the other empty flutes for more relief before glancing back at Kallias.

I never cared for attention.

But his didn't make me want to constantly sneer at him.

I noted his silence.

"What?"

"Every eye was on you."

I flicked my gaze toward a few lingering stragglers at nearby tables, their eyes drifting toward us before quickly looking away. They must have been surprised that I hadn't tripped or fallen on my face like the last Biannual.

"You're a very good liar, Prince Kallias. I don't know how I feel about that in a husband."

The stark change in his face froze me for a moment.

I swallowed.

"It's the dress," I said, flashing a small smile, "and you."

His lips twitched, barely.

"When was the last time you made an appearance at one of these?"

A quiet laugh escaped him—low, rich, and far too easy on my ears. That dimple again.

Another song swelled through the marbled ballroom. Stars spilled in through the distant windows, as if they, too, wished to hear the music.

"It's been a few years," he admitted.

His deep eyes remained on me. It made me slightly lean in.

I needed to lay off the drinks. Any more drinks and I would get more handsy.

"So, then tell me—" I said, straightening in my seat. "What are *your* expectations of a wife?"

I held an empty glass on my lap between us, mildly irritated by the lack of refills.

His lips parted to answer—but a familiar, grating sound interrupted him. I didn't need to look.

Jayce.

"I never thought I'd hear the word *wife* come from *your* lovely lips," Jayce teased as he settled beside me, drink already in hand.

I exhaled quickly through my nose. "*Jayce*...here I thought I wouldn't have to endure you today."

"You should've known better than to wear a dress like that if you wanted to avoid me," he grinned. "Is that not why you picked such a thing?"

I leered at Jayce.

"Why don't you go refill your drink?"

"Why don't you join me?" Jayce grinned. "Help me make all the girls jealous with a dance."

"No. I'm busy."

I waved him off and turned to Kallias. "Continue, please."

"*Fifi...*" Jayce crooned, further poking my irritation.

"Go find my sister to bother," I spat, twisting away.

"But you're more fun to play with," he whined like a drunk child, grabbing my arm. "Now let's go—why are you so skinny?"

I yanked my arm back just as a large hand clamped around Jayce's wrist.

"She said no."

Kallias's voice was like thunder rolling low over the ballroom. He loomed over Jayce, jaw locked, eyes dark. Both Jayce and I leaned back instinctively.

"It—it's all right, Kal, we were just joking," I stuttered.

"He's a friend."

Jayce, for once, was too shocked to say anything. His fingers slipped from mine, but Kallias's grip clasped ironclad. I could feel its rigid force, even from my seat.

Kallias' gaze shifted down, over me. Once he caught my expression, he relented—slightly.

Then, with deliberate slowness, he let Jayce go.

Jayce recoiled, rubbing his wrist while steadying his drink.

"My apologies," Kallias murmured, utterly insincere.

He sat back down, his presence folding back into composed stillness, though the weight of his power lingered.

I looked over to Jayce. "I'll...catch up with you later."

He forced a weak chuckle in response. "You'll have to drink a lot to catch up with me."

He skittered away shakily, nearly tripping over his own feet.

I probably should have been more annoyed at Kallias's reaction. But I was in awe—at his composure, the quiet authority in his anger. So different than my father's wrath.

"Don't mind him. He's always been a little weasel."

Kallias exhaled through his nose. "Would you rather continue talking, or would another dance be preferable?"

"No—please. I've danced enough for the month."

I lied.

I hadn't done enough of anything this month. I clung to this one night of faux freedom like it was the only one I'd have all year.

If I were to be honest, I enjoyed dancing with him. And maybe—just maybe—I'd do it again. A small part of me wondered if my dress truly did make me look as beautiful as I once wished I could have been. Or if it was the ridiculous loss of weight that unfortunately captured others' attention.

"The only reason I'd be on the dance floor is if Jayce had his way, and I was ten drinks in."

Kallias smirked, warmth creeping in my face. "If you keep trying to make me jealous, I just might force you into a dance."

My brows lifted. "Jealous?"

His gaze lingered, unreadable yet pleased. "Well, if you become my wife, you'll have to get used to a little jealousy. It comes with the territory."

I schooled my face again. "Territory?" I squinted at him, waiting.

He faltered—only a little. "Not territory like property—I just meant—"

A chuckle slipped from me as his subtle panic showed. When I covered my lips—an old habit drilled into me—I caught the way his tension eased, his smirk returning.

I waved the moment away. "You didn't finish telling me your requirements of a wife."

Kallias tilted his head at me in what I could only assume was disbelief. "I don't have any. I wasn't sure I'd get this far. Anything's fine with me."

My eyes widened. "Really? *Anything*?" I tapped my chin. "If I demanded we eat nothing but cake every day, you wouldn't stop me?"

He shrugged. "I guess not."

I hummed. "And if I want to paint the palace a bright, blinding yellow–that would be fine?"

He nodded. "I'll hand you the brush."

I smirked. "What if I make everyone in the kingdom call me The Great Princess."

A ghost of a smile tugged at his lip. "I won't stop you."

Too easy.

"And what if I choose to spend every morning running around on my horse until dark–you would let me?"

Kallias tapped his fingers on the table before speaking. "Would you let me come with you?"

I arched a brow. "On my horse rides?"

He nodded.

"Maybe. Sometimes. If you can keep up."

That dimple of his ghosted into view again. I forced myself to look away and change the topic.

"Realistically though—I assume I'll have some duties at your palace? Last I heard your Father doesn't rule, your brother does?"

His casual demeanor shifted. His expression neutralized.

"My parents died a while ago. My brother does his best. The staff is responsible for the upkeep of the palace so he can focus on ruling."

"Oh." I sank in my seat. "Sorry—I didn't mean to bring up any bad memories. If you don't want to talk about it…"

He waved me off. "No worries. As for duties, nothing you're not used to—parties, events. Do as little or as much as you'd like. The staff is fantastic. They practically raised me and my brother. They do more in the palace than I ever could."

I offered a faint smile. "They must be great then."

I'd grown so comfortable in our conversation that I had almost forgotten about the pins digging into my skull. But I itched at them again once I remembered.

"I guess I don't know much about the history of other kingdoms. Our schools mainly teach us of our kingdom and how everything relates to the North in general."

"I'm aware."

"Is it the same for you? Your education?"

"No." He shook his head. "We try to teach the children everything. All of history, despite what the North wants."

My forehead creased. "What the North wants?"

"The Northern Kingdoms have their own version of history and where they want it to go," Kallias said. "Every battle is a triumph, every conquest beneficial to them. They don't speak about the lives lost of those in other kingdoms or the economic toll it took from us to supply them."

"Hence the limiting goods not being traded," I realized.

"Precisely."

I considered the implications. The weight of it settled

over me. There were clear benefits for him in marrying a Northern Princess, but...

"What?" he asked.

I relaxed my face, forcing myself not to gnaw on my lip. "I'm just—" I hesitated. A part of me was still scared to trust him, but I had no reason not to.

"What if we do get married and it doesn't help much?"

My voice lowered as I glanced around the dance floor.

"If I'm honest, I don't know how much assistance you'll get from my father in regard to marrying me. I'm definitely not his favorite—far from it. I don't see how your marrying me would be that beneficial."

It stung to admit, but it was true. I respected Kallias too much to let him believe otherwise.

His eyes stayed focused on me. Even with the glow of chandeliers and firelight, his eyes shone like polished crystal. I found myself staring.

"I doubt that will be an issue. Even if it's only for his image, he would have to supply us with something. It won't look good in his case otherwise."

That was somewhat true. But still...

"I'm not so sure..."

"Why do you doubt he'd provide for you?"

I pushed aside the memories scratching the edges of my mind. *"You weren't there,"* my lips mumbled, but I was thankful my voice didn't extend. I cleared my throat.

"That's just how we've become...slowly. I'm an

inconvenience. It would be easier to rid of me, though he doesn't want me marrying you either, so I honestly don't really know what he wants to do with me. Killing me would be the easiest solution, but it's definitely not discreet. Not with our history." I returned to gnawing my lip.

History proved family wasn't above murder when it suited them. At least, not in the North. I doubted my father would kill me—but he'd nearly beaten me to death before, so perhaps I shouldn't rule it out entirely.

The music swelled.

Jayce had found some poor girl to torment with dance.

"No father would want his child dead," Kallias said evenly.

I scoffed.

"You don't know my father."

"Have you spoken to him? Does he tell you what his expectations of you are? What does he say?"

"The usual," I huffed. "To marry. Not to become a warrior—though he still won't tell me why. I just know I'm meant to stay out of his way. At least that's what I gather through the few words he bothers speaking to me."

It sounded so simple. So dull. Yet those few facts had dictated my entire life.

"Somehow, I doubt he thinks that little of you."

I scoffed again. "My people are different. If something doesn't benefit them, they don't want it. Plus, I don't think I ever fit in here. Just like my mother." My words trailed off.

His silence wasn't uncomfortable—it felt… understanding.

"But sometimes I'm not sure who I've become in this kingdom."

I straightened under Kallias's unwavering attention.

"One more thing—If I marry you, I want access to records, pictures, anything regarding my mother and where she came from. If you have such things. I don't know enough about her, and I never visited her land before it was absorbed. Or after…but it's always been a dream of mine. I want the freedom to explore that."

His gentle smile warmed the space between us.

"Fia, even if you don't marry me, I'll find a way to get that to you. She was a good woman from what I heard—worthy of being remembered. You may visit anytime, borrow as many records as you'd like. You deserve to know where you came from."

A quiet melancholy settled beneath my smile.

Perhaps this arrangement could work. Things could be worse. Maybe that would become my motto from here forward. My life may not be going in the direction I planned in my childhood, but I should be somewhat appreciative for the opportunities he was offering me.

Things could be worse.

"Thank you, Kallias."

I smiled wider. "Sincerely."

The warmth in my chest was something I hadn't felt in months.

TWENTY-FOUR

The long-awaited meal finally arrived, and nothing was going to stop me from devouring every bite of Kivo's famous spicy beef. Across from me, Kallias hesitated before standing.

"I should return to my seat."

He hesitated.

I flinched at him, my mouth full of food. "Why don't you just sit here and we can finish speaking."

"That's all right. You should enjoy your food. I'll find you later."

I returned to my breathtaking meal. It was just as delicious as I'd hoped.

Libby soon joined me, rambling about my dance, how lovely I looked, and how people stared.

I gave all credit to her dress, then mentioned Jayce, only briefly touching on Kallias—until she pointed out how long we'd been speaking. That led to my brief explanation.

"He might be my only way out. I might have to marry

him..." I whispered between bites.

"What do you mean you *have* to?" she asked with a skepticism I wasn't expecting from her. This was what my family wanted—in a way. If anything, I expected her to be ecstatic.

I explained that he'd ensure my warriorship if we wed.

"You shouldn't marry a man simply because of what he offers."

"Why not?" I scoffed a laugh. "That's the main reason people get married at our age. It's never for love."

"But it can be."

Libby was always too optimistic. I loved that about her, but I feared she'd waste her life searching for a perfect love story that didn't exist in our world.

"No. Libby. It can't. Not for everyone."

I turned to her, taking her hands in mine. "But if I do this, one of Father's children will be married—meaning you'll be free to marry someone you do love."

She pulled her hands away. "The man I love died long ago."

"Right. I'm sorry—but you know what I mean. This would be beneficial to everyone—even you and Taroh. You'd both have more freedom. I always wanted to become a warrior and protect you. This is another way to do that—through my actions, through marriage." I hid the bitterness of the truth.

Her skepticism didn't waver. "No. Fia, are you insane? If Father locked you up for months just for the idea of marrying him, imagine what he'll do if you actually went through with this. He'll…" she gasped. "He'll kill you, Fia."

I looked down at my gloves, picking at them once again. "I'll kill myself if I have to stay there," I spoke quietly, because I knew I shouldn't have said it, but the sooner she accepted it, the quicker she could be on my side in all of this.

"No you won't! How dare you say that? Stop saying these stupid things!" Libby's voice rose louder than I'd ever heard it go at a public event.

I glanced around, trying to shush her. "Libby, quiet—"

"No! I won't be quiet. Who do you think you are making such drastic decisions on your own? I'm saying no. You'll be fine. I'll marry someone and we'll move and you can live with me. Don't worry about it. Tell him no. Now." Her hands nearly pushed me off my chair.

"Libby," I exhaled, staying steady in my seat. "I have to make this decision for myself—for us."

"*Don't* pretend this is for us. Leaving me is not *for us*, how could you think that?"

"Well, forcing me to stay and live a meaningless life isn't *for us* either."

Her face hardened in a way I couldn't remember if I'd ever seen before. "Staying with me would be *meaningless*?"

Her bitter voice was a tone I never heard from her. It was as painful to my ears as it was to my heart.

"Libby—"

Then she bolted out of the ballroom.

After my initial shock at her outburst, I followed her. She stomped out of the ballroom, ignoring the eyes on her—not a good sign when it comes to her. When she stopped caring about appearances, her anger had gone beyond a quick fix.

She shoved open the courtyard doors, the night air biting sharper than expected.

Our guards followed, but I gestured for them to stay inside. To my surprise, they listened, lingering near the entrance.

I caught up to her at the bottom of the brick stairs, before the large fountain. Wind cut through like a blade.

She hugged her thin arms, her ears turning red from the breeze, or maybe from anger.

"Libby, stop."

Wind howled as a barrier between us.

"I will not! Who do you think you are taking this upon yourself? It is *my* duty to marry—I'm the eldest, not you. I'm sorry I haven't delivered yet, but just give me a little bit more time."

Clouds of warm air whirled from our breaths.

"It's not just duty for me, it's also about the path I want to take for my life."

"You can still have it. Father—"

"*Father* made his feelings clear!"

Her volume only matched mine. "Yes, he did! And who knows what he'll do when you tell him this. Fia, I lost you for two months and I barely survived that, I don't want to think about what he'll—"

My voice found its volume to match hers and keep our screaming match filling the courtyard. "You wanted me to marry Kallias in the first place! How could you change your mind now?"

Birds startled overhead as our argument swelled painfully.

"Just like this—" I shrugged. "I changed my mind! When I knew what it was like to spend one birthday without you, I realized I wanted that to be the last one. What if you *die*, Fia? Do you even care about what that would do to me? To Taroh? You're so set on pushing Father that you're risking your life or willing to let some stranger take you away—"

The door creaked open. A shadow fell across the stairs as Kallias stepped out, emerging in terrible timing. I winced.

Libby's fury shifted instantly. She bolted toward him as the door shut behind him.

"You are not going to marry my sister."

Libby jabbed a finger at Kallias. I followed her, grabbing her wrist before she could say more. Kallias stood patiently, blankly observing the two of us. I ignored him for now.

"Libby, I would have left at some point. Whether for marriage or to become a warrior—I was never going to stay."

"Temporarily!" she shot back. "You were supposed to leave for a little while and come back. You were always meant to come back."

She didn't know how much those two months had changed me—how close I'd come to making her fear a permanent choice. She didn't need to know. But she had to accept that, one way or another, I wasn't staying.

"You can't change fate—Libby," I said, knowing it was something she valued.

She yanked her hand free. "This isn't fate. You'll see. The matches will prove that, and until then, we're going to find a better solution."

Her breath huffed in quick, uneven bursts. "I hated every second we were apart. I thought you did too, but I guess I was wrong."

A droplet of water pooled in her eye, catching in the moonlight. She was too beautiful to cry. But I was too hurt to cry.

"Don't act like you have a clue what I went through the past two months." My tone was quiet, but the hurt bled through.

She glared between Kallias and me before turning on her heel, storming back inside.

As soon as the door slammed shut behind her, I buried my face in my gloves, trying to catch my breath for a second—trying not to cry.

I knew this would be hard, but not like this. I didn't think she'd be *this* upset. The last thing I wanted for us to do was fight. I had ruined our first night out together.

I hated seeing her heart broken—especially if I was the one who had shattered it.

Warm fabric pressed over my shoulders. I looked up to see Kallias adjust his tunic around me.

His strong arms were now bare, save for the short-sleeved tan undershirt clinging to his frame. My earlier suspicion was right—he *had* grown stronger. It was as if the past month had drained every ounce of my strength and given it to him instead.

"I'm starting to get the feeling that your family doesn't like me," he murmured.

His words were light, but the weight of his presence unsettled me. Not because it was unwelcome—but because I wasn't used to it. Grieving alone was my specialty. I didn't know what to do with comfort freely given.

The warmth from his breath tickled my nose.

I forced something like a smile. "She's just emotional. She'll get over it. Once I leave, she'll go back to her life and her friends, and she'll be content with that."

"She's going to miss you."

I curled my fingers into the fabric of his tunic, pulling it tighter around me and smelling the same musk of his when I had borrowed his shirt from our first encounter.

I wasn't ready to go inside—not yet. Not when I knew the looks waiting for me. The quiet judgment. The silent blame. Not that they would be wrong.

"I'll miss her."

The pins in my hair stabbed at my skull, the ache suddenly unbearable. I reached up, tugging at the sharpest ones, pulling them free.

"Reconsidering?"

His breath clouded in the cold.

I looked at him. We were closer in height when I had my heels on, making every expression of his even more evident.

He was being too kind, too steady. He didn't have to stand here with me. He didn't have to come out at all. Maybe he was doing this to convince me. Or maybe—just maybe—he would make a decent partner for life, if he kept all his promises.

The moon cast a pale halo around him, catching in the waves of his trimmed, dark hair. I pulled out another pin, letting my hair spill onto my shoulders for warmth.

"Actually...I think I made up my mind."

He straightened, tension locking his frame. A line creased between his brows. I wanted to smooth it away—to bring back that quiet, knowing smile of his.

"If you win the matches," I said, voice as ever as ever, "and the Well permits us to be together...*and my father doesn't kill one of us in the process,*" I mumbled. "Then...I will marry you."

His eyes searched mine, waiting. For me to take it back? To hesitate? But I stood firm.

There was something about the stilled night. The

distant birds flitted across the sky, their wings cutting through the moonlight. A strange sort of peace settled in my chest.

The crease in his brow faded, but his jaw tensed. He gave a single nod. "And if the Well doesn't permit?"

I hesitated. The wind stirred, rustling the trees. The pins in my palm bit into my skin. Despite everything—despite him being a warrior, a prince, a man—everything I'd grown indifferent to, I still felt like being honest. Felt like telling him the truth.

So I did.

The three words I hated admitting. The words that made me feel small. Defeated. They rolled off my tongue like the confession they were.

"I don't know."

Part 3
The Matches

TWENTY-FIVE

The matches were held in a sports field that was typically used as a racing court during Quintennial pre-qualifications. The last athletic pre-qualifications were held last year. Aside from that, the field was only used for matches.

The court sat on the outskirts of the palace, a landscape of plains and tracks lined with wooden risers for spectators.

It provided ample space for whatever elaborate challenges my father had devised for this match. Only the speaker and those who prepared the arena were given any details about what it would entail.

Father's choices were rarely difficult. In our early years, he devised grueling competitions for suitors, but over time, I suspected he grew desperate for Libby to marry, making the challenges fairly simple.

Some were easy enough that even I could have completed them myself if that had been an option. The Well at the end was the true decisive factor—I never understood why it wasn't the first match instead of the last.

Perhaps Father believed suitors should at least prove themselves capable of surviving a basic set of trials before facing fate. Marriage was likely harder than a few tests—especially a marriage to someone from the North.

Libby, on the other hand, had never been pushed toward marriage, not because Father was protecting her, but because he hadn't yet decided which political alliance would serve him best. I always assumed it was more beneficial for him to lead alliances on.

Still, Libby believed she could find true love, even within our small pool of options. Her blind faith was admirable. I tried to appreciate the parts of her I had missed while locked away, but this was a dream she would never let go of, and I always wondered if she'd be better off if she did.

The past few months leading up to the proposals were a bore. Father was gone for half the time, traveling to locations he refused to disclose—not that I tried very hard to ask.

I hadn't tried very hard to do anything regarding my father, besides avoid him. In that aspect, he was unquestionably successful in his fear-instilling. I was more terrified of his threats now than I'd ever been before.

Instead, I spent as much time outside the palace as I could—walking the grounds or disguising myself to go to the market with Mattok at night.

At least I got to spend more time with Libby and Taroh around the palace. Libby's attitude gradually improved after countless conversations and endless sleepovers in her room. But it seemed a part of her still seemed to believe this was all some elaborate joke on my end.

One night, she told me she didn't think the Well would ever permit us to marry, despite its unpredictability. She'd read enough folklore that made her believe that perhaps that was never the purpose of the Well at all.

I wanted to believe her.

When Father was home, he and his wife avoided me like the plague, but since I was so often ignored, I had plenty of time to indulge my newfound love of snooping around and avoiding my father.

Our carriage arrived early to the arena, dragging us into the stifling morning heat. I fed Libby some excuse about needing to use the chambers right away, giving me a chance to look for Kallias.

Luckily she was quickly swept up in a group of *friends* that doted on the intricate shine on her flowered, pink dress.

Rosette was among them, and I was beyond relieved she didn't see me first. I wasn't in the mood for whatever snide remark she had about my absence from Libby's birthday party.

In an effort to stay in Father's good graces, I wore something similar to Libby's dress. A small, pointless gesture, but any effort counted. At least mine was more subdued—

fewer flowers, less pastel, and sheer belle sleeves that would probably suffocate me in this heat.

Confining sleeves in the summer was my limit. Most of them ripped anyway. Not that it would be an issue now. My body hadn't fully returned to its usual size yet.

The theatrics of my attire felt so childish.

The dried trees around the plain hadn't fully bloomed into summer, yet the cicadas' song stung so strongly into my ears I cringed. Heat and cicadas—possibly the worst combination for a day like today.

The suitors' holding quarters weren't far from the toileting chambers, and with few people around, only stable boys and servants passed by. My guard slipped into the chambers too when I promised to stay put.

Once the last few stable servants in their noticeable brown passed, I crept behind the tented chambers and jogged toward the suitors' holding tent.

Retrieving the dagger I always had strapped to my thigh, I carefully slit a small opening in the white fabric—just wide enough to peek through.

I glanced around before fixing an eye on one suitor sitting on one of the wooden benches in the tent—the boy whose hand I had accidentally accepted.

I really hoped this wouldn't kill him. Few suitors died at the proposal matches, but it wasn't completely unheard of. The couple times it had happened had scarred me for life.

Two suitors of Libby's entered the tent next. Jayce

floated in behind them, tossing some ridiculous joke at the boys. I still rolled my eyes, even if he couldn't see it. Maybe he could feel it.

Jayce had tried for Libby's hand once before, so I wouldn't be surprised if he was trying again. I thought it was a joke though, but maybe this was one of Libby's pathetic solutions to me not marrying.

The tent opened again and Kallias stepped in.

He stood tall, clad in just enough of his warrior garb to assert his position. His presence was commanding, as imposing as a bear on its hind legs. Stubble dusted his jaw, and his hair had grown slightly longer, brushing past his ears.

Any warmth he'd once shown me was gone, his face still, his gaze blank, but lethal.

I needed to get his attention without drawing any to myself.

He sat on an empty bench, elbows on his knees, staring at the grass just opposite where I was crouched.

I considered waving a bit of fabric from the tent, but the slight wind carried it away unnoticed.

He sat too close to the entrance of the tent, where I couldn't go unnoticed either. The few shrubs around the tent were my only protection on the side I crouched beside.

I didn't have time to waste. If my guard realized I was gone, Father would send someone for me soon. We'd been civil enough today. He still avoided me, but that was preferable to his attention.

I turned and slipped away.

A nearby tree scattered with needles and twigs caught my eye. I scooped up a few twigs, considering whether to throw one. Not the best plan, but it might work. A few more tents stood nearby, forming a small triangle around the trees.

A faint burst of laughter erupted from the tent behind me. I didn't care to know what joke Jayce was attempting.

I moved toward the bundle of tents, keeping out of sight as the crowd grew. The set ahead of me was surely empty.

Slipping into the farthest tent, I found it filled with materials stacked throughout the tent like a maze.

Voices murmured outside, followed by the heavy thud of footsteps along the tent's wall.

I didn't wait to see if it was my guard or a suitor. Instead, I ducked deeper into the tent, carefully weaving through the walls of supplies. Tree roots jutted from the ground near a corner, and I stepped over them as quietly as possible.

This would have been a good place to have met Kallias, if I thought this through better. My thoughts twisted through my mind's own maze as I moved through this one.

Then, the soft flap of a tent closed.

A step inside.

"Hello?" I whispered before my hand immediately slapped over my mouth, regretting the decision to give away my location.

I dropped into a crouch, unsheathing the dagger at my

thigh—something I never should have put away in the first place. They became a normal part of my uniform since that first night I met Kallias in the forest. I used to always pocket a small knife for whittling, but most of my whittling knives broke during my two months in prison.

This dagger was bigger, deadlier. I had brought the largest one I had, the one Libby had given me.

The wavy pattern on the blade looked effective enough to inflict a generous amount of pain. I almost feared using it, after losing my first one, but I'd be lying if I said I wouldn't enjoy using it—only if someone truly deserved it.

My back pressed against a tall stack of wrapped wood as another step crept closer. I raised the dagger to my shoulder, gripping the handle tighter while staying low.

Steady.

I'd been more skittish around crowds since last week. Matty and I had sneaked into the town square, only for me to be pit-pocketed by a foreigner that I just had to start a fight with. I barely got away—left a dagger buried in the man's hand as I ran.

I slowly rose as another step clicked too close—so close I could have reached out and grabbed the person around the corner.

My grip tightened on the dagger as I held it to my chest. My pulse pounded against my fingertips.

Fear from the uncertainty of what was to come slithered over my skin.

Why was I stupid enough to hide here?

What if someone had followed me again?

The hummingbird in my chest wouldn't stay still. Another sound forced me into action—I leapt around the corner, unwilling to be caught off guard again.

A hand stuck to my wrist.

Another shoved me against the wall.

My mouth opened to yell—but a quick, firm hand silenced me before I could.

Wide-eyed, breath hitched, I met a familiar scruffy smirk.

My body relaxed, recognizing, remembering his touch.

I scanned his face, searching for the hidden dimples I hoped to see. Kallias appeared even taller than before—if such was possible. But I didn't mind.

He stood closely over me, glaring down with those impossible blue eyes.

He found me.

His hand lowered, lingering briefly on my neck before retreating. As royalty, he could touch another royal, but as a suitor—I wasn't sure what punishment Father might devise if we were caught alone in a tent, this close.

"*Lias?*" A muffled, rugged voice shouted from outside the tent.

Kallias scanned the tent before locking eyes with me. I opened my mouth to scold him for scaring me half to death, but his finger pressed on my lips, the rest of his hand cradling my face, holding me still. His touch was surprisingly soft, gentle against my quivering lip.

His other hand gripped my hip, guiding me deeper into the little maze. Even as he turned toward the sound, his fingers remained ghosting against my skin.

In quiet precision, he moved his hands to my shoulders, lowering us into a crouch. I bit back the nervous tang on my lips, gripping my knife tighter, running my thumb over the handle's edge.

He stared into the distance, pressing a hand to the ground as he listened to the growing silence around us. I was ready to bombard him with questions—what he had learned, what he wanted, what he was thinking—but then he looked back at me so casually that my mind cleared.

His blue eyes held me in place.

We stared, searching for something in each other. Heat rushed through me as he studied my face.

My reaction was purely because we were alone. I hadn't seen him in a while—his face, his eyes, his lips—

"You look better."

His voice, low and humming, sent a thud through my chest. I swallowed hard, blinking back into our usual banter.

"What does that mean?" I softly hissed, using the opportunity to jerk away from him.

A shadow of scruff lined his strong jaw, but he was well-groomed—likely making an effort for the proposals. It suited him—this balanced look.

His throat cleared as he leaned away from me. "You appear to have been fed normally."

I nodded in a truce. "Thanks. You too." My eyes narrowed.

A pending smile grew on him while I bit back mine.

I attempted to sheathe my dagger, but his grip caught my wrist. My lips parted to protest, but he dipped his chin, shooting me a glare.

"If you're going to face someone with a knife," he said, moving my dagger closer to my chest, positioning the handle near my throat and the blade forward, "keep it close to your body. Or—" He plucked the dagger from my grip, effortlessly twirling it. "Make it harder to be disarmed."

My eyes flickered from my dagger to his eyes. It looked useless in his large hands. He flipped it once more, extending the handle back to me. "I see your Academies don't teach you combat either."

I scoffed as I sheathed my dagger, because he was right, I knew very little besides a few sword positions.

"Who are you hiding from?" I muttered, keeping my voice low. I forced myself to look away from his overbearing eyes.

"My guard can be...a little overprotective."

"At a proposal match?"

He rolled his eyes in a childlike annoyance before settling them back on me.

"You'd be surprised. There's a reason I prefer my

Warrior duties to my royal ones."

It was easy for me to forget that Kallias wasn't born into this life. He had a whole different life before royalty. Who might he have been if his family had never married into the crown? Who would I have been if I wasn't royal? But if neither of us were, we wouldn't be here. We wouldn't be in this moment.

I pushed myself to stand. He offered a hand, but something about our closeness made me hesitate to touch him again. Even just his hand. So I stood on my own.

We were never this unnatural before. I wasn't sure what had shifted between us, but I caught his lingering glances. Part of me wondered what they made me feel.

Another part of me didn't want to think about it.

Not today.

"What's your plan today?" I whispered, leaning back against the wall of supplies.

He sighed, the softness in his face hardening back into the warrior I knew.

"I was going to ask you what you thought the matches might be during the proposals. I'll make it to the end, the rest is up to you after the Well."

I picked at my fingernails.

"Right."

I hesitated, debating whether to ask the question clawing at my mind.

What if the Well rejected us?

What if everything we had worked for resulted in nothing?

What if we lost our reason to see each other?

"What if you don't make it?" The words slipped out, and I tensed, surprised at the weight of my own worry.

He scoffed, maintaining his composure. "Don't worry about me." And that was that.

I couldn't deny the small cushion of comfort his tone provided. I felt inclined to believe him.

"Tell me what you can about the matches. I will handle the rest," he asked.

I sighed, fully aware of my own uselessness.

"I haven't heard too much. I've asked–*a lot*–but all I can tell you is that the matches aren't *usually* overly difficult. But...still, the amount of secrecy around them has been suspicious. I'm sure you can handle whatever it is, but my father has never been this secretive before. I have this feeling he has something up his sleeve... but I don't know if you should trust me and my discomfort alone—"

"I trust you."

His low timbre returned.

I swallowed.

"Would it be the same match for all the suitors?"

My forehead bunched after a sigh.

"I'm not sure."

I stood tall to pace in the little space between us. "He did seem odd today. I wouldn't be surprised if he threw

something unexpected at everyone. I can't be sure. He's been…
civil towards me lately, but I can't exactly trust him from
pulling the rug out from below me. Still…"

I rubbed my chin thoughtfully.

"We've managed to make it this far. I should count that
either a victory…or a reason to stay on guard."

Kallias nodded. "I'll adapt."

Before I could respond, his head lifted at the sound of a
familiar voice.

The voice wasn't just familiar—it was my guard,
standing right outside the tent.

My breath hitched—my stupid reflexes betraying me,
leaving a gasp in the silence, giving away my location.

My eyes widened, pulse roaring in my ears. Kallias
mirrored my panic as we both snapped our heads toward the
entrance. My heart thudded wildly.

I was about to be caught.

Caught alone, in a tent, with him.

My guard would tell my father. And then—

Strong hands clamped down on my shoulders.

Silver eyes locked onto mine. Another step echoed just
beyond the canvas walls outside the tent. There was no time.
Nowhere to hide, not when I'd exposed our location. I had to
think—

The same strong hands quickly slid up, rough fingers
skimming until they held my neck.

I lost my breath again. My hands flew to his wrists

instinctively.

"Sorry–" he whispered, voice barely formed–before he crushed his lips against mine.

Shock hit me like lightning.

My brain short-circuited.

This was his plan?

Sure, warriors were supposed to think fast. And this was...fast. But all reason vanished the moment my eyes fluttered shut.

I might have gasped—or whimpered—but whatever sound I made was lost against his mouth.

Stubble scraped my skin, his grip unrelenting, and the force behind his kiss was...powerful.

Powerful enough to make my knees weak. Powerful enough to erase every coherent thought from my mind.

He pressed forward, deeper, harder, until my back met a solid wall of supplies behind me. And in front of me—

A wall of heat. Of strength. Of him.

Whatever world was around me dissolved the moment he tilted his head to open his mouth more into the kiss, deepening it with a hunger I could feel in my bones.

I wished I could think—could process—but my mind was lost, consumed by sensation. My body moved on its own— fingers tangling into his hair, chest rising to press against his as our breaths grew uneven, searching for somewhere to go.

It was so commanding, and yet—the way he kissed me– if *kiss* was a strong enough word–carried a tenderness I had only ever known from him.

"Hey!"

A voice cut through the haze, but neither of us pulled away.

If anything, Kallias pressed even closer, shielding me as if I needed protection from everything but him.

The voice called out again—louder—before our kiss broke with a sharp smack, and all of his warmth vanished.

I inhaled deeply, eyes still closed, trying to regain some sense of reality, because that...was...

A second *smack* yanked my attention toward the two figures before me.

I was too late. My guard had already driven his fist straight into Kallias' face.

"Stop it!" I surged forward, planting myself in the middle of Kallias and disaster.

Again.

"Are you crazy?"

Slater—one of my newer guards, barely two years in service—reached for his sword.

"Not only are you running away from me, but you're running off to do—this. With *him*—" he sneered, jerking his chin toward Kallias.

I flicked my gaze to him just in time to see him swipe his thumb across his split lip. Wiping away blood. Or maybe wiping the kiss off of him. I couldn't tell.

Slater's tone towards Kallias was as if he was nothing.

It sent heat flashing through me.

"Your father will be quite pleased with me bringing both of you to his feet."

Oh no.

Think–think–think.

I forced a breath, barely sparing Kallias a glance. If I wanted to get out of this, I needed to do it myself.

"All right," I said with a shrug, crossing my arms. My glare stayed locked on Slater. "Let's go."

"What?" Both men said in unison.

I stepped toward the entrance, slow and deliberate, making sure they both felt the weight of my movements. "You want to talk to my father, let's do that–"

I knew how men like Slater worked—how they lived for the king's approval, desperate for a chance to prove themselves, to claw their way up the ranks.

I took another step. "Father would love to know how a trusted guard of his let his daughter slip right through his fingers where she could have been anywhere in the worlds before she was found. Alone. With a man. A *Southern* man."

I turned back to them, my expression betraying nothing but disinterest. "Would you like me to be the one to tell him? Or will you?"

Slater's jaw clenched so hard I thought he might crack a tooth. I stood firm, watching him *think*. Watching him *seethe.*

He finally tore his glare away from me and aimed it at

Kallias instead—like *he* was going to help him.

But Kallias only met him with an arched brow, making it painfully obvious that this was not his mess.

Slater exhaled sharply through his nose, stepping toward me. His grip closed around my arm. "Fine. But you're not leaving my sight."

I barely had time to react before his gaze flicked back to Kallias. And then—curiously—his fingers loosened.

I turned, wondering what exactly Kallias had done to make Slater hesitate, but when I met his eyes, he just blinked.

A brief, silent moment passed between us. After everything, after all of this, it felt like a pause. A small, stolen second where we could just exist in each other's company until—until I wasn't sure when.

"I guess I'll see you after the matches," he said in a way that calmed me almost as much as that kiss did. The kiss that still had my heart beating out of its cage.

"Sounds promising," I tried to tease, but the fire in his eyes—the sight of him, freshly kissed, with that split lip, had me biting my own.

His gaze flicked to my action before straightening. "I *will* see you after the matches," he promised. Not hoped or wished. But promised. And I believed him.

At Slater's shuffling, my eyes were forced away from his before moving towards the entrance of the tent. Every step a hesitation, because I knew his gaze was still on me and maybe I was a little wary of leaving it.

My fingers gripped the flap of the tent.

I paused.

I couldn't admit that I didn't want to say goodbye.

A knot of fear twisted in my stomach—the quiet, persistent dread that whispered the temptation of believing this might be the last time I saw him.

My gut was filled with it. Fear and...something else.

"Good luck."

I stole one more selfish glance.

He stood there patiently. An effortless confidence in his form. He was strong, capable. He would win.

He wasn't me. He wouldn't be blindsided by something unexpected. I assured myself something like this would be easy for him.

Kallias nodded.

Then, with the barest tug of a smile—

I disappeared.

TWENTY-SIX

Our usual booth atop the four-story stand seemed even higher than I remembered. The climb up the four sets of stairs left me fanning myself in this dress I was growing to hate.

It had been so long since my mother died, yet every year, these steps served as a reminder of her. Of where she died. Of how much I missed her. Of how grateful I was that she never saw who I had become.

Although I wished she had been there. I always wished she was here.

Perhaps I would have ended up better—more like her. Perhaps.

"You were gone a while," Libby whispered to me.

I shrugged off the comment, narrowing my eyes over the field, hoping to distract her from further questioning.

As long as she kept her distance and didn't near my still-rapidly-beating heart.

"What were you doing?" she pressed.

I swallowed, hoping she couldn't see the remainder of blush on my cheeks.

We were seated side by side at the step below Father's seat. Taroh and Erie never needed to attend the matches, as we weren't her children. Erie probably thought it all a bore anyways.

Father personally approved the selection of matches every year, sometimes aided by his many advisors. They typically consisted of some combination of physically grueling tasks and tests. The final event was usually a fight, duel, or jest of some sort.

Occasionally, he'd switched that up, but Libby and I knew nothing beforehand. Libby never cared to ask. I didn't either—until this year.

"Just sizing up the competition," I whispered. "Which gentleman are you hoping to win your hand?" I asked her once I settled into the same frail, makeshift wooden throne—the same one I had sat in as my mother died behind me.

Libby sighed, exposing her indecisiveness. Her one flaw peeked out of her perfectly, consistently sun-kissed skin.

I turned toward the arena as a group of men entered the mouth of the gated field.

"Those eyes would be adorable on a little baby king," I teased, nudging her arm as I nodded towards one of her suitors.

A tall gentleman with flowing, straight black hair— longer than mine and Libby's—was stunning over his hooded, light green eyes that sparkled, even from the distance. The perfect depiction of Daerom.

His olive skin bore nothing but two golden bangles on each wrist, one on each bicep, and a waistband that held a drape of short, maroon cloth over his shorts.

Libby let out a quiet giggle—the most relaxing sound I could hear right now.

Matches always made us tense, so any distraction was a lifeline to pull us through the day.

"Yes, his eyes were definitely the first thing I noticed about him," she joked, as we both eyed the specimen head to toe.

With a body like his, I could only assume he was an athlete of some sort. No royal, besides those with military training possessed such features while being so slim.

We sat, mesmerized by the smooth skin of taut, lean muscles, polished to perfection. The men of Daerom were almost as cocky as those of the North.

It was a shame they didn't line up geographically. Father would have easily made that alliance long ago. Perhaps he was doing that today.

"Stop making it so obvious," I jested.

Her brows creased as I struggled to keep my composure.

"Look at something other than the loincloth, Libby. You're embarrassing us both."

Her jaw dropped in comical aghast. Then her eyes

motioned to Father behind us. I cringed as we both carefully turned our heads to find Father in conversation with one of the masked guards. Higher ranking guards wore masks. Slater didn't, which was why I shot him a glare before turning back to Libby.

She sighed with relief, then quickly redirected her attention back to the arena.

I jumped into routine, adopting a specific pompous tone for the first suitor—who was only half listening to the speaker while he devoted the other half of his attention to waving at the crowd.

"Ooh—look at me," I acted out. *"I have the attention span of a gnat because I spend my days rubbing oil on my muscles to make them look bigger."*

Libby kept fighting back a laugh while I continued on, refusing to let her win the silent battle we embarked in every year to see who'd laugh first. *"And if I don't win these matches, then Daddy will take away even more of my clothes."*

With that, I earned a faint snort from her—one that was tragically cut off when Father cleared his throat.

We whipped our heads to him, straightening under his scrutiny before slowly returning our attention back to the matches. But not before I shot her a silly eye roll.

Her scrunched smile was enough to steady me before the rest of her suitors were escorted into the arena.

We waited in silence as they conferred with the

speaker.

After a few minutes I leaned towards Libby.

"I'm sure Father would be thrilled with a Daeroman alliance. Perhaps *you* can convince him to go easy with the matches?"

Libby's nose twitched. "I didn't realize you wanted him to go easy."

She cocked a brow, leaning in with me.

"Are you worried about a certain Warrior Prince?"

I scoffed. "*Please*. I'm not worried about anything."

"Lie!" She said at full volume, causing us both to freeze.

We glanced back at Father in horror. Luckily he was occupied once again with his advisors.

Libby turned back to me, too smug for my liking. "You always give the smallest shrug when you lie."

Damn my shoulders.

I cringed at my pathetic giveaway. "*No*. I was just shrugging you off. You misinterpret everything."

She hummed, too pleased for my liking, before setting back into her throne.

Trumpets sounded.

The three of us stood and offered a quick wave to the crowd gathered on the risers flanking us, one story below our main central platform in the middle of the field. The entire arena stretched several blocks long and a few wide, forming a narrow, ovular field.

Once we were announced and seated, the speaker

turned to Libby and loudly introduced each suitor to the audience.

One by one, they waved to the crowd, each adding their own flair—a wink, a bow, the blow of a kiss.

"At this time," the speaker boomed, his voice naturally thunderous in the deadly silence of audience members, "any overlooked suitors may come forward now or remain on the sidelines for the duration of the matches."

To no one's surprise, two more men entered the field.

These last-minute additions were almost always non-royals. They rarely made it far, but because it had happened before in other kingdoms, many poor families clung to the hope that their son might be the exception—the one to lift them out of poverty.

I could only recall a single non-royal who had made it to the final match. He had come so close—only to be rejected at the Well.

The first round of the matches was a rite of passage: the suitors presented gifts to the princess.

The prince from Daerom presented an intricately designed, breathtakingly crafted glass sword.

He launched into a speech about its history, but I barely heard him. My focus was entirely on the shiny toy I would soon beg Libby to get my hands on.

Another suitor offered a gilded jewelry box, a piece I was sure Libby would love. Even from this height, I could tell it was unique enough to suit her tastes.

One of the common boys brought a beautifully sculpted, painted clay pot. It was the sweetest gift, and Libby's favorite, I could tell.

The other commoner presented a necklace, though I doubted the jewels were real.

The final suitor, a man who said he was from Pasirfi, gifted yards upon yards of golden fabric, woven from the leaves of a rare tree hidden, and native to his region.

Once all four suitors had presented their gifts, attendants collected them, and the men were ushered to the far end of the arena, closer to our platform.

The speaker then announced the first trial: a simple sword fight between the three royal suitors. The winner would advance to face the remaining two, and from there, the last two would compete in a final round until only one remained.

The suitors drew their swords, blades gleaming in the midday sun.

The trumpets soared again.

The match had begun.

The prince from Daerom—Doa, I believe—moved freely across the arena. Barefoot and barely clothed, he had all the movement he needed to maneuver his thin-bladed sword. It wasn't the most appropriate attire, but the women in the stands didn't seem to mind.

A distant non-royal relative of Jayces that I recognized from Nerstradt, Teck, wore the typical Northern tunic— unbuttoned at the top, sleeves rolled up against the heat.

The third suitor, an older man—too old for Libby, whose name I'd already forgotten—drew a heavy metal sword that required both hands to wield. His simple clothes bore no insignia from Pasirfi. His shaved head made him look more common than royal.

The men took their stances, circling each other in a tense triangle before Doa struck first, swinging toward Teck.

Teck dodged swiftly, blocking the blow with a practiced ease. Doa seemed impressed by the response, tilting his head toward the older man.

Doa and Teck gave a quick understanding nod before both lunging at the man. The older man was more skilled than I'd expected, parrying their attacks with surprising precision.

Libby tensed beside me. I wanted to catch her attention, to lighten the moment, but with Father watching as intently as she was, anything I said would be overheard. She wasn't as amused this year the way she had been in the past.

Minutes passed in a brutal exchange of slashes and strikes. Blood trickled from fresh wounds across the older man's arms and legs before he finally collapsed, his body marked by a dozen shallow cuts. Doa stood over him, blade pointed at his chest.

"Truce!" the man gasped, raising a hand.

If any man called for a truce, he would be escorted away to the holding quarters, given the choice to return to his kingdom or accept Father's invitation to stay at the palace for the weekend.

Just as the speaker announced him off the field, Doa kicked Teck to the ground and held the blade to his throat before he, too, screamed for truce before it could go any further.

With only two victors left—the match was over.

Doa stood victorious, smug as he raised his arms to the crowd. The cheers that followed were respectful, restrained— an appreciation of the lethal beauty below.

He finished with a blown kiss to Libby, who barely managed to return a cordial smile.

Around us, commoners in the rafters exchanged gambling papers and tickets. Cheers and groans tangled together into an eerie, buzzing melody in the background.

The final match was simple. Hand-to-hand combat. Doa had the advantage—strength, speed.

It was a quick transition, thankfully. I was ready to move along. He was the clear winner and I had already moved on, thinking about Kallias's matches.

Until the commoner boy pulled off his shirt and threw it over the fence to give himself more agility.

"*Damn*," Libby and I both whispered before exchanging glances.

Not bad—my eyes indicated.

I know—hers said back.

The boy was no mere commoner. No, he was quite the equal to Doa. He also removed his shoes and took a stance that was quite confident for a common boy.

The trumpets sounded.

The three circled before Doa struck first, dropping one opponent with a swift kick. The boy kicked himself up before lunging, sending them both tumbling. They rolled, limbs locked, until Doa kicked free and rose to fight.

The remaining commoner charged, but Doa spun, landing a knockout blow to his face that made him stumble enough to nearly fall back. But he shook it off, recovering quickly before trying again, but Doa avoided a punch, smiling and taunting with each ducking movement.

It was turning into more of a battle than originally planned.

This wasn't uncommon.

Whenever lesser-folk had a chance to show the royals what they were made of, they didn't hold back. Neither did the royals, apparently.

It was one of the reasons Father never let us mingle too much with commoners. Which was a shame for me, whose only companions were the common children when I was very young.

But the same year Mother had died was the same year commoners were banned from the royal-only Academy.

The commoner fell after another failed attempt to grab Doa. Doa seized the moment—not to finish him, but to flaunt his victory, grinning for the crowd.

The women cheered as Doa reached down and threw a fistful of dirt into his face.

As the women cheered, the boy recovered faster than anyone expected and leaped onto Doa, locking his head in a vice grip.

I flinched.

The movement didn't only look and feel like a move, but an intentional, maddening attack.

Doa's face reddened deeper than his cloth. He clawed at the man's arms, struggling, choking. The commoner didn't budge, instead turning their bodies—showcasing Doa's helplessness to the crowd. And to us.

The man's face darkened deep red too—not from strain, but fury.

"You see me now, Your Majesty, don't you?" the boy barked, tightening his grip on Doa, stepping closer to us.

"You won't give your people the time of day until they have one of your own at their mercy, isn't that right?"

The pain dripping from his voice outweighed the fury. He didn't want to kill Doa—not really. He wished it were my father in his grasp.

"We slave for you and your kingdom. We pay tax to your trades—trades we are shut out of. Our children die in the hospitals you refuse to fund. Our women break their backs when their sons are stolen for your military."

Doa thrashed, choking louder, hands flailing.

"You couldn't protect your wife. How can we trust you to protect your people—King?" He spat the word like poison.

I couldn't find it in myself to look away from the boy

and see my father's reaction, though I could almost feel it.

Silence.

Only Doa's strangled gasps filled the air.

Then, the man spoke again. "How many royals should we kill before you see us? Before you stop leaving us in the cold? My brothers and I will rise—we will take what we deserve, and We. Will. Win—"

A flash of light.

It took only a second for his throat to slice open with Doa's bracelet. It took less than five seconds for the man to cough so much blood that it choked him to death.

TWENTY-SEVEN

The screech of an older woman tore the crowd's attention from the dead man. Several others leapt from the risers, rushing onto the field.

It didn't take but ten seconds before guards sliced most of the aggressors in half—the rest were dragged away. The bloodbath was the shortest in history.

Doa hadn't moved an inch.

When he finally caught his breath and the color returned to his face, he turned to the crowd, thrusting his fists into the air, his golden bangle still in his grip.

I couldn't tell how sharp it was from a distance, but the blood dripping down his arm from where he held his weapon made it look far deadlier than any bracelet should be. A deadly accessory. For blood and show.

His victorious turn was met with a deafening roar from the high risers. The bodies of commoners were invisible, their corpses nothing more than pieces shuffled across the arena floor. Nothing more, nothing less.

Doa looked up at us and pointed a conquering finger at Libby, treating this like some great act of love and not the disgusting carnage before us.

I pried my eyes away with a mechanical force, my head rotating stiffly. My eyes landed on Libby's lovely face—now ashen. I almost reached out to make sure she was still breathing. Frozen in time, she stared ahead blankly. I have her a moment before glancing at Father.

"That's cheating," I forced out.

He didn't move. He didn't even blink at the slaughter before him. I had the nerve to yell at him, to give him a piece of my mind. I had a better mind to jump off this rafter and tell it all to Doa—the bastard that will not be marrying my sister.

Over my dead body.

Libby's breathing was the only sign she was alive. Had this been any other proposal match, I would have caused a scene. But the woman in the riser beside us was already doing just that.

I also couldn't stop myself from the tear that pooled in my eye for the woman who must have been the boy's mother. But I tried to force it down.

I still had Kallias to think about.

I couldn't have been more thankful that he wasn't in the arena with the two of them. Any pleasant feeling I had earlier today was overpowered with fear.

I bowed to the cowardice.

My stomach twisted at what might happen next.

The arena was cleaned out in minutes and set up for my suitors. It was different this time. Clearly, the test for my hand would not be the same as Libby's.

I fought to remain calm, not to look at my father in question as I aggressively scratched at my thumbnail, silently praying to the ghost of my mother to protect Kallias in this next match.

I couldn't watch his life end while accepting mine would too.

"Kallias Asherah, Warrior Prince of the Kingdom Lyen, fighting for the hand of Princess Fiadh Alepha Dagny, Jewel of Sevaire," the speaker announced, still projecting louder than usual, in an attempt to corral the crowd. Though the crowd seemed to not know how to react to all that had transpired.

I didn't either.

Kallias stepped forward, finding his place next to the speaker. He was so far away from this high up, yet I could still make out those piercing eyes. I could still see the small red speck of his split lip that made me lean forward in concern.

I wasn't sure if he could see the fear in my eyes: the worry. I wasn't sure if they had heard of the massacre that happened five minutes prior, or if it was already swept under the rug, forgotten.

I gnawed on my lip as my eyes didn't know whether to dance to Kallias or watch the uneasy faces of the spectators. Some worried, some terrified, some still focused on their betting papers above everything else.

My eyes narrowed in on their whispers. Rippling through the risers, something caught their attention. My father clearing his throat behind me caused me to fix my eyes back on the arena.

My jaw slowly dropped at who was joining the speaker's side.

"Prince Jayce Tove Avrone, Son of Desica."

I froze.

I don't believe it.

TWENTY-EIGHT

Why in the world was *Jayce* here?

The weasel smiled up at me after a brief nod, clearly reveling in my irritation before taking his place beside Kallias.

My eyes rolled for what I expected would be the first of many today.

The last competitor was announced—a sweet-looking boy, clearly younger than me, clearly in over his head.

I didn't catch his name. My attention was fixed on the silent exchange between Kallias and Jayce while I tried to steal a glimpse of Libby's statue-still expression.

The first match was announced between Jayce and the boy. I couldn't have cared less about the two, but at least it would save Kallias some effort.

I had never seen so many men at my proposal matches. It was unnerving. I didn't care for this much attention—especially after what had just happened.

For some reason, Father chose to begin with a joust

instead of saving it for the final match.

It seemed strange, not that anyone would question it.

The competitors mounted their horses, handed lances far heavier than seemed reasonable. The victor would move on to face Kallias.

As inept as Jayce was at most things, he was a master on horseback. The boy never stood a chance.

They weren't that contrasting in figure. But Jayce was the quicker, more conniving type. The boy already looked unsteady in the saddle, and Jayce wasted no time exploiting it.

After the trumpet rang, he ducked low, twisted his lance, and struck the boy's shoulder, sending him crashing to the ground.

The joust was quick and painful.

I exhaled, relieved when the boy managed to limp away. As long as no more blood was shed, I could consider it a victory.

Even if Jayce was the victor.

Jayce dismounted with a flourish, arms stretched wide as the audience erupted in cheers. Rustling papers flickered through the stands.

"What is he doing?" I seethed at Libby. But her face hadn't changed.

I kept talking, hoping something—anything—might snap her out of her haze.

"I didn't think he'd ever do something this stupid. Then again, it's Jayce. I shouldn't be surprised."

I turned back to the arena, glaring furiously. A small part of me hoped he'd finally learn his lesson. But Jayce never did.

A simple obstacle course was being set up as the men were led back to the arena's entrance. I tried to catch their eyes, but neither looked up at me.

Instead, I watched Jayce speaking to Kallias—probably joking, teasing—but Kallias stood motionless, his face unreadable in the fading heat.

The sky was shifting, the scorching sun now softened by drifting clouds.

Both men stood sweating, though neither seemed to acknowledge it.

The obstacle course seemed massive as it was being set up. It took several men to assemble, their deliberate pace teasing the restless audience.

Once everyone resettled and the course was in place, a large wagon was pulled in front of the entrance of the arena. It turned, backing into position. A thick rope bound its doors shut.

The carriage driver jumped down and began untying the rope.

"Is the wagon...shaking?"

I leaned towards the arena.

I hadn't realized I'd spoken aloud until Libby leaned forward beside me, eyes locked on the trembling box.

Jayce and Kallias stood a safe distance apart, but I

could have sworn I saw Kallias tense.

The closed box of the wagon *was* shaking. It jerked—just slightly, then again, harder. Inside, something moved.

The course itself looked standard at first: barrels and walls leading into rows of smooth logs. Then came the sound.

A high, pitching roar escaped the wagon, tearing into the silence of the field.

Wind stilled for only a moment while the people were more silent than I thought possible. Then, as if determined to ruin the moment, cicadas buzzed in the distance, their droning cry thickening the tension in the air.

Both men took careful, vigilant steps close to the obstacle course as the speaker's voice rang out.

"For this match, all the suitors need to reach the end of the obstacle course first."

My fingers dug into my knees, fabric twisting under my grip. The speaker continued, voice heavy with practiced grandeur.

"We are all privileged today to be in the presence of a real-life, full-scale, *dangerous*, and riveting *creature*."

His hand swept towards the wagon. My forehead pulsed at how tightly it squeezed.

The crowd gasped.

My eyes widened as my head shot back to my father.

A creature?

A real-life, skull-crushing, human-eating creature?

"The victor—or should I say, *survivor*—shall be granted passage to meet the Princess and her family at the Well."

Father didn't even blink.

I snapped my head back just in time to see Kallias looking up at me. Our eyes met, locking in shared horror. He stepped back, yelling something at Jayce, but Jayce didn't move. His feet were frozen.

"No need to worry, spectators! *You* are all safe. The rope will remain secured on the Creature, and this one cannot fly."

The speaker strode to the other side of the fence, placing himself safely behind a wall of guards.

I couldn't believe Father did this.

I couldn't believe I didn't see something like this coming.

The weight of my failure crashed down on me.

I had promised Kallias there was nothing to worry about. And I had been so, so wrong. I had failed him.

The crowd didn't settle. A nervous, rattling hum swept through the stands.

Libby's hands gripped the seat so tightly her hands turned white. Her lips parted in shock as something tumbled out of the wagon and hit the ground.

At first, it almost looked like a rabbit. Hairless. Towering over two full-grown warriors. Then it moved.

Kallias didn't hesitate. He ran.

Jayce didn't move.

The rabbit—if it could even be called that—peeled its

mouth open. A cavern of brown, dagger-sized teeth stretched wider than any animal's jaw should. It stumbled as it unfurled itself, then let out a screech—high-pitched, ear-piercing, unnatural.

The sound ripped through the sky, louder than anything I'd ever heard. Spectators clamped their hands over their ears, wincing in pain.

"Jayce! Run!" I yelled out, rising to my feet.

I desperately needed to not see my friend mauled to a million pieces by something as disgusting as that.

Eyes turned to me—those that could look away from the creature.

My favorite set of blue eyes landed on me too, watching my eyes widen in all their fear.

Kallias looked back, hesitating, but then he bolted toward Jayce. Grabbing his arm, he yanked him forward until the two sprinted toward the first wooden wall of the obstacle course.

The creature's eyes flared red beneath drooping, wrinkled skin. It tracked their movement, then dropped to all fours with a sickening thud.

My hands were gripping the ledge so tightly, my nails ached from digging into the wood.

That thing was revolting.

It was evil.

It radiated pure anger.

And yet, somehow, it felt...trapped.

I felt the creature's rage in my core. It vibrated through me, raw, consuming, and painful.

"Stop this. Now."

My voice came through gritted teeth, directed at Father.

He didn't blink or bother acknowledging me.

"Father!"

The crowd gasped so loudly it snapped my attention back to the arena.

Kallias was still dragging Jayce by the arm, running. He crouched at the base of the wall, kneeling to boost him over the wooden wall before climbing up after him.

At the other side, Kallias yanked Jayce down before saying something to him.

Jayce crouched against the wall, arms wrapped around his knees.

The rabbit leaped forward.

It soared over the wall just as Kallias began darting away, leaving Jayce in the depths beneath its monstrous shadow.

Please don't die.

My thoughts willed themselves to Kallias.

Even weighed down by armor, he moved effortlessly. Any other man would have lagged behind, but he was showcasing his warrior status with ease.

I could see him on a battlefield, slicing through anything in his path. Death running. Stronger, faster than anyone I had ever seen.

I couldn't withhold my jaw from dropping at the sight.

He was a marvelous spectacle. I was amazed, enthralled, and a little threatened. I was starting to understand why Westerners loved watching their sports so much.

The shriveled rabbit launched itself over another obstacle with gut-wrenching ease as Kallias ducked underneath. Another field of logs stretched ahead. Kallias leaped lightly onto them, barely disturbing their balance.

The creature wasn't as lucky.

It tumbled onto the platform. Its gangly limbs tangled in the rolling logs.

Kallias staggered too but dropped to all fours, gripping for balance. The thick rope binding the creature's leg whipped against the wood like a snapped rein, the only sound in the field.

The logs kept rolling. Almost comically.

Then Kallias jumped down from the logs, while the creature flailed, struggling to regain control.

Kallias didn't waste a second.

He snapped into motion, moving as a blur as he seized a log that lay on another part of the course. It took two men to roll those into the arena, but he gritted his teeth, screamed with effort and hauled it up with his straining muscles.

The sweat on his face gleamed as he strained, gripping the boulder. I hadn't blinked since the match began. My eyes fixed only on him as I watched his legs struggle to settle him back up. His chest heaved as his face, red from heat and effort. I couldn't believe it.

He was lifting it above his head.

Kallias lifted the beam with the force of his entire body and something other-worldly as he slammed the boulder over the rabbit's neck, pinning it against the logs. Even through his garb, every muscle of his back moved with precise, impeccably unrelenting control.

The creature thrashed. The ground trembled beneath its struggle, but I couldn't look away from Kallias. I thought intensely at what my chances would be in helping him if I jumped down from here and ran to help.

But my feet wouldn't move.

My lungs wouldn't expand.

My eyes couldn't look at anything but Kallias.

A cowardly Jayce scrambled over the logs, sprinting away from the creature like the weasel he was. If he won, I'd do more than punch him in the gut.

"Jayce!" The roar tore from my throat before I could stop it. A different type of worry in my voice. A worry I no longer had reserved for him.

He flicked his gaze up for a single second but didn't stop.

"Help him!"

My fingers dug into the railing so hard they went numb as they fused into the wood.

Kallias threw himself onto the beam, using his body

weight to keep it down, but the creature fought harder. Its ear-splitting wail rattled my ribs, shriveling the air in my lungs.

I wanted to help. I needed to help. But I couldn't move.

Jayce kept running as the rabbit jerked and squirmed from under the log.

Kallias's red, sweat-slicked face deepened with rage as the beast wrenched free.

It shook off its head, wheezing. Its sunken red eyes locked onto Kallias, who clawed desperately for anything around him—anything to use as a weapon. Fear burned in his gaze, but so did fury.

The creature reared back, dragging in a massive breath. The wind stilled.

Then, it shrieked.

The air itself seemed to ripple from the force of it. The audience clapped their hands over their ears, faces scrunching in agony. The beast's rotten, dagger-sized teeth rattled in its gums, its rage rolling over the field like a tide.

Kallias turned from the creature as it lunged on top of him.

"No."

The word barely left me, little more than breath—begging to be a scream but lost into the air.

Jayce slammed himself behind the fence, ramming his body against a beam below our riser.

My hands flew to my stomach, gripping at nothing. Pain knotted inside me, hot and sharp, like my body had split open.

For one fractured second, I thought I was about to meet my mother's fate—dying at a proposal match in front of the entire kingdom.

A searing heat struck my chest.

I gasped, dragging in the first real breath I'd taken since I set eyes on the creature.

But anger clenched my ribs tighter.

My entire body flushed with heat, burning beneath my skin. I had to look down. I had to be sure no blood or wound appeared on my chest.

Just my mind, playing cruel, cruel tricks. My hands clenched over my abdomen.

Silence.

The world was deathly still.

My eyes slowly glazed over the course. The creature lay unmoving. My vision blurred—tears or sweat, I couldn't tell.

"What's happening?"

Libby's voice barely reached me, a whisper of disbelief. She was suddenly beside me, staring just as I was.

Slowly, I turned my head—to my father.

Unmoved.

Still.

How dare he?

My fingers flexed, about to reach for the dagger I'd longed to throw at him.

I had nothing to lose now. No home. No future. Not one

I could see. Not one where I wouldn't be driven to insanity—to death.

My eyes bore into his, wondering if they would look the same in death.

My hands just about brushed my thigh when the crowd erupted. The risers shook with the force of their voices, roaring, pounding like drums at war.

I whipped over to see the commotion, nearly pitching over the ledge.

The creature rolled onto its side. A wooden stake jutted from its torso, splattered up to the crown, streaked down to his knees. The crowd howled in triumph, the riotous sound consuming the arena.

Kallias wavered on his feet. Blood coated him, smeared across his torso, splattered up to his crown, streaked down to his knees. The crowd howled in triumph, the riotous sound consuming the arena.

My breath hitched.

His gaze found mine.

Alive.

He was alive.

I hadn't killed him.

Speckles of blood that sprayed on his face began darkening. The sun almost completely disappeared, causing the blood on him to blend into a shade of black. I've never seen blood that black before.

My worried look must have alerted him. He slowly

lifted his arms, staring at the stains riddled on his body. The entire arena followed his gaze.

Kallias shook his hands like this was just some minor inconvenience.

He began walking towards the finish line with a march that made everyone gawk in amazement. Clouds thickened in the sky, and the smallest drops of rain began misting the arena.

I'd never seen so many people have the exact same reaction to something. Conquering and triumphant, he walked nobly to the end gates.

Everyone's attention was now on the creature. Not because it was a dead creature—or a disgusting one for that fact. They started because the corpse began to wither.

Not decaying—withering.

It was the most unnatural, repulsive thing I'd ever seen, and yet, I couldn't look away. Its flesh shrank, curling in on itself, drying into a twisted, skeletal husk. Then—

It melted.

The creature slowly sizzled, turning into a withered skeleton.

Melted.

The pile of flesh somehow oozed into the ground, vanishing like a mist, leaving nothing but a slick pool of black ink in its wake. The rope, once tethered to the creature, was the only evidence that it ever existed.

Chatter rippled through the crowd. The speaker

stumbled forward, grasping for control of the moment.

"...the Well will decide," he announced, voice unsteady.

Papers flew through the stands as bets were hastily settled. The world shifted back into motion, but I remained still, lifting my chin as I turned to face my father.

The rain picked up behind me, cool against my burning skin.

He stood now, his gaze fixed on the ruined course.

I stared up at him, my voice steady, unwavering.

My chin lifted as high as it could at him.

"I'm ready to choose my suitor."

TWENTY-NINE

Father's decorated chest puffed at my word, swelling the shining metals and pins even larger than they were.

His gaze quickly shifted to Libby, who stood frozen beside me.

She hadn't moved, or breathed, it seemed.

I was relieved she hadn't thrown up over the ledge.

Father didn't look shaken, not in the way any human would after witnessing what we had.

I turned towards the stairs, not bothering to wait for him.

As measured as my steps were, every fiber of my being screamed to run—to leap down the flights of stairs—to push through the crowd and find Kallias myself.

But I fought every pulsing instinct tooth and nail to appear as unbothered as possible. Despite the gut-turning terror threatening to make an appearance.

I reached the bottom of the stairs and waited, trying to

ignore my pulse hammering beneath my skin.

Countless eyes bore into me, assessing every inch of me, speculating every expression.

I kept my chin lifted, my breathing steady.

The crowd blocked my view of anyone I needed to see. Of Kallias.

Father descended with his usual, infuriating and steady pace, his guards behind him.

Libby took her place beside me. Her pale face was slick with sweat, and her shallow breaths were only perceptible by me.

I linked my arm through hers, fearing she'd collapse if I didn't.

The walk to the Well stretched too long. Feeling worse beneath the thickening rain.

Droplets pricked my skin, cool against the heat burning inside me.

I held Libby tighter, hoping the rain would wake her from the daze she had sunk into.

But she remained rigid, eyes unfocused.

Who could blame her? If I were in her position—if I knew a cocky, murderous snake awaited me at the Well—I wouldn't be at peace either.

The crowd followed, a surging wave of whispers and expectation pressing in around us. Their anticipation misted the air like smoke. Father walked even slower, a deliberate pace that set my teeth on edge.

I could have crawled faster.

The small hill rose ahead, marking the Well's place. The speaker already stood at its crest, his concern vanishing the moment we arrived. In its place, a wide, artificial Northern smile stretched across his face, as insincere as possible.

"Your majesty," he greeted, his hand out to us. "Princesses."

I would have spat in his face for the facade he put on, but this job gave him a run for his limited money today.

He bowed to us, moving out of the way to reveal all the suitors standing beyond the Well's rounded stone edge.

I gasped at the sight of Kallias.

This close, he looked worse—drained, battered, his wet hair clinging to his forehead, drenched from sweat and rain.

Ink shaded blood streaked his face, smudged and uneven. The rain caught in his lashes, carving thin rivers through the black staining his skin like tears.

The sky darkened. The rain intensified.

I wanted to reach for him and wipe off all the dirt and reality from his face to bring back his dimples. I'd do anything to see his smirk right now.

Yet, even through the grime, his eyes burned, striking yet untamed. Nothing could dull such a unique color. As he stood there, battered and unbowed, I swore he commanded the crowd with his presence more than my father did.

No one spoke.

No one even shuffled their betting pages.

The entire crowd stood frozen, straining to hear, unwilling to move.

A tight ring formed around the Well, every person close enough to witness, yet too cautious to step forward.

Even Doa watched Kallias with wary calculation.

Kallias didn't look like a prince anymore. He looked greater—something untouchable.

A warrior.

A conqueror.

A king.

I could already see the title draped over him like a mantle, heavy with power.

Warrior King Kallias. A name that could command armies, bring kingdoms to their knees.

The rain was now pooled at our feet, but no one raised an umbrella. No one shielded their faces. The tension was heavier than the downpour pressing down on us all.

I wanted to give Kallias some look of endearment or silent apology, but all I could muster was a look of regret.

And then, my gaze found Jayce.

Whatever pity existed in me evaporated.

His light green eyes met mine, glinting with something infuriating.

Reason escaped me. I just moved—stomping over to him without a care.

Libby reached to grab me, but my hands were already gripping Jayce's wet, white collar.

"What is *wrong* with you?" I seethed, my breath hot despite the cold rain. "Were you trying to get him killed?"

The bastard had the audacity to smile.

"I see I've got your attention," he muttered, leaning in like we were sharing a secret.

The man would never take anything seriously. All his fear from the arena had dissipated back into his stupid, smug self again.

I drew back my fist, ready to wipe that smirk clean off his face. But Father's voice silenced the land.

"*Fiadh.*"

The ground itself seemed to flinch.

A warning.

Reminding me that he was still lord over this land. I was still his subject. It didn't matter who survived the matches.

I froze my fist, trembling as I kept a glare at Jayce. I saw his stupid smirk, but a part of me could read the regret behind his eyes.

That he could never hide from me.

For a split second, I debated whether to release my fist and risk it all for one good strike.

But my qualms weren't all with Jayce. Not really.

I dropped my arm, pushing Jayce away before turning on my heel to find my place next to my father.

I tried to mask my relief that *that* was all he said. Perhaps I'd get the brunt of that later, but I would put up with it for now.

My glare fixedated on Jayce, letting all the fury my fist couldn't release filter through my eyes like smoke through a crackling fire.

If looks could kill, Jayce would be the one withering in the dirt alongside that creature's corpse.

The rain came harder now, thick and steady, pooling in the crevices of the stone.

It fell down my face, my shoulders, seeping into the earth. The very land itself couldn't breathe as it waited.

The speaker's voice wavered as he attempted to recover.

"A-And now..."

He cleared his throat. "We call upon the Fates to determine the final round of suitors." The crowd stirred. "One drop of blood will be required from the princess, then the suitor. One at a time we will see if the Well blesses the pair with a decision they are free to make—blue. A pair unable to ever form—white. Or a pair destined to become—black. Let us start with—"

Libby and Doa were called first.

I watched her throat bob before walking up to the speaker.

A small knife was presented to her. Small and unassuming, yet she stared at it as if it might strike her on its own.

Her hand trembled at her side before she forced herself to take it.

Rain droplets beaded along the dark, golden streaks in her hair, trickling onto her hand as she pricked her pinky.

A single drop of blood fell into the Well.

Doa followed suit, stepping forward like the predator we now all knew he was.

Water sluiced off his form, yet his eyes remained locked on Libby in a way I wasn't fond of, and I didn't think she was either.

Her eyes remained on the Well.

The water in the Well remained still for a moment. Then, the surface rippled. A faint whirlpool formed, spinning lazily before fading into a clear, sky blue.

A murmur of applause rustled through the crowd, light and distant. Behind their faint claps, the rain grew louder and louder.

Then my name was called.

Jayce and I were summoned forward.

I didn't acknowledge the speaker as I stepped up to the Well, planting a foot firmly on the stone ledge.

My eyes remained on Jayce when I lifted up my skirt to retrieve my dagger.

My eyes didn't falter.

My hands hovered over the Well's surface. I waited a moment, making sure Jayce watched every movement I made before I sliced a gash into palm in one swift motion, unflinching. It burned through my entire arm, but my anger was a motivator like no other.

I held my open palm over the Well and let the rain spill my blood into the water. Jayce's face morphed into that of a scared weasel as he walked over to take the knife offered by the speaker, who also continued to gawk at me.

A drop of his blood later, the water began to swirl, but I didn't watch.

I walked back to my post next to Father and Libby, ignoring whatever result might have appeared.

Those around the Well watched for a moment before they all gasped.

My heart sank at the sound, thudding in an unknown fear, and I prayed it would be any color but black.

I gripped my bloodied hand and tried not to make my worry evident. Heads all around the crowd either leaned forward or lifted higher on their toes, trying to see into the Well.

"It's just...clear," the speaker said, but tried to quickly recover. "Should we try again?" he asked the King.

"No," I answered. "If it's not black, that's answer enough."

I prayed to whatever Fates would listen.

Please be on my side.

I walked back up to the Well, not awaiting my father's command, and looked at Kallias.

I wished I could talk to him, ask how he was, inquire about what he wanted after all that had occurred—but all we could do was look at each other.

His eyes blinked gently, and there was something behind them I'd never seen before. Something cold.

My bloodied hand unclenched for a moment, and I let another drop fall into the water from my still-bleeding palm.

It faded beneath the surface as the pouring rain splashed into the bowl.

I felt my father sigh behind me, but I wouldn't look at him. I wasn't even sure how I knew it, but I felt the tension—thicker than the gash on my hand. I watched Kallias glance over to him before stepping up to the Well.

Maintaining a similar stare to my father, Kallias ignored the knife he was offered. Instead, he gently leaned over the stone and spit in it.

A glob of bloodied saliva splashed into the Well and slowly sank into the clear water, speckled with raindrops.

I smiled.

The water instantly swirled, faster than I'd ever seen before.

It was so quick, I had to step back from the force of its movements.

I stared at that water as if my life depended on it. Because it did.

My breathing quickened as the whirlpool stopped abruptly—faster than water should have been able to halt.

I feared it would be clear again.

Or worse, I feared it would be white.

I wouldn't know what to do then.

Water flooded down my face. My entire dress was soaked. My hair hung like a wet rag. My shoes sloshed in the watery grass beneath me.

The bottom bowl of the Well began to fade into a deep black. Not just the water—the stone. The water turned darker than the ink on Kallias' face.

The black seeped into the base of the bricks like ink on paper. The white stone soaked it up, spreading until every sliver of the Well looked like an onyx goblet.

It shined, even in the heavy rain.

Sparkled.

People gasped, but I had no idea what it meant.

The uncertainty provoked an entirely different kind of concern.

I wasn't sure how Father would react to something like this. I was terrified of what it could mean.

"*Unbelievable*," the speaker breathed, stumbling over his words again, trying to announce something—but Father interrupted.

"Results are inconclusive. Each suitor is to return home and wait to hear from the Princesses for an outcome."

"*No.*"

I spoke the word straight from my soul. My eyes frantically searched my father's face. I couldn't remember the last time I had said no to him and was left physically unscathed.

Still, I had to risk it.

I had to do something.

If Kallias and I parted, Father would guarantee I wouldn't marry him.

The second we slipped away, it would be the final signature on my death warrant. Marrying Kallias—Heavens, even Jayce—would be a preferable alternative. Because I wasn't sure Kallias still wanted to marry me—not after everything that transpired. I didn't know if we were fated or not, but I couldn't let my father take my choices away.

Not again.

He wouldn't win this. If it was the last thing I did…

Time seemed to slow.

My lips stuck together like wet tar. My eyes blinked so slowly I thought I'd faint.

I looked back at the Well.

There was no saying what this meant.

What could be powerful enough to alter an entire Sigil? What force, what fate, would allow such a thing to happen? Was the Well broken? Altered? What if results from now on were inconclusive?

What did a broken Sigil mean to the world—to the Fates?

My eyes lifted to Kallias.

He blinked slowly.

I struggled to breathe. Underwater.

No one could help me right now.

I stepped closer to the Well, my eyes fixed on the

darkening water. It reflected an image of me back. It scared me how different I looked. How old I looked.

Fear trickled into my mind—fear of the decision I was about to make. Of letting go of the little girl I'd always been.

Maybe I was letting her down. But I would be letting her down more if I obeyed my father for the rest of my life.

I didn't want to remain this scared child.

I didn't want to stay trapped like the water in this Well.

I'd had no control over my life, and this probably wasn't the best time to turn against my father—but it might have been the last chance I'd get.

I took one more glance at the water.

A small tear slipped away when I realized who the shaded reflection below me looked like.

My mother.

It was the last bit of courage I needed.

I looked up at Kallias, watching the heavy rain pour onto his still face. Unmoved. A rock of his own. My breaths grew deeper and deeper until I found the strength.

My lips moved to say something. The speaker asked me to repeat what it was.

So I cleared my throat and dug my nails into my palms.

"I have chosen!"

THIRTY

I didn't wait for any objections or gasps that I was certain would follow.

Instead, my feet hauled me up onto the ledge of the Well.

I stood atop the Sigil.

It was surely disrespectful, judging by the sharp inhales from the crowd, but nothing could stop me now. Not the worried look on Libby's face. Not the trepidation in my father's eyes.

Nothing stopped the words that were about to leave me.

"I will marry Warrior Prince Kallias Asherah, Prince of Lyen."

The words spilled from me so quickly they felt more like vomit than a declaration.

Shakily, I stepped onto another brick, speaking directly to the crowd as rain and sweat coated my clenched fists.

My chest hollowed under the weight of all those eyes on me. But I needed witnesses—hundreds of them.

Perhaps Father could command them all to forget what I'd said, just as they forgot the men whose blood was being washed away in the arena.

Or this was how I would secure my future.

My nails dug into my palms as I swallowed a breath and addressed those around me. "In one week's time, we shall wed here...in Sevaire."

Words wouldn't stop spilling from my lips. I wasn't sure where all this courage came from. Maybe it wasn't courage at all—perhaps it was desperation. But something inside me clawed to break free. It took all my control.

The gasps reduced into a moment of silence. Nothing but rain and the pounding in my chest.

Then—a rupture of applause.

Libby stared at me, eyes wide and shaken.

Her wet hair clung to her face, and I'd never seen her care so little about a ruined dress.

Jayce's expression was unreadable, his face taut with something restrained. But I barely registered it before turning back to Kallias.

I wanted to say so much—to give him a choice. But right now, I couldn't do anything else.

It was this, or maybe it was death. Or maybe the Fates would smite me where I stood for the desecration that had happened here today.

Whatever this now was, I would figure all of it out later.

Right now, I needed Kallias to trust me. And I needed the Fates on my side.

His words echoed in my mind, and I prayed they still rang true as I stepped down from the Well.

I trust you.

I willed a thought toward him.

Forgive me—

All of this was so selfish of me, but he had expressed his opinion before, and I prayed to everything beyond our world that his mind hadn't changed in the last few hours.

I gave him a curt, worry-filled nod. It was the only thing I could offer him before the speaker stepped between our gazes.

"A—a wedding in the kingdom..." he fumbled, brushing back his short, wet hair, mustering an excitement he wasn't sure he should have.

"And so soon!"

The speaker successfully rallied the crowd, flashing his toothy, far-too-white smile at those around us.

In a thunderous boom, cheers drowned out my thoughts, roaring even louder than the rain. I couldn't react fast enough to the commotion. I couldn't express my shock at their boisterous response.

My shoulders flinched at their sound, and I didn't realize my hands were threatening to shut out the noise until I felt Libby's hand press gently on my shoulder.

I looked at her and forced an unnerved smile.

"We should go," she yelled over the noise—the people, the rain, the emotions. I barely heard her.

I ignored Father as we passed him and joined the guards pushing us through the crowd of hollering people closing in around us.

I couldn't remember the last time I saw the common people this happy.

I couldn't believe something as strange as a marriage would excite so many.

After everything that had happened, they were beyond ecstatic.

Was it just the idea of a party? Something to celebrate?

Either way, I couldn't help but smile—just slightly—at the beaming faces turned toward me.

Was this what it felt like to be Libby?

It was unsettling, but the taste of it—of attention that meant the people had heard—was entertaining, to say the least. They heard me, and they were excited.

Surely, my future would be secure if this many witnesses encountered my proclamation. It had gathered this much excitement, it had to happen. My wedding was guaranteed. They had to guarantee it.

The crowd pressed in, meeting me with hands of congratulations and smiles of delight. Betting wages littered the ground, floating in the inch of water below us.

Women hollered at me, and men thrust their fists into

the air. Questions flooded toward me before I could process
them—

What will you wear?

Will the common people attend?

Will you live here or in Lyen?

You'll make a beautiful bride!

It wasn't the kind of attention I was used to. I still
couldn't quite put a pin in the reason for their excitement. I
had assumed everyone expected Libby to be the first to marry.
And if anything, I thought they wouldn't approve of my
marrying a royal from the South.

But with this reaction, it felt so much bigger. Bigger
than me. Bigger than all of this.

Beyond the crowd, I could barely see Kallias. His head
peeked out above the sea of people. He wasn't part of the
commotion. He was staring at the Well—not in fascination or
curiosity, but in fear.

I had never seen him fearful. Not like this. Not so still,
so statuesque.

I waited for him to meet my eyes before I turned to
walk with the guards.

The common people beamed and waved before me, but
I couldn't look away from Kallias. I needed him to look at me
just once more.

Just in case I'd be locked away after this, too.

I waited as I was pulled back toward the arena. It was
only a split second, but just before I was pushed toward the hill

and out of view, his eyes finally met mine.

My breath escaped me as I kept walking, the image of his expression burned into my mind. Maybe I had misinterpreted it. Maybe I hadn't seen it correctly.

But if I had—

The look I saw petrified me.

It felt like regret.

EPILOGUE

The Prince of Lyen stared into the endless depths of the dark Well before him. The water shimmered with specks of heavy rain, drumming against its surface.

His eyes couldn't stray from the water—darker than any he'd ever seen. But it wasn't the color that held him captive.

It was the reflection staring back at him. A beautiful woman, shaded beneath the veil of falling rain.

"You shouldn't have done that."

The soft, feminine voice whispered against his ears. His eyes widened. A trick of the mind, surely.

He tore his gaze away, scanning the people around him. The speaker had begun following the crowd, disappearing into the shifting mass.

Kallias' eyes found the princess among them—her face tilted slightly, her expression caught between confusion and something else.

She was almost smiling.

It was rare, that smile. One he wouldn't have minded seeing more.

Her eyes, the lightest shade of sage, met his. Beneath her thick, dark brows, they gleamed with something fragile.

Hope.

That look locked them both in place, even as regret crashed over him—heavier, harsher than the rain.

What had he done?

What fate had he sealed—for her? For the continent?

What had his selfishness, his own agenda, his own powers wrought?

How had he forced this into being?

His gaze darted back to the Well, to the voice he thought he'd imagined.

"Only you can hear me, King Kallias."

The word struck deeper than the stake he had driven into the creature minutes ago—minutes that felt like days.

Never in his life had he wanted that title. Never had he envied his brother's crown.

It was a title he had revered.

A title he would give to anyone else, if he could.

But it was what bound him to the princess from the North. The princess who had unraveled his carefully laid plans after the night they met.

He didn't speak. He didn't move. His eyes remained fixed on the Well.

"The Fates do not look kindly upon those who destroy a Sigil as easily as you have."

The smooth melody of her voice did little to soften the weight of her words. He might have spoken—might have pleaded his case, might have explained that it had been an accident.

An accident, yes. But one that had come from a power deeper within him than even he had known.

"You must pay the penalty of the Fate assigned to the Well."

Kallias swallowed. The sound of her voice was so final, so ancient, it tickled his bones. It terrified him.

He began to pray to the Only, begging to be spared from whatever punishment the Fates would decree. Begging to believe that this was all in his head—a hallucination brought on by exhaustion, by battle, by too many blows to the skull.

"You may never tell the princess you love her."

His brow twitched in confusion. *That* was his penalty?

Certainly the Fates wouldn't trick him into binding himself to some cursed destiny.

Even if he wanted to, he couldn't speak.

I do not love the princess. I have no trouble with this penalty—He would have said it—if breath had not caught in his throat.

"If you tell the princess of your love for her before she tells you, when the time comes, you shall pay the penalty with your life."

He still could not react. Could not comprehend. Yet he tried to feel relief. It was an easy punishment—too easy—for a crime he had expected to be punishable by death. Or worse.

Through the mist of rain, he thought he saw the woman in the water smile at him.

"The Fate of this Well has smiled down upon you fondly. She grants you a gift—one no other has received."

The voice paused.

"Would you like to accept?"

He felt the presence of that smile again.

His voice was hoarse, barely a whisper, but he forced the word through his lips. *"Yes."*

"Make your wife the queen. Stop at nothing to do so."

There were many stories about the wisdom of the Fates. People from all corners of the world sought the Sigils, each granted a single answer to a single question.

The Well was different.

It seemed to favor the princesses and their quests for love. It was unlike any other Sigil. But few knew the true extent of its power.

The King of the North had ensured its protection. Yet Kallias had not asked a question. And still, he had been given an answer.

It was unheard of. Unspoken of. The Fates were already too much of a mystery, but something this different—this deliberate—meant more than he could comprehend.

Kallias turned back toward the crowd, now gathered at the bottom of the small hill where lines of carriages awaited them.

Who was this girl? This girl who claimed to have no powers. The girl whose eyes had haunted him since the first night they met. Who was she, to stir the Fates awake?

A sizzling burn ignited across his chest.

Kallias hissed lightly, fingers tugging at the fabric of his tunic. The pain was quick but sharp, unnatural—like a hot branding on his skin.

When a scratch to it brought no relief, he yanked down his shirt just enough to see the source, his breath catching at the sight.

A burned mark branded his chest.

It was fresh and angry and deep. The type of burn that would leave a lasting, brutal scar.

Rain slid onto his skin, sizzling the mark as they touched the wound.

He inhaled sharply at the sting, pressing a tentative finger to the center of his chest. His breath shuddered as he gently traced the shape of the mark.

It was a swirling pattern—similar to the whirlpool that churned within the Well moments ago.

"Tell nobeing about this."

The words rang in his skull.

His eyes snapped back to the Well. Still. Too still. Not a ripple disturbing its surface, defying the rain pouring relentlessly onto it. The water seemed like it turned to glass, or stone, swallowing every drop before it could cause a ripple.

The air was thick and wet. Suffocating. He could smell something uncertain beneath its surface.

With the little knowledge Prince Kallias did have about the Fates, he knew better than to dismiss this. Knew that nothing they did was small. Nothing they touched affected just one life.

This was not just about him. This was a thread—woven

through the past, the present, and the future. And now, he had pulled it, unraveling everything it held.

His stomach twisted.

He had never meant to use his power against the Fates. But he had. And the reaction was greater than anything he had imagined. Because nothing the Fates did was simple.

Nothing they did was ever out of mere punishment. It was a correction.

A balance.

A cost.

A carriage rumbled forward, wheels kicking up water as it began its journey through the rain. His breath was shallow, pulse unsteady beneath the cursed mark scarred into his chest.

Inside that carriage was the princess–his princess. His future.

He could do nothing but watch as she was taken away. Doors slammed shut. Horses lurched forward. She was gone.

The weight of her absence and all he had just caused to break in her life sank him like a stone.

Rough hands grabbed his arms. He didn't resist. Didn't react. Even as the guards threw him into another carriage his mind remained on the burn on his chest.

The mark.

The symbol that wouldn't disappear until the penalty was paid.

ACKNOWLEDGMENTS

I can't believe I get to write my own acknowledgements page! They really let you write whatever you want on this page, it's crazy…lol.

There are too many people to thank, and as much as I'd love to, I'll never be able to actually dedicate a book to each and every person in my life who I love, so this will have to do.

First, I am nothing without my Lord and Savior. He has blessed me beyond what I deserve and everything I do I owe to Him.

Starting with my husband, I get way too emotional when I think of all the ways you've loved and supported me. I never would have finished that first book if you never continued to push me and believe in me when I didn't believe in myself. Your unconditional love has changed me as a person and has bled into every love story I have ever written and will continue to write. I can't wait to watch you become a father as I try to hold back having seven more children with you. Also, I still think your butt looks really cute.

Then to my mother. My first love. The first person to put up with my creativity and insanity. You are the coolest person I will ever meet and I am truly honored to be your daughter. I owe so much to you and everything you've sacrificed for me. All single mothers kick ass, but you're so classy when you do it, you're just #goals.

To the rest of my family and friends, thank you for listening to me ramble about this book and doubt myself and change my mind one hundred times.

Smile, JJ, and Justine, you three have been annoyed by this project more than anyone and I cannot thank you enough for being so invested in this. You are my sisters.

Christel, you are the first person to ever read this story when I was first drafting it, and I credit your enthusiasm for keeping me going in the beginning.

Aaron, thank you for being the creative, wise, wizard I go to for council.

Kimberly, I'm so blessed to have you as a friend and an editor. I can't believe our lives have led us here, but I couldn't be happier.

Thank you also to Jennifer Rees for such flawless execution in editing.

To my beta and ARC readers, I am too lucky to have you all. The book community I have found is so loving and accepting. I hope all artists encounter people as awesome as you.

Finally, to anyone who's read this book, you have no idea what it means for me to know anyone at all has read this makes me want to break down into ugly tears and sob like a baby. I thank you all for taking a chance on me to help me take one little step closer to my dreams. If you take anything away from my love for this story, it's to never give up on your dreams. If you've been given a lifelong passion, don't do yourself the disservice of not pursuing it.
God bless.

ABOUT THE AUTHOR

When she's not lost in a fantasy world of her own making or someone else's, Avi can be found in many of the amazing, local Minnesota coffee shops.

Avi has written genre's ranging from crime to romance. Fantasy, however, is her way of tying everything up in a beautiful, unique, out-of-this-world bow.

You can find Avi spending her time eating amazing food found in the hidden corners of Minnesota, or the cuisine crafted by the talented hands of her husband.

If you would like to support Avi as a new writer, or just see what she is up to, follow her on Instagram or Tiktok at @avipinkerton.

Stay tuned for the release date of book two in the Pact of Fate series.

Enjoyed the book?

We as authors thrive off of reviews.

Consider it a tip for the book you read and all the hard work the author and artists put into it. Except this tip only costs your time!

I would appreciate if you took your time to write a review on Goodreads, Amazon, and anywhere you bought this book to help support a self-published author.

* 9 7 9 8 2 1 8 7 2 7 9 7 0 *